I

MW01125616

Book Seven
Kaiju

Published by John Van Stry

P81525G

ISBN-13: 978-1533688514

ISBN-10: 1533688516

Portals of Infinity Series:
Portals of Infinity: Champion for Hire
Portals of Infinity: The God Game
Portals of Infinity: Of Temples and Trials
Portals of Infinity: The Sea of Grass
Portals of Infinity: Demigod and Deities
Portals of Infinity: Reprisal
Portals of Infinity: Kaiju
Portals of Infinity: The Seven Worlds
Portals of Infinity: Consequences
Portals of Infinity: Vis Major
Portals of Infinity: Bridge of Sighs

I would like to thank the following people for their support:

Sean Kennedy via Patreon

And my Beta Readers:
Eric Rice, Jennifer Toplitz, Pat Patterson, Francis Turner, Denise Howell
Also Dane at ebooklaunch.com for his wonderful covers.

SERIES SYNOPSIS

There are an infinite number of worlds, or realities if you prefer, and they are all interconnected in a vast network of portals often referred to as 'The Infinite'. No one knows exactly why the portals exist, but the gods claim it is to balance the power and energies between the different realities or 'spheres'. Worlds tend to be connected to ones that are similar, but not always.

A few select people are able to perceive these portals, and travel through them. Traveling through a portal remakes you, if necessary, so that you fit in to the world you have entered. Because every world has its own rules, be they rules of physics, metaphysics, religion, or magic, and every world has its own time, history, and politics. This means that even though some may appear similar, each is unique, and some can be very different than others.

All worlds contain gods and goddesses, and they too are bound by the rules of both their realms and the Infinite, as they play their own games, for their own reasons, and seek to increase both their power, and their religions. Some of these gods have Champions, people who have sworn themselves to them, and in exchange, have gained power and powers, for as long as they stay. Some of these gods even enter into alliances with other gods, even ones in spheres beyond their own, to further their goals and gain advantage.

In the center of this is our hero William, a portal traveler from the sphere which contains the Earth, but who after a series of adventures now finds himself the Champion for the god Feliogustus, a newer upstart on the sphere of Saladin, William's new home.

ONE
HILLSHIRE
SOUTHWEST MOUNTAINS

It was mid-April and as usual for Hillshire in mid-April it was raining.

I was wearing a much better cloak now than the one I'd bought all those years ago when I'd first come here, better as in warmer and more waterproof. So I was staying relatively dry, though the horse I was riding wasn't, and I don't think it appreciated the rain anymore than I did.

Currently I was following my sister and leading a packhorse through the mountains along a very narrow trail that twisted up along the side of a rather deep ravine. We'd left Riverhead two weeks ago, after she had come to ask me for some help with a problem she was having.

We were about a half-day's ride to the south of the southern road that connected eastern and western Hillshire, not far from where it came down out of the mountains. Apparently a well-organized and possibly large bandit company had set up somewhere on the border between Hillshire and the Atolian nation to the south.

They'd tried to send in a small group of guardsmen back when they'd first realized that there was a problem, that group however had not survived. Apparently the camp was well hidden up in the mountains and rather well defended. But being in a disputed area, if either country sent in their army, it could lead to complications that could lead to war.

So this had presented King Andrew with a problem, and after considering his options, he'd approached the temple and asked if he could borrow Aryanna's champion to deal with this issue.

Nikki thought about it, then came out to Riverhead to ask if I would help, seeing as I was currently there visiting Darlene and my children for the winter. I'd agreed of course, because it made sense. If the bandits saw a single woman riding in on a horse, they would suspect Aryanna's champion, but if a man and a woman were riding in, with a packhorse, they'd suspect either hapless travelers, or more likely, a couple of criminals on the lam from the guard.

In either case, they were more likely to allow us to ride right into their camp, and then they'd deal with us there. Rather than ambush us out here in the rain and mud. After all, why spend hours getting cold, wet, and dirty, when the people you were worried about could be slaughtered in the comfort of your own bandit camp, right? Bandits were notoriously lazy by all accounts.

"So, what are your plans for the summer?" Nikki asked as we rode along. We were keeping our voices low, so they wouldn't carry.

"Rachel mostly," I replied. "Though if she or Fel don't have any pressing plans, I was thinking of taking a week to visit Mom and Dad."

"Sure that's safe?" She asked.

"Yeah, I think things have cooled down enough by now. Besides, the 'Executive Assistant Director' of the FBI is my friend now."

"Must be nice," Nikki chuckled.

"Too bad I can't ask him to fix some traffic tickets for me," I replied. "Still, it's been a couple of years now, and Rachel has been asking me to take her flying, so I may just drag her home and introduce her."

Nikki laughed, "That would be a trip! I don't think Rachel will be able to survive without a household of servants."

"Eh, it would only be for a few days if I do. She can't be gone for too long, people would ask questions."

"So, she wants to fly, huh?"

"Yup, always been a dream of hers. When she found out about home, she made me promise to take her one day."

"And of course, you did."

"Of course I did. She's my wife. So what's with you? Any current love interests in your life?"

"A few, nobody really special though. Well, maybe Joseph a little bit."

"Joseph?" I said surprised, "You mean four-legged and furry Joseph?"

"You're rather furry yourself," Nikki chuckled again, "and he's only four-legged when he wants to be, or when he's at home."

"Wow, first Dezba, now you. Joseph obviously has something going for him." I teased.

"Maybe you should ask for lessons, he did land a goddess after all!" Nikki bantered back.

"How often does he visit?"

"Couple times a year, seems Circe keeps him busy with little chores, so he gets around quite a bit. Still, it must be different being able to actually live with your god like that."

"As long as he's happy, that's what matters. How are things going for you and Aryanna?"

"Pretty good actually, she was right about me and this job. I love it."

The trail turned into a rather wide cleft in the rocks then, wide enough for two to easily ride abreast, so I moved my horse up next to Nikki's as we rode through the cleft.

"Well, looks like we're almost there," Nikki said.

"I wonder how far we'll get before they figure us out."

"Guess we'll see," she replied.

A minute later we rode out into a box canyon with a fairly large pond to the north, forty or so acres of pasture with dozens of horses grazing in it, and what looked like an old inn with a lot of tents and one small house scattered around it rather haphazardly.

There was a fence of sorts across the end of the cleft here, and there were a couple of men standing behind it.

"Who be you?"

"I'm Clem, this is my woman, Gail," I said looking them over.

"This ain't no homestead, what're ya' all doing up here?"

"Hiding from the guard, whadda ya' think?" I asked him. "We heard there was a group up here, might be looking for more hands. If nothin' else, we have some things we can trade to yer boss, iffen' he'll let us stay awhile."

"What's on the horse?" He asked nodding to the packhorse.

"Trade goods."

"What kind of trade goods?" He asked looking at the bundles from behind the fence.

"Armor."

He laughed, "We got plenty of that!"

"Guardsmen armor," I added, and smiled.

"Guardsmen armor? Where the devil did you steal that?"

"Offen' a dozen guards, whatca' think?" Nikki said piping up. "So, you gonna jaw, or ya' gonna let us in?"

I could feel her using some power when she said that, pushing on the guards to let us in.

"Keep an eye on them, boys, while I look," the one in charge said, and coming out the gate he walked over towards the packhorse and pulled back the covering on one of the bundles. Sure enough, there were several sets of guard's armor underneath, though a few of them were a little cut up with bloodstains on them. None of them looked new.

"Well, I'll be," he said shaking his head, "A dozen you say?"

I nodded, "Some are in worse shape than others, but most of them are good, once you clean the blood off," I laughed.

"Well, iffen you can do something like that, you just might have a place with us." He turned to one of his men, "Toby, take 'em to Jared."

Toby nodded, "Follow me," he said, so we rode through the gate and then after dismounting we led our horses towards the inn as we followed him.

"Get much visitors up here?" Nikki asked our guide as we crossed the pasture to the inn.

"Eh, a few stragglers show up now and again, not unlike you two."

"How many you got up here?"

I could feel her pushing with her power again.

"Umm," He stopped a moment, "Hunert or so I think? Course that's not counting the whores and the slaves."

"Course," Nikki agreed.

We stopped in front of the inn, and tied our horses to the rail out front. I took off my cloak and draped it behind my saddle. I was wearing a loose shirt and pants, with what looked like an ill fitted set of leather armor on top of that.

"So, introduce us to your boss," I said and we followed Toby inside.

Walking through the door, I was surprised that the place wasn't a complete sty. It was run down and a bit of a mess, but overall the place was mostly clean, and didn't smell all that much. There were a lot of tables in the room with men and even a few women sitting at them. From the way they were dressed, I guess they were members of the bandit company.

Glancing around it looked like there were about forty of them in the room, and in addition to them there were almost as many slaves, all of whom were women, and from the way they were dressed, their role was rather clear.

Toby led us up to a table by the far wall, at which a rather large man sat, with a slave to either side of him. Both were rather attractive, and both looked like they would rather be anyplace but here.

"So, you be Jared then?" I asked looking at him.

"Yes, I'm Jared, and this is my domain. Who are you and what are you doing here?" Jared said rather smoothly.

"Huh, and here I thought you'd just be some uncultured criminal slob," Nikki said walking up to stand before him.

"You had best behave yourself," He said starting to stand, "or I'll add you to my harem."

Nikki threw off her cloak, "In the name of Aryanna, you are sentenced to death!" She said and invoking her champion's aura, she ran her sword through his head without any further preamble.

I shifted into my own champion form and the ill-fitting armor now fit just right on my larger frame as I got the speed boost that all champions got during combat. Drawing my swords and turning to my left, I attacked the people sitting there, running my swords through the necks of the first two, and stabbing a third one through the heart.

The other six at that table all pushed back their chairs and started to scramble to their feet, two of them however losing their balance and falling back onto their butts on the floor.

I stabbed two more, gutted a third and jumped on a fourth, one of the ones who had fallen onto the floor, ripping his throat out with the claws on my foot as I took yet another in the head with a sword.

They were still trying to draw weapons and attack me back, it didn't help that they'd all been drinking and several of them were rather drunk.

It also didn't help them that quite a few of their slaves were now pulling the daggers off of the belt of whichever man was closest to them and stabbing him with it.

I started taking off arms and hands, stabbing whenever I could, dodging around tables and stomping on anyone who was already down but didn't look dead. While I had claws on my hands, the ones on my feet were considerably larger and I wasn't afraid to use them.

It quickly became complete bloody chaos and I was wreaking mayhem through the men and even the women bandits, while Nikki was doing the same on the other side of the room.

Eventually, they started to get coordinated, but only because it had taken us a good ten minutes to kill most of them, and all the tables, chairs, bodies, and blood on the floor was making it difficult for anyone to move around.

At that point the smart ones ran for the exit and the stupid ones charged Nikki. Everyone avoided me, or at least tried to. I guess a seven-foot tall cat-man covered in blood passed for a demon here. So I went after the ones running for the door, several of whom looked at me in complete and utter fear as I ran them down. They were so focused on trying to escape the room that I managed to cut them all down easily.

Turning around I looked at Nikki who was talking to one of the slave girls. The men who had charged her were already dead and there no longer any living bandits in the room. I could see that there were a few dead slaves as well, sadly. Spying a wounded one however, I quickly walked over her to heal them.

"I won't hurt you," I sighed as she cried out in fear and tried to move away. I guess I looked like a demon to her as well.

"Be at ease!" Nikki commanded using another cantrip, "He is one of mine, and I am Aryanna's Champion!"

They all relaxed then, and I healed her and one other that looked to be in a bad way.

"Come, Will. There are a lot more outside still."

"Lead on, Sis," I said and followed her out of the inn.

Surprisingly no one who had gotten out the front door had decided to warn the rest of the camp, they were all too busy running away.

I walked over to my horse and got my bow, I'd strung it when we'd set out this morning.

"Is that Toby?" Nikki asked, and pointed at a man running for the gate.

"Probably," I said and grabbing a handful of arrows I quickly took aim and sent two in quick succession his way. Looking around there were a lot of people standing about the tents looking at us. I wasn't sure if that was because I was in my champion form covered in blood, or because I'd just killed Toby in front of them.

Probably both.

"No rest for the righteous," Nikki smiled and I noticed she had her own bow out as well.

Turning I started picking off men as fast as I could. After the second one, the others all got the idea and started to run for their tents as everyone began to yell and shout that they were being attacked.

We both mounted our horses then and drawing swords once more we started to lay into them with a will, using our height and speed advantage while attacking from horseback to ride around the tents and take them out, one at a time.

Several times a group would make a break for it, either trying to gather up their horses, or run for the gate, and one of us would ride off after them, cutting them down from behind as the other kept attacking and moving, doing their best not to let the bandits get organized.

I guess we'd taken out the leaders inside the inn, for while there were almost twice as many of them running around outside, it didn't take all that long to kill most of them as very few of them tried to fight as a group. The hardest part was going tent to tent, finding which ones had slaves in them, and which ones had cowering bandits after we'd eliminated the majority of them.

The sun had set, not that it mattered all that much, as someone had set the inn on fire and the resulting blaze shed more than enough light on everything.

"That's the last of them," Nikki sighed as she got all of the former slaves settled down on the far side of the small box canyon.

"What happens next?" I asked her.

"I'll open a portal to Aryanna in the morning and start sending them through. There's only forty-three of them, so I think I can get them all through in one shot, if they hurry."

I nodded. We'd lost about twenty of the slaves to the bandits. Once they had the opportunity to turn on them, many had not hesitated to do so, even if it meant their own life. All of these women had been captured by the bandits during raids in the last year and used rather harshly. So many of them had not hesitated at all when the opportunity for revenge had come their way.

I had returned to my local form, and put on clean clothes from the pack on my horse, after taking a short bath in the pond, but most of the women were still rather wary of me, not that I blamed them.

"When are you leaving, Bro?" Nikki asked.

"I'll stay until you've sent the last of them off. Some of the bandits who got away might come back."

Nikki nodded, "Thanks."

"Sure thing, Sis," I said and finding a nice place to sit, I got out some food and watched the fire as I ate.

"So, when was the last time you stopped by and saw Mom and Dad?" I asked returning to our original conversation.

"Oh, I went home for Christmas, I even dragged Joseph along and told them he was my current boyfriend."

I laughed and looked at her, "Really?"

Nikki grinned, "Yup. Mom loves him; Dad isn't quite sure what to make of him."

I shook my head, and wondered what our parents would say if we tried to tell them the truth? That I was a champion on a medieval world where the dominant race was based on evolved felines, that Nikki and I both worked for gods? That Nikki lived in a world where technology was impossible and kings and queens still ruled the earth?

Assuming that we could even get them to believe us.

We talked a bit more, and then split the watch between us. In the morning, after she'd taken care of everyone, I'd be heading off to Hiland and Rachel. Winters were slow times in Hiland due to all the snow, which was why I usually spent them here with Darlene, giving her the time and attention she deserved.

Last summer in Hiland had been pretty easy for a change, Barassa was in the midst of an economic crisis after losing the war, so they weren't causing us any problems, and Rachel was still rebuilding the treasury after not only winning the war, but growing her kingdom once again.

I looked around the valley, the place reminded me of someplace but I couldn't quite place it. Maybe it was those city-states to the south in the mountains that Rachel was thinking about adding to her kingdom.

Whatever it was, if it was important either Fel or Rachel would remind me when I got home tomorrow. I'd traveled to so many places, both in this sphere, my home sphere, and a couple of dozen others in the last decade that it was hard sometimes remembering just where I'd been.

Two
Saladin - Hiland

"Hi, Fel," I said as I stepped out of the portal I'd opened to gate back to the temple, letting it collapse behind me. The ability to be able to gate directly back from anywhere was a pretty handy one.

"Hello, William," Fel's disembodied voice responded. While he could manifest his image in his main temple, he rarely did so when I was involved.

"So, what's on the schedule for this year?" I asked walking to the back door. I knew Narasamman, the high priestess, would be annoyed that I went straight home to Rachel, without visiting with her first, but I missed my wife and I could visit with Narasamman later. As it was, I wasn't even planning on chatting with Fel until later, and he was the god to whom I was sworn.

"Nothing terribly important, and not until more of the passes have cleared. So go have fun."

"Thanks, Fel," I replied and left the temple and headed up to the small 'castle' that Rachel and I lived in. It only was called a castle really, because Rachel was the ruler of the Hiland Kingdom. It was really more of a glorified estate with some government buildings on it, and a low defensive wall.

I caught up with Rachel in our quarters; she was seated with her scribe Telran going over records of some sort. As soon as she saw me she got up and came over and we hugged and kissed, just spending a few moments enjoying each other's company.

"You're late," Rachel said to me when we stopped, looking up at me.

"I had to help Nikki with a problem she was having," I said and sitting down in the chair she had just vacated, I pulled her down onto my lap.

"Ah, so how is your sister doing?"

"She's doing well and pretty happy with things. What's all this?" I asked nodding towards the paperwork on the table. Telran was watching us, looking a little bemused. I liked Telran, he wasn't afraid of me in the slightest.

"Budget issues, requests for gold, the usual," Rachel sighed.

I nodded, "Well, I'll try not to interrupt you too much then," I purred and put my hands on her shoulders and slowly massaged them as she turned back to Telran and the documents, still seated in my lap.

Yeah, it wasn't the most exciting way to spend time together, especially after being apart for the last four months, but any time spent with the one you love is worth it. Plus I had an engineer's understanding of public works she could call on, and I had dealt with most of the people making the requests, so I knew them at least as well as she did. She might be the Queen, and I just her consort, but I was also her husband, and the champion of the god Feliogustus, the one the vast majority of her subjects followed. So knowing what she was doing and wanted done was always helpful, especially if she needed me to twist an arm or two.

"My advisory council is meeting tomorrow, I want you to be there," Rachel told me later, after Telran had left and we'd sat down to dinner with Laria and all of our children.

I nodded, "What's the topic?"

"Holse and Rigel have some things involving Barassa and the northern kingdoms they want to share with me and the other members."

"Not another war I hope," I sighed.

"No, or not for us at least, now, let's eat."

I looked around the table as I sat down next to Rachel in the council chambers. After the war last year she'd been forced by necessity to reorganize her council, as it had grown rather large, and several of the people now on it were close to a week's ride away.

So the full council only met twice a month, and representatives were allowed to be sent in your place.

Rachel's advisory council however met twice a week, more if necessary. It only had six members on it; Diament's son Brandt, and Ramert were the only two from the nobility on the council, Ramert because of his loyalty and Brandt because his house was still the most powerful of the noble houses. Holse was on the council, as the leader of all of the kingdom's armed forces, Jezza as the one in charge of all of the public works and any other construction projects, and Rigel, our intelligence head and spymaster.

Narasamman was also on the advisory council. There had been some discussion about that, mainly because I was there fairly often as well. But I couldn't speak for Feliogustus or Fordessa, or their followers, and Narasamman could.

Rigel was going over the intelligence reports that he'd just received.

"So, from what we've been able to learn, Langhir, Ronshir, Stadhir, Yamland, Metina, and Bronsard, have all combined their armies and are marching south as we speak. Based on the latest reports I received, I would estimate that they've either crossed, or will soon cross, the northern border of Barassa's kingdom."

"What united them?" Rachel asked, "Do we know for sure?"

Narasamman spoke up, "It's a holy war. The priests of Roden, Keiss, Tiremenentan, and Quzelatin have been pushing for war against Tantrus because the temples he had established in their domains were found to have been engaging in assassinations."

"But that was ten years ago now," Rachel said looking at Narasamman. "Surely they can't still be upset over that?"

"Yes, but ten years ago Barassa was too strong to attack. After their failed attack on Marland two years ago, and last year's economic collapse, they're much weaker now," Rigel pointed out.

"But still, how do you whip the people up for a religious war over something that old?" Rachel asked again.

"The followers of Roden, Keiss, Tiremenentan, and Quzelatin have been making inroads with the population of Barassa," Rigel said. "A lot of the populace has been becoming less enamored with Tantrus over the last few years, and well, with the economic collapse last year those other religions sent in their people with food and other relief to try and gain followers."

"Which Tantrus's temple guards, with the help of Stivik's guards, then either slaughtered or sold off into slavery," Narasamman continued.

"Exactly," Rigel said picking back up. "So the head priests leaned on the leaders, the leaders looked at Barassa, saw much easier pickings, and agreed."

Rachel looked at Narasamman, "Where does Feliogustus and Fordessa stand on this?"

Narasamman shrugged. "Officially both are doing nothing. Feliogustus has no followers in any of the Kingdoms involved, though my priests are instructing the Mowoks to steer clear of the invading armies and not get involved with any from Barassa unless they cross into their lands.

"Fordessa, however, does have followers in all of the cities, except of course Barassa. Some of them have joined with the armies to provide entertainment and to write songs of any great deeds they may observe. However, none of her clergy have joined."

Rachel nodded and thought a moment.

"What do you estimate Barassa's army to be now, Rigel?"

Rigel consulted his notes, "About fifty thousand, including the levies. They no longer have any mercenaries working for them, and after the war recriminations and then last year's near collapse of the government, I'm not sure how effective what they have left is. General Holse and I have spent a great deal of time discussing this matter."

Holse nodded, "They had a lot of desertions in the upper ranks after the war. Whatever command structure they have left, has got to be lacking in experience."

"And how big does the invading army look?" Rachel asking looking back and forth between Holse and Rigel.

"It's eighty thousand, with two champions," I said speaking up for the first time.

Rachel turned to me, "And you know this...?"

I smiled at her, everyone else was looking at me now too, "Feliogustus told me this morning when I was down at the temple. I was going to bring it up, but Rigel beat me to the punch," I rubbed my leg up against Rachel's under the table and she just nodded.

"Okay, you're forgiven," she said.

"Do you know what the dispositions of those troops are, William?" Holse asked.

"Well Langhir, Ronshir, Stadhir, and Metina each contributed ten thousand foot soldiers, mostly regular infantry, but they've all contributed some heavy units as well. Yamland and Bronsard contributed twenty thousand each, of which probably half are heavy infantry. Bronsard mainly because they're the ones who have been having to deal with Barassa's aggressions over the last two years.

"As for champions, Roden's and Quzelatin's are with the army. Keiss and Tiremenentan do not have champions currently."

Holse and Rigel both nodded, the later making a few notes.

"So," Rachel said looking around the table, "What do we do?"

"Do we need to do anything?" Ramert asked, looking around the table. "I say just let them go at each other."

Brandt nodded, "As much as I'd like to see Barassa trampled under the feet of our troops for the death of my father, I agree that a wait and see approach would be best for us."

"The church has no comment," Narasamman said.

Jezza shook his head, "I am never a fan of war, Your Highness."

"I see nothing to be gained for us at this point, Your Highness," Rigel said, "However I would like to send a few spies down there to keep an eye on things."

Holse sighed, "We're going to have to send out the army, Your Highness."

Rachel looked at him, "Why?"

"Well first, with an army of that size running around, we just can't choose to ignore it. We'll have to reinforce Tradeson, just in case anyone gets 'lost.' We'll have to move significant portions of the army to both Rivervail and Marland as well. Those will be more to deal with the flood of refugees we'll undoubtedly see, but also, if Barassa does fall, where will its army and leadership flee to? Increasing our presence in Marland will help to convince them not to come this way."

"You think they would?" Rachel asked, "After all, we beat them last time."

"Desperate men take desperate measures, Your Majesty. There are several hundred thousand people living in the city of Barassa alone, if we see a flood of refugees, they could easily hide an army in it, and attack us when and where we least expect. So we need to deal with the inevitable results."

Now it was Rachel's turn to sigh. "I really need to appoint a finance minister. Okay, figure out who has to go where, I'll summon Holden's ambassador to let him know what we're doing, I'm guessing king Charles will be willing to donate some troops and I'll send a messenger to Duke Eklin as well to let him know you'll be talking to him. I'll also let the representatives from Tradeson and Stongshold know tonight."

She looked around the table again, "Anything else?"

Jezza spoke up, "Your Majesty, if General Holse's suspicion on refugees is correct, we should probably figure out where we want to put them, and build some sort of shelters or something."

Rigel nodded, "That's a good idea, Your Highness. That would let us check them out and determine who we want to keep, and who we want to move on."

"Put it in eastern Marland," Brandt said, "I understand that we still have a lot of open property there since the war?"

Rachel nodded, "Good point. We can settle them there, and if they want to go back after this is over, they'll be close to home. Anything else?"

Everyone shook their heads.

"Good," Rachel said and stood up, holding out her hand to me. I stood up and took it.

"Dismissed," She told them. "I'll want to see numbers on what this is going to cost me come the full meeting on Thursday."

Rachel and I left then as the others gathered their things and stood up to leave.

"So, what do you think, Hon?" Rachel asked me after we left the room.

I shrugged, "I honestly don't know. Fel thinks that the army is just going to go down there and lay siege to the city and try and starve them out."

"Barassa is on the river and has a port," Rachel said shaking her head, "I don't see that working very well."

"Well, after what happened last year, Barassa's coffers aren't very full. They're not going to have a lot of money to buy food or other goods. Besides, this isn't a war against Barassa; it's a war against Tantrus."

"Like that matters," Rachel sighed.

"You never know," I said giving my head a shake, "Stivik could wise up and toss them out and let the other religions in. That would end it right there."

Rachel gave me a sidelong glance as we walked along, "Really, Will?"

I laughed, "No, of course not. Stivik's an idiot; he should have moved his economy off of the slave trade when it started to crash. No one would even think of attacking him, if he wasn't so weak now."

"Tomorrow I want you to ride down to Eklin let him know what's going on, then ride east until you're across from Barassa and keep an eye on things for me."

I sighed, "So I'm the messenger you're sending to him?"

Rachel nodded, "You've got a good knowledge of the area, you know Roden's champion, and everyone respects you." Rachel stopped and rose up on her toes to give me a kiss. "You are my husband after all," she purred.

"You do know that Roden's champion is a crazy woman who scares me half the time, right?"

"Yes, but you trust her," Rachel said.

I looked at her, rather surprised. "What makes you say that?"

"I've heard you talk about her, and I've heard Jane talk about her. You admire her and you trust her and you're afraid she's smarter than you."

I blinked, and I was sure I heard Fel laughing at me.

"So, anything else I need to know, before I leave, dear?" I asked her.

Rachel didn't say anything until we were in our quarters and she started to remove her official raiments.

"I don't know, Love. I just have this feeling that something unexpected is going to happen. King Stivik and the Priests of Tantrus have to be on edge right now, after everything that's happened. Holse is right, desperate men do desperate things. Stivik has to be desperate. Tantrus is probably getting desperate as well.

"Once they have the city under siege, they'll probably pacify the rest of the country, so what will Stivik and Tantrus be left with? A walled city that can't feed itself?"

Rachel shook her head, "They're not stupid, if they have any tricks left, it's in their best interest to pull them out and use them immediately. And that's what worries me."

I nodded and gave her a hug, then kissed her.

"Don't worry, Love. I'll take care of it."

THREE
SALADIN - MARLAND

I left early the next morning with Laria in tow. I was a bit worried about taking her along as her child, or to be more honest our child, wasn't quite a year old yet. But Rachel had been rather firm on Laria going with me, and Rachel was rather fond of Keith having confided in me that it was nice having a baby around without having to go through all the problems of having one yourself.

Laria wasn't exactly thrilled with the decision, but she knew her child would be well cared for, so she didn't complain.

I resolved to make it up to her as much as possible, and when we arrived in Marland city five days later, Laria was back to her usual cheerful self.

"Will!" Duke Eklin said coming up to Laria and I as we left our mounts at the castle stable. I guess someone had sent a runner to tell him I was here, and rather than wait for us, he'd come down himself.

"To what do I owe the honor?" He asked.

"There's an army marching on Barassa, if you haven't heard anything about it yet, you probably will soon. Queen Rachel is sending Holse down here to make sure no one gets any ideas."

Duke Eklin nodded, "We've been hearing rumors from some of the merchants coming in to our port. I passed them on of course, but I had no idea.

"Please, come inside, it's late and I'll have a room made up and some food sent up as well. I'll send a squad out immediately to ride east down to the coast and back, to see what intelligence they can gather and I'll warn my commanders to prepare for a deployment, once we have an idea of what's going on. Sound good?"

I nodded to Duke Eklin as he led us inside, "It sounds very good. I doubt we're going to be forced into anything right away, but Rachel is worried about refugees, as well as just what Stivik's reaction is going to be."

"How big is the army marching on him?"

"We believe it to be about eighty thousand, with two champions."

"I don't know what kind of reaction he could have," Eklin said thinking about it a moment. "Stivik's army is smaller than that, however, I doubt eighty thousand is enough to do more than sit outside the walls and throw insults. With Barassa having a port, they really can't starve them out."

"What if they were to block the port?" I asked, curious.

"Well, if they could do that, it would be a huge problem for Stivik, but I don't see how anyone could do it. The river is too wide, and the port too well shielded.

"Where is the army coming from? I didn't think any of Barassa's neighbors could put together that large of a force."

I gave him the run down of the forces then.

"So, Stivik just needs to sit tight until the fall, when they'll probably all give up and go home."

I nodded, "Probably, but the whole time Stivik's bottled up inside his walls, they'll be wreaking havoc on the rest of his kingdom, and probably cutting pieces of it off for themselves. So he has to do *something*."

Duke Eklin shrugged as we stopped outside of a doorway to what looked like a guest room. It was late and the idea of bed after riding all day was rather attractive.

"His last chance to do something was after he lost the war," Duke Eklin said. "I think he's out of options at this point. Other than putting his family on a ship and sailing off across the sea and never coming back, I don't really see any options for him that don't involve his head on a pike."

"Agreed," I said nodding. "But better safe than sorry."

"I'll let you eat and get some rest. I'll send for you in the morning and you can discuss it with my commanders and me."

"Thanks, Eklin," I said and touched palms with him. I then I escorted Laria in to the room. Servants were already bringing in food, so we settled down and had dinner.

"I think I've been spoiled traveling back in your home world," Laria said to me sitting down a little gingerly. Several long days in the saddle was something she wasn't exactly used to.

"It does have its benefits," I admitted. "But I like the women here more," I smirked and leaned over to give her a kiss.

"So what do you think this King Stivik is going to do?" She asked. Up until this moment, I don't think she'd really heard anything about why we were even coming here.

I shook my head, "I have no idea. Like Eklin said, I don't think he really has any options. Personally I think he's an arrogant self-centered jerk, but he must have had something going for him to have been king this long."

"Obviously, Rachel thinks so," Laria pointed out.

I nodded, "Obviously."

"Then he does," Laria declared, "Rachel is very wise and she understands all of the other rulers around here very well. If she thinks he's going to do something, then you can count on him doing something unexpected."

"You think so?" I asked looking at her.

Laria smiled, "Well, she is smarter than the both of us. So yes."

"Smarter than the both of us?" I asked with a smile.

"Oh, surely you realize that she doesn't keep you around for your brains!" Laria said smirking.

"Oh really, now..." I started to reply when the door suddenly flew open

"Will!"

I looked up and tried not to face-palm. It was Goth.

"Is that anyway to refer to your father?" Laria said without missing a beat, bringing Goth up short.

"Who are you?" She said looking from me to Laria.

"Goth," I said standing up. "This is Laria. Laria, as you guessed correctly, this is my daughter, Goth."

Laria smiled and gave a little nod; Goth looked at her and bristled just a little bit, but then turned back to me and gave me a rather strong hug.

"I just found out you were here, Will, and I..."

"Goth," I stopped her, "I'm your father, and you will address me as such."

"But...."

"No buts," I warned her, letting my voice drop down an octave.

Goth "Harrumphed", but released me from the hug and took a step back. I hadn't seen her since just after the war, when I'd spent a few days visiting with her. With everything that happened after that, well I'd not had a lot of free time. Fel had spent over a month 'putting me back together' as I liked to think about it, though really it was just more of a breathing space.

When I'd finished with that, I owed both Darlene and Rachel a fair bit of my time. Then there was Laria, Narasamman and even Tareassa. So, unfortunately Goth had gotten the short end of that arrangement.

"Where have you been, Father?" She said and looked at me rather imploringly. "You said you'd visit."

"I was very busy, Goth. I've been away from the kingdom for quite a bit of time, and when I was here, I was off to the west, taking care of tasks that Feliogustus had assigned to me."

"And, who is this?" Goth said looking over at Laria, "Where did she come from?"

I looked over Goth, again, I had to admit she'd turned into a good-looking young woman, and she'd dressed rather attractively, no doubt hoping to attract the kind of attention she wasn't going to get from me.

But for as good looking as she was, Laria was better looking. Laria's whole life had been based on her being attractive, and as she had started with rather impressive looks, even after a few days of travel sitting at the table she looked better than Goth did right now. Because looking pretty was really her job when you got down to it.

"I said, this is Laria."

"I'm his concubine," Laria purred, smiling up at Goth.

"His what!" Goth exclaimed, looking both shocked and angry.

"I was his reward for one of the tasks he was sent to do, of course," Laria said smiling. "Your father really is such an impressive male, so they felt they had to reward him with the best, you see."

Laria then just leaned back in her chair and smiled rather beautifully.

I grabbed Goth as she lunged forward growling.

"Does your wife know about this?" Goth said angrily.

"Yes, Goth. Rachel knows about Laria, she lives with us after all."

"What?" Goth looked at me shocked, and I could see tears starting to form in her eyes. "She, she let you have this, this *tart* and she wouldn't let me have you?"

I sighed and pulled her into a hug. "Goth, you're my daughter, I've told you that before. It doesn't matter that I adopted you, to me you're my daughter."

I grabbed her shoulders and pushed her back a bit and looked her in the eyes, "Now apologize to Laria for what you called her."

"What?"

I just gave her a hard stare to make it clear I was serious.

"I'm, I'm sorry for calling you a tart, Laria," She said looking at Laria, and then looking back at me when she was done.

Goth sniffed then, and started to cry softly. "I'm sorry, dad. I'm sorry."

I hugged her close again and patted her on the back.

"I'm sorry I've been away, hon. Life has been hard on me the last few years. Now, sit down, and you can tell me about everything while I eat."

Goth sniffed and nodded, then sat down on one of the chairs in the room while I sat back down next to Laria, who leaned up against me as I started to eat again.

It was a little strained at first, Laria was clearly staking out her territory and I don't think Goth missed the fact that Laria was younger than her. But after a while Goth seemed to accept the situation.

"So, any men in your life?" I asked Goth.

"Umm, well," she blushed.

"You were going to cheat on your boyfriend with your *father*?" Laria giggled and Goth's ears went flat and all the fur on her face bushed out.

I was surprised; I don't think I'd ever seen Goth that embarrassed.

"Well you can introduce him to me tomorrow," I said to Goth. "I'm going to be here for at least a day or two, maybe more. Are you staying at the temple?"

"I'm in the building next door, with the other acolytes," she said, still embarrassed.

Finishing dinner, I stood up and went and gave Goth another hug as she got up and then escorted her out the door.

"I'll try to come by around lunch time. Say hello to Felecia for me, and Jane too if you see her. Goodnight, Goth."

"Night, Dad," Goth said and looking down at her feet she left.

I closed the door again and made sure it was locked this time, leaning back against it and sighing rather loudly.

"She's a nice girl, why didn't you just sleep with her?" Laria asked.

I looked at her, a bit surprised. "She's my daughter."

"She's your adopted daughter; she's not really your daughter."

"Did they do that back in Hidden Vale?"

She nodded, "She's not really from your family, so no one would really care all that much."

I shook my head, "Where I come from, an adopted daughter is the same thing as a real daughter. You don't sleep with them."

"I gathered from Rachel that it's frowned on in Hiland as well. And to think Rachel says you can't resist attractive women."

I grumbled a little at her, "The idea of sleeping with Goth really does not sit well with me. Maybe if I'd never had kids I wouldn't have made the strong association that I did with her being my daughter, but in any case, I'm *definitely* not interested."

"Well, then how about coming over here with someone with whom you are interested?" Laria purred, giving me a wink as she stood up and walked over to the bed, swaying rather seductively.

I smiled at her, "Now that I can do."

FOUR
SALADIN - MARLAND CASTLE

"So there you have it," I said to the small cadre of officers that Duke Eklin had assembled. I'd told them everything that we knew about the army coming to attack Barassa, what we estimated Barassa's strength to be, and most of Queen Rachel's concerns.

"If I may, William?" One of Duke Eklin's senior officers asked. I didn't know his name, though I recalled seeing him during the war. I hadn't worked with Eklin's staff much back then, so I really didn't know many of them, except for Third Adams, who was now a second.

I nodded, "Go ahead."

"It seems to me that the real concern right now is dealing with any refugees that might make it across the river. I don't think Barassa has the will, nor the army, to come at us again. Further for the northern army to try it, they'd be splitting their forces rather dangerously and thus allowing the Barassan forces to sally out and destroy them."

"I agree that seems to be the case. However, by making a show of force on our side of the river, it should discourage any ideas anyone might be entertaining of future adventures.

"Plus," I continued, "as you noted, if we see a major flow of refugees, we'll probably need quite a few soldiers down there to corral them and keep them from flooding into the city."

Everyone around the table nodded in agreement.

"There is however, one thing that worries our queen, and that is plain and simple that Barassa is in a desperate situation, and she is worried that they will act on that desperation and do something that may affect us."

"What could they do?" The same officer asked.

I shrugged, "I have no idea at all. Militarily and economically they're still smarting and still recovering. But there are two things I have learned in life: The first is to never second guess your queen, and the second is to never ever, *ever* second guess your wife."

I smiled as everyone got a chuckle out of that, while bringing the point home that it didn't matter what I believed, or even what they believed; I had my orders and we would all work to carry them out.

"So, what are your orders?" Duke Eklin asked, causing everyone to quiet back down.

"Tomorrow I'm going to ride down to that city we ran Barassa out of at the end of the war, what is its name?"

"Edgemire."

I nodded, "I'm going to set up there for a while, and see what I can learn. I'd like for a couple of companies to be sent down there as well. I'm not sure how big a force General Holse is going to send, but we should scout out some suitable encampment sites, not just for his men, but to deal with any refugees that we end up with."

"Second Adams, take your men down there, you'll be in charge of all our forces in the area," Duke Eklin said.

"Yes, Sir!" Second Adams replied.

"How long will it take you to get the men there?" I asked him.

"It's about a two day march from here, to the garrison there."

I nodded, "How big is the garrison?"

"We have a small company stationed down there," Duke Eklin said. "With Adams's battalion, that would give you over a thousand men."

"Good, I think that should be enough to start with. When the rest of the troops get here, I'm sure they'll have new orders for us." I looked around the table. "I don't really have anything else, Duke Eklin, would you like to add anything?"

Duke Eklin shook his head, "Other than to tell everyone to keep an eye on the situation, just in case something does happen? No. Thank you, William."

I nodded, "In that case, I'll see you in the morning, Adams. Have a good day, everyone."

"So now what?" Laria asked me as I came back to our room.

"We need to run over to the temple, so I can visit with Fordessa, check in with Jane if she's around, and spend some time with Goth so I'm not breaking my promise to visit with her."

"And after that?"

"After that I think we're just going to re-supply so we can leave in the morning."

Laria nodded and accompanied me out of the room.

"So, where are we headed next?"

"Further east, to a town on this side of the river across from Barassa that has a good view of it."

"And after that?"

I shook my head, "I have no idea what comes after that. I really don't want to spend all summer watching Barassa," I sighed.

"Oh, I don't know. That doesn't sound all that bad." Laria smiled.

"Trust me, when it starts getting hot and humid, and the insects are buzzing all around you, you'll be thinking it's pretty bad."

The walk to the temple wasn't a very long one; Fordessa's temple had been set up here long enough ago that her followers had been able to procure a building in the old walled section of town. Unlike the Tantrus one we'd trashed years ago.

"Greetings, Fordessa," I said when we walked inside and bowed to the altar. Fordessa may be the junior member of the pantheon she had joined with Fel, but this was her main temple, so I felt it only fair that I pay my respects.

"Greetings, William!" her voice replied, causing Laria to give a slight start. She was still far from used to the casual way I had with the gods.

"Felecia and Jane are in Felecia's office waiting for you; they would hear your plans."

"Thanks," I said and bowed to her altar again, "So just how bad has my daughter been behaving?" I asked in a much quieter voice, "I know Felecia and Jane would never tell me the truth!"

Fordessa's laughed, "She's only trouble when you're around. Otherwise she's well behaved and rather talented."

"That's a surprise," I admitted. "But a good one I admit."

"Well, after Jane had a few words with her, she became quite the model student."

"I don't think I want to know what happened," I sighed.

"Which is for the best," Fordessa agreed.

I took Laria's hand and led her back to Felecia's office. She'd already met Jane, so introductions were brief, and then we all sat down to discuss the situation once again.

"So, is there anything new that we know?" I asked after we'd all sat down.

"The army should be outside of Barassa's walls within the week," Felecia said. "They've been dealing rather carefully with the towns and villages they've come across. Bronsard and Yamland are expanding their borders into what is no longer Barassan territory, so they're trying to sow as much good will as they can."

"I wonder how well that's going to work?" I asked.

Felecia shrugged. "It's hard to say, all of these nations used to be on very good terms, which didn't get rocky until Barassa was forced to turn its eyes to the north in its search for new slaves for its markets. While King Stivik still maintains that the raiding parties that were hitting Bronsard's southern towns and villages had nothing to do with him, it's obvious that Bronsard didn't believe his denunciations.

"And seeing as he never did return any of the kidnapped people to their homes but instead allowed them to be sold off in his markets, it did make his words rather hollow. So the rest all decided they didn't want to be next and joined forces."

"I think it's more the prospects of easy pickings," Jane said. "Plus they're probably afraid that Rachel will send you down there to take it for her before they can take it themselves."

I nodded, "It would be nice. But from what Holse tells me, and from what I've learned over the years, it will be a while yet before we can take that city on."

"Do you think they'll succeed?" Felecia asked.

I shrugged, "No one I've talked to thinks they have a chance. Everyone thinks this is just an attempt to takeover some of the outlying lands."

"Then why even bother?" Laria asked.

"Because it will weaken Barassa further, especially if they can't regain the lands that they're losing this year. Barassa is on a downward spiral, if nothing happens to alter that, eventually they will fall."

"And if these attacks keep up every year or two," Jane added, "It will fall sooner than later. A lot sooner."

"Which is why Rachel is worried," I replied. "Stivik is a lot of things, but stupid isn't one of them. He has to know that if things go badly this year, eventually he's done."

"It's not just Stivik who you should be worried about," Felecia said softly, and we all looked at her curiously. "Tantrus is going to be desperate as well. I've been getting reports that the army is burning down his temples and churches, while putting his priests to the sword and converting his followers. This is a holy war after all."

"Well, Fordessa," I asked, "Do either you or Fel have anything to tell us?"

"No, William," Fordessa's voice said. "We can not see into his places, or see what his people are doing. However we do both agree that Felecia's words have merit. Tantrus is an elder god, far older than either of us. That temple has been there a very long time and we know nothing about it. It is best to be concerned."

I looked at the others as I nodded in agreement, seeing them nod as well.

We discussed the refugee problem after that, it was decided that a number of clerics from Fel and Fordessa would be sent down to convert any refugees that showed up, as well as to put us on guard for any of Tantrus's who might try to sneak in. Felecia would also talk to the local priests of Roden and see to it that they were included in the task. Roden's faith had grown considerably in Marland since the war and relations between the churches had been good. Fel had made it clear that he didn't want that relationship disrupted.

I had no idea if Fel was planning on inviting Roden into his pantheon, nor was it really my business to ask. I wasn't even sure which of them had the larger religion.

After we finished that up, Laria and I went off to a local tap house and restaurant that Jane had recommended. Felecia had sent an acolyte to fetch Goth to meet us there.

"Goth!" I said and stood to hug my daughter when she showed up. "I'm glad you were able to join us."

Goth rolled her eyes and hugged me back, "Like I would miss seeing you, Dad."

"Well, I wasn't sure if you might be busy or not."

"Do you really think anyone is going to stop me from seeing my father?" She said with a touch of sarcasm. "Especially when my father is Feliogustus's champion?"

I gave a small shrug, she had a point.

"So, where is your boyfriend?" Laria asked.

"Oh, he's busy, but he said he would join us in an hour or so. Apparently something important came up that he has to see to."

"More important than meeting your father?" I asked surprised.

"Apparently," Goth shrugged, sitting down and joining us. She had a cased instrument with her.

"Are you any good with that?" I asked nodding at it.

Goth smiled, "Surprisingly, well at least to Felecia, Jane, and myself, I am," she said looking rather proud. "Everyone thought you had just sent me here to get rid of me. Who knew I had talent?"

I coughed suddenly at that comment; *I* hadn't sent her here to get rid of her, that was more Narasamman's idea. I'd sent her here to keep Rachel and Narasamman from killing her.

"Let's hear it, while we wait for your boyfriend to show up," I told her.

"Sure," Goth smiled and uncased the local version of the guitar and after tuning it, she started playing. I was impressed, she was rather good.

When she started to sing, even Laria looked impressed.

We drew a lot of attention after that, and we got a round of ale on the house from the barkeep, who was appreciating the sudden increase in customers. I was surprised that there wasn't a performer here already. Then again, it was still early in the day yet, only an hour or so after lunch. I ordered food for the table, and put an arm around Laria as I enjoyed Goth's performance.

When Second Adams walked up to the table I stood up and greeted him.

"Second Adams, what brings you to our table?" I asked smiling at him.

He looked at me, then looked at Goth, whose facial fur bushed out slightly in a blush, then looked back at me.

"I'm dating your daughter, Sir."

I could feel my eyes widening a little and looked down at Goth, who looked even more embarrassed as she stopped playing and put her instrument away.

"I guess she wanted it to be a surprise," I said and motioning him to a chair a sat down as well.

"You're not upset, are you, Sir?" Second Adams asked taking a seat.

"Call me Will, Adams, this is a social setting after all," I said and smiled at him, and then at Goth. Second Adams was probably ten years older than Goth, either she liked older men, or was testing me.

"And actually, I'm not upset at all. In fact, I approve." I said and with the way Goth's face lit up, it was pretty clear she wasn't testing me; she actually did like Second Adams.

They moved closer together at that point and exchanged a kiss.

The food I'd ordered showed up then, and we just discussed things in general while we ate. Goth and Adams related how they'd met last year, and then talked about the city and how things had been going since the war.

Overall it was a nice time, and when it was over I felt a lot better about things with Goth. Last night had apparently been her last 'play' for me, probably more out of habit than anything else. It seemed fairly apparent to me that she was finally moving on.

"So, no comments about older men?" I asked Laria when we'd finally gotten back to our room after replenishing our supplies.

"Well that would hardly be fair," Laria grinned at me, "Considering that I'm younger than Goth and you're older than Adams."

"Well not everyone has such discerning tastes as you do," I grinned.

"By the way she looked at him, don't be surprised if you're a grandfather soon," Laria said grinning back at me.

"Adams is a good male; I'm glad she's found somebody and is happy."

"You mean you're just glad she found somebody and you're off the hook!"

"Well, yeah," I said trying not to look too embarrassed, "but at least it's someone I'm okay with."

"Good. Now that we got that over with, how about we enjoy our last night in this rather nice bed before we leave in the morning?"

"No arguments there!"

FIVE
SALADIN - EDGEMIRE

We rode into town about an hour after the sun had set, even though we'd gotten an early start it was still a fairly long ride. I had met with Second Adams before we left; he was getting his men ready to march then, and was fairly certain he'd join us tomorrow night.

I had no idea when to expect Holse's troops, or how many he would be sending.

"Champion William," the garrison commander said when I rode in.

"Third," I paused a moment and burned a cantrip to help with my memory, I recognized him then and it came to me quickly, "Hicks, right?"

Third Hicks smiled and nodded, "Glad to see you remembered, Champion William."

"Took me a moment, that's all," I smiled and touched palms, "and please, just Will, you should remember I'm not much on the formalities off the field."

Third Hicks nodded, "Yes, Will. So, is the queen really that concerned with Barassa?"

I nodded, "She thinks that if Stivik is going to play his hand, he's going to play it when that northern army shows up, rather than wait. So she wants to be ready if it should be something that will affect us.

"This is my companion, Laria," I said introducing her, "Laria, this is Third Hicks."

Third Hicks smiled at Laria and greeted her, another male taken in by her rather striking beauty.

"Well, let me show you to your room," he said to the both of us. "Then if you want we can go up to the lookout tower and take a look at Barassa."

I had noticed the large wooden tower that had been erected since I'd been here last with the army. It reminded me of the forestry towers that used to be put up for spotting fires; it looked like a watchtower set up high on a wooden framework. Probably not anyplace you'd want to be in a storm or when the wind got blowing.

"That sounds good to me," I said and after handing the mounts off to a groom we followed him first to our room, where I dropped my pack and Laria's, then we both let him lead us to the tower.

When we got there I looked up the ladder that went up the hundred feet to the enclosed platform on top, and then looked at Laria.

"You don't have to go up, if you don't want to, Hon."

She smiled at me and shook her head, and started up first.

I followed her up with Third Hicks coming up last.

"Well, at least we can enjoy the view," he whispered.

I snickered and Laria just gave her tail a rather rude flick.

I was surprised that the ladder didn't sway all that much, nor did the tower once we got up there. Obviously it was better built than it looked.

Once inside the watch platform we found two men who were already there, looking out towards Barassa.

"Seen anything?" Third Hicks asked as he climbed in after me.

"No, Sir. Looks about the same as always," the guardsman replied.

"Champion, Sir," they both said, and moved out of the way so Laria and I could take a look.

There really wasn't much to see. The river was maybe two and a half miles wide here, I knew that currents could be rough in it during the spring thaw and during tide changes. Tonight it looked fairly calm, and I could see the lights of Barassa on the far side now that it was getting late.

Making much more than that out was hard in the darkness, perhaps I'd come back after the moon had risen, or just wait until morning.

"Any increase in shipping traffic that you've noticed?" I asked the guards.

"No, Sir. It all seems to be about normal, at least as far as we can tell from here, Sir."

I nodded, "Thanks."

I looked around the area for a couple of minutes, and then took a last look at the city.

"Well, I guess that's it for now. Know of any place we might find a meal this late in the day, Third Hicks?"

"Definitely," he said and after we climbed down the tower he led us off to a small inn that was still open, and then left us to our own devices until morning.

I took a look at Barassa again after the sun had risen, but there really wasn't anything unexpected to see. Second Adams showed up with his brigade the next morning and I directed them to set up out of sight of anyone watching from Barassa.

I didn't think it was the Barassan army we needed to impress, at least not yet. The following day and the day after that were quiet, but then the besieging army showed up.

I had gotten up in the tower early that morning, along with Laria and Second Adams and we all sat up there and watched all day long. I knew they'd be showing up, because Fel had told me in a dream before I'd woken up.

That early in the morning, you could hear the actual alarm being raised in the city, and it was possible to see people streaming into the gates for the next hour, until they were closed and the people who hadn't gotten in by then, realized their situation and fled.

We couldn't tell when the leading elements of the army arrived, because they showed up on the far side of the city, but when a company came marching around on the west side first, and then a second on the east side. It was clear that the siege had started.

We watched all day as more and more forces showed up, there were a few exchanges of arrow fire, but the attackers made sure to set up out of range. When the Barassan defenders let loose with a few of their heavier weapons, the attackers just picked up and moved their encampments further away.

"When will they attack?" Laria asked me.

"Not until they're ready," I told her. "First they have a lot of people to get into position. Then they'll either have to move up siege equipment, or build it."

"Siege equipment?" She asked looking at me.

"Ladders to climb the walls, battering rams to break down the gates, weapons to toss rocks, balls of fire, dead animals, whatever they want, into the city."

"Dead animals?" She said surprised. I noticed a couple of looks from the guards, but Second Adams just nodded.

"To spread disease. Sick animals or ones that died from being sick. You want to try and either make the people sick, or kill off the livestock they have penned up inside the city."

"And that works?"

"Sometimes," I said. "Sieges can last for years, though I'll be surprised if this one runs past the fall. Barassa's port is still open, so they can still get food and supplies. While this will hurt Barassa economically, I don't know if they can do much more than that."

We watched all day, only taking breaks for meals, then when the sun set Adams, Hicks, Laria and myself went to the inn for some ales and to discuss what we saw. Which really wasn't much.

Holse arrived with several brigades and a small cavalry detachment two days later and joined us in the watch tower.

"What are they doing to the west of town, Will?" He asked as we settled down to watch that morning. So far, there hadn't been a single attack made on the city, at least not that we could tell.

"I think they're building siege towers or something," I told him. "They've been cutting down trees there for several days now."

"Then why not do it on the east side as well?"

I shook my head, "I honestly don't know."

"Third Hicks," Holse asked looking at the garrison commander, "When does the tide go out?"

"I don't know, General. Let me go find out."

I looked over at Holse while Hicks quickly climbed down the ladder.

"You think they're up to something?"

Holse nodded, "To make this siege work, they have to block that port."

I looked back at the construction that was going on to the west of the camp, then looked at the opening to the port. Barassa had grown up along the river; the sea was about twenty miles east of here. But the riverbank wasn't all that straight along the side where Barassa was located, it was more like a lake that the river had cut one side off of, which made it a natural harbor, with a very wide mouth.

A mouth that was close to a half-mile wide.

"You think they're building something to block it, don't you?" I asked looking back at Holse.

"Wouldn't you?"

I thought about that, a chain on floats, large floats, would be ideal. But I don't think the ability to forge a chain like that existed anywhere near here. And the cost of it would be fantastic, it would have to be iron or steel, both of which were not in that great of supply yet.

But rope, with the grasslands to the east, and the many fields all of the countries had, they could make a hell of a lot of rope. But they would have had to have started on making it months, maybe even years, ago.

"Have we heard anything about an increase in rope making?" I asked Holse.

Holse shook his head. "No, but who would think to look for such a thing?"

I shook my head, "My sister would, Evean might, she's pretty smart but I don't know if she's studied that much about naval blockades."

"Well, I figure once the tide starts to turn, we'll see."

Third Hicks came back while we were mulling it over.

"The tide should turn at noon today, General."

"Good, well why don't we all take a break now, and come back then?" Holse suggested looking around.

"Sounds good to me." I agreed and the others followed suit.

Three hours later we were watching when the first small boats were launched.

There appeared to be two dozen rowers in each boat, and they were pulling a thick line, which had a large float attached to it, every forty or so feet.

Using the current to help them along, we watched as they pulled the rope from the west to the east, hundreds of soldiers working on the shoreline, moving the rope and floats into place. It took hours, but by the time the sun was starting to set, the rope was in place.

And that was when the army attacked.

The attack ran all night; siege weapons were tossing rocks and burning pitch over the walls and into the city. Twice we watched as troops charged the wall under the cover of their shields and tried to put up ladders to scale the sides.

Each time they were easily repulsed. I was surprised they hadn't built any siege towers yet, and commented on it to Holse.

"Too much of their effort was used to build the rope," Holse told me. "I'm sure they'll start on building them now, however."

"Then why attack now?" I asked. "Why not wait?"

"Scare tactics," Holse replied. "Everyone inside the city knows that they're now cut off. This attack was probably more of an attempt to hurt morale and try and inspire a panic and riots in Barassa, than to try and take it outright."

"What do you expect to happen next?"

"I expect Barassa to send out a ship to cut that rope." Holse paused a moment, "But not until after sunset tomorrow."

I nodded, it made sense.

Things were quiet all the next day, except for the constant barrage on Barassa by the catapults. When the next morning came, sure enough, the rope had been cut. But apparently the besieging army had been ready for this. They reeled in the broken part on the eastern side, pulled it out at a landing that some of the troops had been working on, and then they spent a few hours transporting it back around to the other side. Once there they attached it to the moored section, and then let the whole thing play out as the boats from before rowed out to the end, and towed it towards the anchorage.

The next morning, when we awoke there was now a small ship lashed to the center of the barricade, flying the flag of the allied army.

"Apparently they laid a trap for the rope cutting party last night," I observed.

"And got themselves a nice prize in the process," Holse agreed. "Someone apparently has given this a lot of thought."

"It looks like they're building a fort now," Laria said, pointing to the western anchorage of the rope barricade.

Holse stopped and watched for a while, before saying anything.

"I don't think they're going to be leaving when the winter comes, William." Holse said after awhile. "In fact, I think they mean to stay until the city has fallen."

I nodded slowly. If King Stivik hadn't been desperate before, he'd be getting desperate now.

§ §

"Hi Fel," I said picking up my beer and nodding to him. "What's up?"

"Well, I wanted you to know first of all that Holse's observation was correct. The allied Army is settling in for a long stay. They've been planning this for some time now."

"And you knew this, of course?"

Fel smiled, "It's another one of those god things, William. I knew but couldn't act on it, until I was 'made aware' of it."

"So, what is King Stivik going to do? Think he'll make a stand of it, or will he gather up his family and try to make a run through the blockade?"

"Stivik is weighing his options, what few he still has."

"What about Tantrus? Surely his priests and followers are not very happy about this situation?"

"What Tantrus does in his temples and with his priests is beyond my sight, you know that, William."

"Well, aren't there anybody else's followers or priests inside the city? I'd expect there to be some! That place is huge after all."

Fel shook his head slowly, "Tantrus's priests and champion have been very busy for the last two years. They scoured the entire city, from one end to the other, killing any rival priests, and any followers of any rival religion. Large sections of the city have now been blessed and warded. Tantrus has been moving to keep the eyes of the other gods and goddesses from seeing into the city for some time."

I thought about that a moment, "That's not good, is it?"

Fel shrugged, "Tantrus is about to be forced out of the game. It's only natural for him to do everything he can to hide his followers' moves. I don't see what he can possibly do, but whatever it is, it won't involve us."

"Is that why we're not part of this holy war?" I asked wondering.

Fel laughed, "No, we weren't invited to the party because everyone else thinks I'm strong enough already. The other leaders feel the same way about Rachel. They didn't want her to have any claim on the city either."

"I'm not sure she would have wanted it," I paused and took a sip of my beer. "She's mentioned to me more than once that she's worried about being overextended. She'd like to spend a few more years consolidating and get Holden secured via Baron's wedding before moving on again. I think her eyes have been looking more to the south."

Fel nodded. "I'm going to have a task for you in a few weeks, for now you can stay and keep an eye on things. But it looks like the situation here is going to be static for a very long time."

I nodded, "Static is good. Besides, it's nice for Barassa and Stivik to be somebody else's problem for a change!"

Fel smiled and reaching over gave me a pat on the shoulder and I fell into a deeper sleep.

Six
Saladin - Edgemire

I woke up with a start; there was a loud noise, a very loud noise.

It was hard to describe, it was primal, and full of anger and terror, but it wasn't natural. It sounded like a cross between the monster of all elephants, and the sound you'd think a large warship would make if it sailed across a reef and tore off its metal bottom.

I could hear the frightened shouts of people as they awoke, Laria was suddenly clinging to me in confusion and fear.

I grabbed my weapons harness with one hand, her with the other, and I ran outside of the officer's barracks into the pre-dawn light.

The sound came again, clearer now that I was outside, and I could hear echoes from the earlier noise. Whatever it was, it wasn't nearby.

I threw Laria over my shoulder and ran for the tower. Officers were starting to spill out of their quarters and started trying to make some order out of the mess of confused and panicking people.

"Are we under attack, Will?" Holse yelled as I ran past him.

"Not yet!" I said and slinging my harness over my other shoulder I climbed up the tower ladder as fast as I could.

When I got there, both of the guards on watch were standing, transfixed, looking to the north, towards Barassa with their mouths hanging open.

Setting Laria down I turned to look as I donned my weapon's harness, then froze myself.

Rising out of the center of the city was a monster. A large monster. A *Huge* monster.

"What... what is that, thing?" Laria asked, seizing my arm in a death grip and trembling against me.

"I'm... not sure," I said slowly. At first I thought it might be a dragon, the thought of that scared the hell out of me, and I remembered to do the eyes and ears things for Fel, whatever it was, he would surely know!

As it rose up onto its hind legs, its body reminded me more of a t-rex than a dragon, though it had much larger and thicker arms. Something about it looked familiar, but I couldn't place exactly what.

It reared its head back, and let out that horrible cry again, then bending forward a beam of, *something*, came from its open mouth and it started to scour the city in front of it.

"It's destroying the city!" One of the guards said.

"The attackers must have summoned it!" The other one said.

I watched as it jumped forward and started to stomp its way towards the east end of the city, its massive tail slamming into buildings in its wake.

When it got to the wall, it kicked it down, then stomping out; it started in on the army that was gathered to the south.

"I don't think the army summoned it," I said.

"What in the name of Feliogustus is that thing?"

I turned and saw Holse panting hard and looking with the rest of us. He must have come up the ladder right behind me.

"I don't think it's a dragon," I said.

"What's a dragon?"

"Something like that, only with wings."

"Well, thank Feliogustus that it can't fly!" Holse said fervently. "I hope it can't swim either!"

We watched for the next hour as it chased the troops to the south of Barassa around, breathing on them, stomping on them, bending down low and apparently even eating them.

Many of them fled before the monster, how many died I had no idea.

It turned then and stomped westward, around the outside of the city, which obscured our view of what happened to the army stationed there, though from the number of times it used its breath weapon, I'm sure it was fairly nasty.

Then suddenly, it turned south, and stomped through Barassa, once again doing massive amounts of damage from what we could see, until it reached the harbor, where it jumped in, destroying or swamping all of the ships, as it sunk out of sight, beneath the water in a massive wave.

"Do you think it's coming this way?" One of the men asked.

I shook my head slowly as I watched; it was big enough that if it started swimming this way, we'd see the water move.

"I think its resting," I said.

"What is that thing?" Laria asked.

I looked at my arm, where she was still clinging to me tightly. Her claws had sunk in fairly deeply and my arm was rather bloody. We'd been up here for hours and I hadn't even noticed.

Laria noticed me looking at my arm then, and she gasped and slowly withdrew her claws and let go.

"I think we need to have a staff meeting," Holse said looking at me, and then looking back at Barassa. A number of fires had broken out in the city now, and what was left of the army to the west was pulling out rather quickly.

"I'll be there soon," I said and healing my arm I gave Laria a hug, "I just need to check on a few things first," and then I followed Holse down the ladder.

I'd hoped to be able to go take a nap and talk to Fel about what was going on, there was a small church here, but I didn't think it was big enough for him to be able to manifest his voice and talk to me.

But the camp, the town, and even the army, was still in chaos. The sound of the thing, whatever it was, was quite fear-inducing, and the sight of it stomping around and destroying both Barassa and the army attacking it, hadn't been very reassuring either.

So I found myself having to call on my champion's aura and had to spend the next hour improving morale of the army and then calming the general populace down. When I finished with that, I went and joined Holse and the other officers.

"Ah, finally," Holse sighed as I joined the meeting. "I didn't want to bother you, whatever that thing is, the effect it had on morale needed to be dealt with first."

"Which leads us to the next question," Second Adams said. "What is that?"

I shook my head, "I have no idea. I haven't been able to talk to Feliogustus yet to see what he can tell me about it."

"Where did it come from?" First Mossic, who had come down with Holse asked next.

"I'm not sure, but I have my suspicions, and they're not good."

"Oh?" Holse asked.

"Remember that wyvern that we had to deal with up in Hidden Vale?"

Everyone nodded.

"You think it's from the same place?" Holse asked.

"The same, or similar; and that's bad because most of our weapons can't hurt it."

"But you killed it, didn't you?" First Mossic asked.

"The thing that I killed was a tenth the size of this monster," I said looking around the room. "Killing this thing isn't going to be easy and I have no idea where to even start. Right now, it's not our problem, thankfully. But that's not the worst of it."

"It gets worse?" Third Hicks said looking rather forlorn.

I nodded, "I'm afraid so, if the portal that thing came from is still open, we may be seeing more of them."

Holse nodded and sat up straight and looked around, taking stock of everybody.

"Okay," he began, "here are my orders. Mossic, take the army and leave, immediately. I want you to wait up at Rivervail for further instructions. Send one rider back to the Capitol with the information of what happened here, a second to Duke Eklin in Marland, and a third to King Charles in Holden.

"Now go."

"Yes, General," First Mossic stood up, saluted, and left, taking his aides with him.

"Second Adams, you are to return to Marland immediately with your brigade."

"You're leaving us undefended?" Third Hicks said his eyes wide in surprise.

"You saw what that thing did to the Northern army!" Holse said looking at him. "I'd rather not draw its attention here to us with lots of soldiers milling around."

"You have your orders, Second Adams."

"Yes, General!" Second Adams stood, and saluted, leaving the room with his men in tow.

"Now, Hicks," General Holse said turning back to him. "I want you to take your men, and go around town and see who you can talk into leaving until this problem is resolved. Take those that are willing to go, and have your men escort them to one of the towns south of here. Keep a guard in the tower at all times, and if that thing starts to cross the river, send out riders to warn us, then evacuate the town.

"Understood?"

Third Hicks stood up and saluted, "Yes, General. Sorry for doubting you, General." He then turned and left the room.

Holse looked at me and sighed. "I'm leaving with Mossic. If you have any suggestions, Will, I'm all ears."

Standing up as Holse got up to leave I shook my head, "I haven't a clue, Holse. Not a single one."

I went and found Laria; she was in the room, packing our things and obviously more than ready to leave.

"When are we leaving?" she said to me as I came in and sat on the bed.

"Not for a while yet," I said stretching. It was mid-afternoon and I was starving.

"Let's go find some food."

"Food?" She said and looked at me.

"Yes, food. Everyone is still rather panicked, including you. That thing isn't going to be coming over here anytime soon. So I need to take the time to calm everybody down, and my sitting down and eating will hopefully do just that. Plus, I'm starving." I said and standing up, I took her hand and led her outside to see if we could find a meal.

With the army packing up and heading out, the mess was already closed, but when I got to the inn, they were still serving food. In fact the place was rather crowded with locals.

"Hey!" One of them yelled as I walked in.

"Yes?" I said while flagging down one of the harried serving girls and looking for a place to sit.

"Why is the army leaving? Who is gonna protect us?"

"If you have family, I would suggest you evacuate to the south. The local garrison is going to be setting that up for whoever wants to go." I said, using a cantrip to make sure my voice was heard by everyone.

"Right now, there isn't anything we can do against the monster, and we felt it would be best to move the army away, so as to not draw its attention. Until it crosses the river, *if* it crosses the river even, it's not our problem.

"There is a huge army on the other side of the river, for now, I'd rather let them deal with it. Anyone here disagree with that idea?"

I looked around and everyone was shaking their heads. More than a few people were muttering that not attracting any attention was the best idea they'd heard so far.

"So, what happens now?" Laria asked as we sat down, several people had cleared a spot for us and a serving girl came over with a platter of food and a pitcher of ale.

I shrugged, "I won't know until I've had the chance to discuss this with Fel. I need to find out how to kill it first. After that, well there are two champions on the other side of the river, so we might not even have to deal with it."

Laria shivered a bit and leaned into me as I started in on the food that the serving girl had left. I was a bit surprised that I wasn't feeling anything urgent from Fel. Then again, there were four different religions involved on the other side of things, and two of them had their champions there. It may very well be that he figured they had this well in hand and that he didn't need to worry about it.

After we ate I returned to the tower with Laria and the two guards normally stationed up there to see what was going on.

There were still a couple of fires burning in the city, the blockade barrier that had been across the harbor had been broken, probably when the monster had settled into the water and caused the wave that swamped or sunk most of the ships. So while the port was now unblocked, there wasn't a single ship floating in the harbor.

I could see some elements of the attacking Northern army were gathering to the west of the city, a lot further off than they had been before. There appeared to be military units to the east going through the wreckage as well, though whose side they were on was anybody's guess from this distance.

Occasionally there would be a disturbance on the surface of the water in the harbor; I guess the monster was still there. What it was doing, I had no idea. Sleeping or eating perhaps? Something as big as it probably burned a lot of energy moving around, so maybe it wasn't active for very long periods during the day.

At least I hoped it wasn't. And if it needed water to live in, that meant it was a lot less likely to come up the river and cause problems. At least not past Rivervail, where the falls were, or so I hoped.

By the time night had come, all of the army units were long gone, and Third Hicks had organized a large group of townspeople who would be heading to one of the towns further south of here come morning.

I had freed Tom and Jeri from the stalls where the wolats were normally kept, and were keeping them nearby, just in case we had to leave quickly. Considering the way they were now acting, I think they were more than happy to stay near us as well. Apparently the cry of that creature had spooked more than just the townspeople.

§   §

"Fel!" I said sitting up in the bar, "What the hell is that thing? Where the hell did it come from?"

Fel shook his head slowly, "We're not exactly sure, but we think Tantrus just went 'nuclear' on us, to use one of your world's expressions."

I looked at him blankly, "Huh?"

"It's a doomsday weapon. Apparently Tantrus's temple was built on top of, or next to, a rather large gate to an underworld sphere. A number of us are starting to suspect he had figured out a way to use it to his benefit, or possibly even had a deal with one of the gods in the negative plane.

"So, when Tantrus realized that the situation was desperate, for him and his religion at least, he had his priests clear the portal entrance, and this is what came out."

"Is the portal still open?"

Fel shook his head, "The monster did so much damage to the city when it came out that we're fairly certain that the portal is obscured for now."

I sighed, "So, what's our next step? How do we kill it?"

"We're not sure."

"What?" I said surprised. "You're a god, how can you not be sure?"

Fel gave a small laugh, "It's from the negative plane, William. We can't see into it, just as they can't see into here.

This is not a common monster; tracking down the myths isn't easy for something like this. We have a lead, and we will be pursuing it."

I nodded, "Who's 'we', anyway?"

"The rest of the gods on the plane of Saladin."

I blinked. "I thought you weren't on speaking terms with the other gods?"

"William, this monster could destroy the entire world. Our armies can't stop it, and if anymore come through that portal, we're in serious trouble. This thing isn't like a dragon, where you can reason with it, try to bribe it, without having to resort to killing it.

"This monster isn't much smarter than a wolat, if that. It's the most dangerous and toughest life form on the plane it came here from. All of the other gods see how dangerous it is, and are willing to do what they can to help."

"What about Tantrus?"

"Considering the monster kicked over his temple and ate half of his priests, including the high priest, Tantrus isn't capable of doing much of anything. Not that anyone wants anything to do with him anymore," Fel sighed. "Tantrus over played his hand. Maybe he had been hoping for something else, something he could control, but that thing did as much damage to Barassa as it did to the armies surrounding it."

"How badly were the armies hit?"

"About a third of the soldiers were killed. Evean organized a fairly large pikeman's square that annoyed it enough that it decided to go sleep in the harbor for now."

"Well good for her. Can I talk to her about it? Maybe she can tell me something to help us if it comes across the river."

"Sure," Fel said and suddenly Evean was sitting in the bar with us.

"Wow," She said looking around. "So this is your god's domain?" She said and smiled at me. "No wonder you and he are such good friends!"

"That was quick," I said, "I figured I'd have to wait until you went to sleep or something."

"Nah, I'm dead."

"Dead?" I looked at her surprised.

"Yeah, when the gojira stepped on us, it killed me and half a company."

"Gojira?" I said looking at her, "You know what this thing is?"

"Of course I do, I told you I liked movies, Will. The Japanese made lots of movies about them."

"Wait," I stopped and thought a moment. "You mean to tell me, that thing out there is Godzilla?"

Evean nodded, "More or less. How the Japanese picked up the legend of it, I have no idea. Maybe some portal traveler brought it through, and wrote a story about it."

"That seems like a bit of a stretch to me," I said. "Then again, the sound that it made," I said and shuddered, thinking about it.

"Big lizard with a breath weapon that likes to stomp on things and lives in the water," Evean shrugged, "Sounds like a gojira to me."

"So, how do we kill it?"

"Simple, we just need to find us an Okishijen Desootoria."

"What's that?"

"It's the weapon they used to kill gojira in the first movie."

"And you think it will work?"

"Those of us who know about it," Fel said, breaking into the conversation, "do."

"So, where do we go to get it, and when do we leave?" I asked.

"We?" Evean said looking at me.

"It's a threat to my people as well as yours, besides, I think I owe you one," I smiled.

"After Evean reincarnates, you'll be leaving. A couple of the other gods will be sending people with you."

"Anyone that I know?" I asked.

"Jane."

"Aww," Evean frowned. "If Jane comes along, how am I supposed to get Will in bed?"

"Oh, I'm sure you'll find a way," Fel laughed.

"Gee, thanks," I grumbled. "Will anyone else be coming with us? Any of yours and Aryanna's friends?"

"Suzona, Gregory, and Joseph."

"Why them?" I asked curious. I liked Joseph, Gregory was okay, Suzona however left a little to be desired. Mainly because she had the biggest ego I'd ever run across. It didn't help that she was entitled to it either.

"They're all from high-tech worlds, and we believe the Okishijen Desootoria comes from just such a world."

"You don't know for sure?" I asked surprised.

"That's why were sending so many of you," Fel said.

"At least we know where to start," Evean told me.

"Oh? Where's that?"

"Japan, of course."

SEVEN
SALADIN - HILAND

"You're taking Laria with you!" Rachel growled.

I sighed, this argument had been going on for probably longer than any argument we'd ever had. Not that we'd had all that many.

"No, I can't."

"Yes, you can, and you will, William!"

"There are going to be eight other champions on this quest, eight! Only three of them I trust, and of those three, one of them I'm not even sure of half the time, seeing as I *killed* her once! Three more of them are from here, this plane, and their gods and their countries aren't even on good terms with us!

"I don't need that kind of liability, Rachel! Laria will end up dead, and it will be *my* fault because somebody will try to use her against me!"

"I told you before, William, you will do as I say, and you will take her, or else!"

I growled long and low and I jumped on Rachel pinning her to the bed.

"I've had enough of this, Rachel. You may be the queen, but you are *my* wife! And like it or not, this time you are going to do what *I* tell you, or I'll put you over my knee and spank your royal ass! Do you understand me?"

"You wouldn't dare!" she growled back.

I grabbed her wrists in one hand, rolled over to a sitting position, pulling her with me and dragging her across my lap I curled a leg around hers to lock them in position, and then started to spank her.

She screamed and she swore and the guards stayed the hell out of the room. We didn't have many knockdown drag outs, but when we did, everyone cleared out.

I stopped after six and then waited for her to run down. She was pissed, but then I was pissed as well. Maybe I should have brought her down to the temple and had Fel tell her for me. But dammit, she had to understand that I wasn't doing this just to get another plaything.

"Hon," I said in a much softer voice, "You know I love you, but you have to understand that many of us are going to die on this quest. That's why they're sending so many of us. We have to be fast and we can't be safe, and we can't wait for anyone. Laria isn't able to jump portals, and she's mortal.

"I can't take the time to watch out for her or protect her. If she gets in trouble, I'll have to let her die."

Rachel froze at that.

"You'd let her die?" She asked.

"If it would be the choice between saving thousands of our people, or her. Of course I'd let her die, I'd have no choice. You'd do the same thing, and you know it."

Rachel sighed, and then whacked me in the face with her tail.

"I'm still mad at you," she growled.

"Well don't kill me," I said, only half-joking. "We're leaving tomorrow and Fel will be pissed if I don't go with them. This monster may be in Barassa right now, but eventually it may cross the river and be in your Kingdom."

"Let me up," she growled.

I did and pulled her close, she was being stiff and prickly; all of her claws were digging into me somewhere. Rachel did not like losing, ever, to anyone, even me. Usually I let her get her way, but every once in a while I still took the time to remind her that we were husband and wife first, Queen and Champion second, and sometimes we were going to do things my way. Like it or not.

"You can leave her home," Rachel said still softly growling.

"You *will not* take this out on her, Hon." I said and gave her a hug. "I already had this argument with her last night and she's terrified of what you're going to do to her."

I felt Rachel relax a little, "No, I will not take it out on her. I know it's not her fault. But if you bring home any surprises, you are likely to wake up dead.

"Several times!" She growled.

"Why are you getting so possessive these days?" I asked, a little surprised. "I thought you didn't mind my occasional dalliances?"

"It's nothing," Rachel said and turned her head away from me.

I grabbed her chin and slowly turned her face back to mine. "It's important to me, you're important to me, Rachel. Tell me."

A strange expression ghosted over her face for a moment, anger, fear, sadness, I wasn't sure which.

"I'm not getting any younger, William."

I stiffened a moment, she hadn't said 'love' or 'dear'; she'd said my name.

"But you aren't getting any older," she sighed and buried her face in my chest and started to cry.

"You know I love you more than I've ever loved anyone, ever, Hon. You know that, right?" I whispered softly, holding her and letting her cry into my chest, her arms coming around and clinging to me.

"I'm getting old, old! Eventually I'll be old and gray and you won't! You'll have all of those young girls throwing themselves at you! How am I to compete with that?"

"Do you want me to quit?" I asked softly.

Rachel gasped and looked up at me. "What?"

"Do you want me to quit? I could ask Fel to make me look older, look my age, before I did."

"You'd do that?" Rachel's expression was rather shocked. "For me?"

I nodded, "Of course I would. I've been meaning to ask Fel to make me look older anyway."

"You really do love me, don't you, Hon?" Rachel said, and I lowered my head and gave her a kiss.

"Yes, I really do. If you want me to quit, when I get back from this quest, after we get rid of this monster, I'll quit. I don't care how old you get, or how old you look, Love. I know when this life is over, we'll be together in the afterlife, and if I can't love you here, until the end, how could you love me there?"

I kissed her again and then I pulled her down to the bed and made love to her. I meant what I had said, if Rachel wanted me to quit, I'd quit.

The next morning when I left, Rachel looked a lot happier, if thoughtful. Laria was still a little concerned, but Rachel had taken the time to put her at ease with the situation.

I walked down to the temple, I really wasn't sure where we were going next, just when to show up. I wasn't even sure who was going to be in charge of the group.

"Morning, Fel," I said when I walked into the temple.

"William," Fel's voice replied.

"I'm sorry about what I said last night," I sighed.

"William," Fel's voice was lighter this time, "if you didn't love her, you wouldn't be who you are, or as good a champion as to our people as you are. I'll talk with her, after she's had some time to think about it. I'd rather not lose you, but if it's what the two of you want, I won't complain."

I nodded, I wasn't quite sure if it was what I wanted, there were still a lot of places I'd like to travel to, and things I'd like to see, if the infinite really was infinite. But I didn't want to lose Rachel, ever.

"Thanks, Fel. She was pretty upset and, well, I've been worried about something like this for a while now."

I looked around, no one else was around. I thought Jane would be leaving from here as well.

"Where am I off to?"

"Japan, as I said."

"Where is everyone?"

"You'll all be meeting at the same, spot."

I nodded, "Who is in charge?"

"Evean, she not only knows the most about the item, but she also speaks Japanese."

"Well, I guess I get to finally see just how ugly she is," I sighed shaking my head. "I hope I don't do anything stupid."

"I've found that knowing someone makes a huge difference in what you think about their looks, William."

"Then I'm doomed," I sighed.

"Well, let me open up the portal for you."

"So, just where in Japan am I going?"

"Tottori." Fel laughed then, "Doesn't help much, does it?"

"Nope," I said and stepped through the portal as it opened.

"Will?"

I turned and saw a young woman, the first thing I noticed was she had a rather nice figure; the second was that she was ugly. She had a cleft palate that hadn't been dealt with properly, as well as a weak eye, and several of those 'port-wine stain' type birthmarks on her face.

"You haven't done the cosmetic surgery?" I said walking up to her.

"No 'hello, Evean, it's nice to see you, Evean?'" she grumbled at me.

I shrugged and gave her a hug and a kiss. "It's nice to see you, Evean, I'm glad you're here, Evean, where the hell are we going, Evean?" I said and smiled at her.

She paused a moment and looked at me surprised.

"You kissed me."

I shrugged, "I seem to recall doing that the last time I saw you and hadn't seen you in a while."

"Yeah, but..." she stopped then, looked at me a moment, "boy scout," she mumbled and then moved on. "We're the first here, the others should be coming through shortly, but I wanted to go over the plan with you before they do.

"First, we need to find out who designed the monster for the movie. Then we need to go talk to them, and see if we can find out where they got the idea from."

"Do you think they were a portal jumper?" I asked.

She shrugged, "Maybe, maybe not. Could be they learned of it from someone else. I don't know. But it's the first spot to start. It beats the other option."

"What's the other option?"

"We go through the portal in Barassa and try to backtrack through a portal there to the place that can kill them."

I shook my head; I didn't see that working very well at all.

"Will?" I heard, followed by a string of what I could only guess was Japanese.

I turned and there was a rather tall Japanese woman there, she looked like Jane, so I figured it was her.

"Hi Jane," I said and she looked at me funny. Evean said something to her and Jane nodded and said something back.

"Why can't I understand her?" I asked Evean.

"Jane's never been here before, so her template locked her in as a Japanese woman. She won't know any other languages here. Same for the three others coming from Saladin."

Suddenly I realized why it was so important that Evean spoke Japanese, as well as English. I was from here, so my template was North American and English speaker. Joseph, Suzona, and Gregory had been here before and were locked in as European looking English speakers. As long as we were in

Japan, half the team wouldn't be able to speak to the other half, except via Evean.

Joseph showed up next, followed quickly by Suzona and Gregory. I introduced them all to Evean, Joseph didn't react to her appearance at all, Gregory and Suzona both did, but at least Gregory seemed to get over it almost immediately.

The other three showed up in quick succession then, and as expected they all looked Japanese and spoke only Japanese. Evean introduced them to the rest of us; they were Loomis, Shin, and Teshes, which was the Saladin word for Tuesday.

I looked at Evean, "Her parents named her Tuesday?"

Evean laughed, "Yeah, I know. According to Roden, all of her sibs were named for a different day of the week."

"I can imagine that must have been rough. Are all three of them homegrown then?"

"Homegrown?"

"Native to Saladin."

"Oh, Teshes and Loomis are. Shin comes from someplace else."

I nodded.

"Tell them," Evean waved to the other English speakers, "The basic plan; I need to fill these folks in on Japan and what I need them to do."

"Sure," I turned to Joseph, Gregory and Suzona. "Evean is in charge, I'm second."

"Why?" Suzona asked.

"Because," I sighed and rolled my eyes. "Any other stupid questions?"

"It's not stupid!"

"Actually, it is. She knows the country where we are, and speaks the language. She's also the only one who recognized the monster and knows how to destroy it."

Suzona started to open her mouth and I raised a finger, "So we are going to look for the one person here, who we believe to be connected to the history of the monster here, and see if they can tell us what sphere the weapon that kills the monster comes from."

"The monster doesn't come from here?" Gregory asked.

"No, the monster comes from one of the negative energy planes."

"And the weapon doesn't come from here either?" Gregory asked.

"No."

"Then why are we here?" he asked looking perplexed.

"Because about forty years ago, someone made a movie with a creature that looks, sounds, and acts a lot like our monster. They also had a weapon in the movie that killed it. We think that either the author was a portal jumper, or heard the story from one.

"So we're off to find them, and talk to them."

"It sounds stupid," Suzona said and scowled at me.

"Joseph?" I asked.

He shrugged, "Just how big is this monster, anyway?"

"I'm not sure, one hundred and fifty feet maybe?"

"How tall are you again?"

"Six foot."

All three of them paused a moment.

"That's big," Gregory said, and the other two both nodded.

"Okay," Evean said and turned back to us. "Let's get going, follow me."

"Where are we going?" Suzona asked.

"Into town to catch a train. Then off to a town you've never heard of, to find a man whose name you don't know." Evean said and smiled rather sweetly at Suzona. On her face it didn't look all that sweet however. I could suddenly see why Evean could be such a bitch at times, and I suddenly suspected Suzona had met her match, though *she* might not have figured that out yet.

Suzona grumbled and fell to the back of the group to talk with Gregory, who seemed more than happy to talk with her, Joseph tagged along with me as I followed Evean, Jane and the other three following us.

"So, you know where this guy lives?" I asked softly

Evean shook her head, "Nope, haven't got a clue. But I think the company that made the movie is in Tokyo. So we'll head there first, ask some questions, and go find this guy."

"That easy?" Joseph asked.

"They made like a dozen sequels to the first movie, they were all huge," Evean said. "This guy is probably famous. I don't think we're going to have any trouble finding him."

"Well, at least its not hostile territory." I said.

"But we don't speak the language," Joseph sighed.

"Well, they do," I nodded to the ones with Jane, "and Evean here does."

"Don't worry about it," Evean said. "Almost everyone here speaks English."

"Really?"

"Yup."

"When was the last time you were here?" I asked curious.

"Ten, fifteen years maybe? Doesn't matter." Evean looped her arm around mine and smiled at me. I just shrugged and smiled back. For some reason, I was a lot less paranoid about Evean here. Then again, she didn't look like a sex goddess here, or have the ability to cause my hormones to go on a rampage using pheromones, so maybe that helped.

We walked for a couple of hours, and eventually came to the outskirts of a small city. Evean led us to what was apparently the local portal jumper's trading house, and converted some gems into cash, and then bought us all train tickets to Tokyo.

Next she led us to a small noodle shop of some kind and ordered us all food while we waited for our train, then led us onboard and got us situated.

To be honest, I was impressed. Evean was efficient, decisive, and able to get us to do what she wanted us to do without being offensive about it.

I noticed as we traveled on the train that the locals all seemed to snub Evean, I wasn't sure that it was her looks however, she was obviously *not* Japanese, the only one other than those of us who were Caucasian, on the train. The Japanese looking members of our party were treated with the typical behavior of the locals for another. Polite, but no real interest.

Suzona however they were all over, given her six-foot tall, blond, svelte and busty super-heroine female appearance.

Gregory, Joseph, and I got some attention, a lot of people wanted to practice their English on us, and I left that to the others.

"So why are they snubbing you?" I asked Evean quietly after the other people had left us alone.

"They don't like Vietnamese people," Evean said rather matter-of-factly, "Most Japanese people don't like the other Asian races and worse yet, I'm a half-breed."

"Half-breed?" I said looking at her curiously.

"My father was a Frenchman. Least my mother thought he was French. He was with the French forces that were in Vietnam before you Americans came in."

"Oh, what happened to him?"

"He died in the war when I was still a baby."

"Sorry to hear that."

Evean shrugged a shoulder, "It all happened a long time ago."

"So why are they all over Suzona like flies?"

Evean giggled, "Because they like big tall and very sexy American women here. She's going to be opening up a lot of doors for us."

"I'm not so sure she's going to like that," I warned.

"Too bad for her then," Evean looking at me, and gave me an evil grin, one that really did look evil.

"You know, you really should go for that surgery," I said.

"Why? Don't like looking at me?" Evean said giving me a hostile look now.

"No, it's because I can see it bothers you, a lot. You can afford to fix it now, get it fixed. We suffer enough for our gods, no reason for us to suffer about anything else, is there?"

"No," She said settling back into the seat and losing the hostile expression.

"So, what are we going to tell these people when we get to Tokyo?"

"We're an advance team from a small studio in southern California that is looking to do a documentary on the kaiju movies that were done here in the sixties and the seventies."

"Think they'll buy that?" I asked surprised.

"Well, I have a nice set of counterfeit identification that says that's who we are, and tall, blond, and Viking, over there bears a remarkable resemblance to a rather popular female actress back in America."

I laughed, "Well she's sure insufferable enough for it."

"You don't like her much, do you?" Evean asked.

"Oh, she's alright, most of the time. Her attitude just rubs me the wrong way occasionally."

"She's always the hottest bitch in the room and she knows it."

I nodded, "Exactly."

"Worse then me even?" Evean asked, grinning at me.

I shook my head. "You never copped an attitude over it, Evean. You go into a bar; you buy everyone a drink even though you're the hottest gal in town. She's goes into a bar and she expects everyone to bow down and buy her drinks."

"Want to piss her off?" Evean asked giving me a wink.

I looked at her, "What did you have in mind?"

"This," She said and leaned over in her seat to press up against me.

I noticed Suzona looked up from the man she was chatting with and shot me a glare.

I put an arm around Evean and closed my eyes relaxing back against her.

"This I can do," I laughed softly.

As we were taking a train, I had thought it was going to be a long trip, but it was surprisingly rather quick. The trains here were incredibly fast, as well as comfortable. A little less than six hours after we left, we were in Tokyo. It was late at night, so Evean made a few phone calls and found us a hotel to stay at. So once again we all marched off after her to it.

Suzona was playing up to Gregory, who seemed happy with the attention. I knew that they had slept together fairly often the last time we'd been together, while Joseph had avoided her like the plague and I'd tried to as well.

But she kept shooting me nasty glances, as I walked along with Evean to the hotel. As Suzona and I had only slept together that one time, I was rather surprised by that.

"Somebody is on the warpath," Joseph said to me when we got to the hotel as Evean went up to the desk and booked us rooms.

"I noticed. Any idea why?"

"Because she thinks she's the alpha bitch and that all the men should be sniffing around her, but you're not."

"Well you're not either."

"But I haven't slept with her," Joseph smirked, "you have. And now you're paying attention to a woman who she sees as far below her."

I sighed and shook my head, "Suzona is going to be in for a very rude awakening when Evean lowers the boom on her."

"I don't know, Will. Suzona is a pretty tough cookie."

"Yeah, but I'm not afraid of Suzona."

"But you're afraid of Evean?" he asked looking over at her as she collected the room keys and turned to walk back to us.

"Evean terrifies me. Ask Jane about her sometime."

"Okay, I have four rooms, so who is sharing with who?" Evean said.

Suzona walked up and grabbed a key and started to look at me when Evean continued.

"Actually, make that three, Will and I are already sharing one together," and she just winked at Suzona, who turned on her heel, grabbing Gregory as she stalked off.

Joseph grabbed the next key and then took Jane by the hand and smiled at her. She nodded and the two of them walked off.

Evean handed the remaining key to Loomis, Shin, and Teshes, said something to them in Japanese and then after showing them where their room was, she led me off to ours.

"I finally get you all to myself, and in bed no less, and I look like this," Evean grumbled.

"I'm surprised you haven't switched to your Champion form," I said taking off my shoes and relaxing.

"Would you sleep with me if I did?" She asked, but apparently already knew the answer.

"Not tonight, no," I said grinning.

"Well, I'm going to use the bathroom, then you can have it."

"Sure," I agreed.

Evean quickly stripped, and I had to admit, she did have a nice body. However she had a couple more of those port-wine stains on her upper body, and they were fairly large. I didn't think they looked bad, but I could see how she wouldn't think so, when you added everything else up.

When we finally got settled she turned the light out and cuddled up against me.

"Well, now that it's nice and dark, how about we fool around some?"

I sighed, "Turn the light on, Evean."

"Why?" she said, and I could faintly hear the hurt sound in her voice. She was trying to hide it, but I could tell it was there.

"Because I want to look at you while we make love," I said and rolled over and kissed her.

"Are you serious?" she whispered surprised.

"Very."

The light came back on.

EIGHT
EARTH - TOKYO

Morning came, and Evean was so incredibly happy that it was almost painful. As for me, I wasn't sure I'd ever be able to walk again.

The truth is, I really did like Evean, after the time we'd spent together on Siren we'd developed a fairly close friendship. I knew she wanted to get me in bed, I'd known that for sometime now, but back home, on Saladin, where she probably was the most beautiful woman in the entire world, it was kind of scary to have that kind of woman focused on you.

But here? Looking like she did? Well Fel was right, it didn't really bug me that much and she was now a lot more, I guess you'd say 'accessible'. It wasn't scary having a woman like her interested in me here.

Plus I knew it would make her happy, and again, I really did like her.

The problem now however, was that she hadn't been kidding when she told me years ago that she'd been taught everything the priests and priestesses in her order knew about sex. I'd slept with a lot of women over the years, some of whom were very experienced in the ways of love and sex.

Sex with Evean was, well, to be honest I was at a complete lack of words for it. Amazing, fantastic, and unbelievable just didn't seem to do it justice. She did things that I didn't even know were possible.

"I think you broke me," I moaned as the sun came through the window.

"Want me to kiss it and make it better?" Evean teased.

"I was kind of hoping to get an hour or two of sleep before the others woke up," I groaned rolling over to face her. I don't think I'd ever seen her so happy before, and I'd seen her happy quite a few times. "What's got your motor revving so much? Still trying to kill me?"

Evean kissed me and cuddled up closer. "No one has ever done that before, Will. You're the first."

I pulled the covers up and then put an arm around her; Evean was definitely very cuddle-able. "You expect me to believe no one has ever made love to you before?"

She shook her head, "No, not here, not ever. Oh, I've had sex here, more than a few times. With the lights out, in the dark, with men who didn't mind using my body, as long as they didn't have to look at me."

I didn't know what to say to that, so I didn't say anything. I just gave her a kiss and closed my eyes and got some sleep.

Or tried to at least, Evean still had other ideas.

"What happened to you?" Joseph asked when we all sat down to eat breakfast.

"Evean happened," I said and yawned.

"What, she beat you up or something?" he teased.

"Or something. I think like eight hours straight of 'or something'. I thought taking her on in her original form would be safe. Boy was I wrong!"

"That good?" Gregory asked from next to Joseph, we were all sitting along a counter; eating breakfast. Evean was standing at the far end, talking in Japanese to Jane, Loomis, Shin, and Teshes.

"The term good is an insult in its inability to fully describe what happened last night," I said and yawned again.

Suzona shot us a dirty look. "Men and your bragging."

"I'm not bragging about me," I pointed out, "I'm just telling the truth about Evean. I mean I've heard the stories, now I know the truth."

"Stories?" Joseph asked, "Now I'm really curious."

"Well, understand her champion form is from the same place as mine, only hers is quite incredibly beautiful."

"And?"

"She leads armies into combat ...."

"I lead armies into combat!" Suzona interrupted.

"... stark naked," I finished. "With a sword."

Gregory laughed as Suzona turned red and Joseph nodded slowly. "Yeah, that would scare the hell out of me. A beautiful woman coming at me with a sword, with an army behind her?"

Evean walked back over and sat down next to me and started in on her breakfast with an obvious appetite.

"Somebody looks hungry," Joseph teased.

Evean didn't even look up from her plate, "Usually they pass out after a few hours, Will however, stayed up all night."

She looked up at Joseph and winked, "And I do mean *up*."

I tried not to choke on my tea as both Joseph and Gregory broke up laughing rather loudly, while Suzona just scowled, then stood up and walked to the door.

"I think I need some air," she said going outside.

"I think she needs to get the rod out of her butt," Evean smirked and went back to eating her food.

I took a minute to recover from choking, trying not to laugh at Suzona's behavior.

"She is a nice woman, but she does need to be taken down a peg now and again," Gregory offered.

"That's the truth," Joseph agreed.

"So, what do we do today?" Gregory asked Evean.

"I have identification that shows us as working for a small production company. Today we go to the Toho studios and ask some questions, find out the name of our man, and then go meet him."

"That sounds easy enough."

"Well, yes. But first we must dress the part. Someone go retrieve her royal highness, and as soon as we're finished, we can buy some better clothing."

Three hours later we were at the offices of Toho studios. It was Me, Evean, Joseph, Gregory and of course, Suzona.

Evean was in an understated business suit. Her role was that of our guide, translator, and facilitator. Joseph and I were in business suits, rather nice ones. Gregory was dressed to look like a bodyguard, complete with dark glasses and I had to admit he seemed to rather enjoy the role.

Suzona was done up in a skin tight black leather outfit that was a front and a back with lots of lacing up the side, so you could tell she wasn't wearing either a bra or any underwear, with stockings, three inch pumps, and a black choker.

Men's jaws were dropping as she strutted by, and she did not look happy at being used as eye candy.

"Smiles everyone," Evean said as we approached the door.

Suzona scowled and Evean said without even looking over her shoulder, "Don't make me have to talk to Isengruer, Sue."

"It's Suzona," Suzona growled.

"Of course it is. Now, smile," And with that Evean opened the door and we all swept in. Suzona, I noticed, was smiling. I guess Isengruer was her god or something.

The five of us walked up to the front desk, Evean had set the other four on some other task, as I didn't speak Japanese I really had no idea what it was.

When we got to the desk, Evean started to talk in Japanese to the young woman sitting behind it, switching to English after a brief discussion.

"One moment, while I summon Mr. Takagi," The woman behind the desk said and gave a small bow. "He is most interested in talking to you."

"Arigato," Evean said and bowed, then steered us over to a set of chairs the receptionist had motioned to.

"They're expecting us?" I said.

Evean nodded, "I called yesterday, while you were all eating."

"And they talked to you?"

Evean smiled, "Apparently your god has a rather important contact in Washington. As I understand it, one of his aides called and asked the President of Toho studios if we could visit with their special effects department for this project."

"Whose idea was all of this?" I asked surprised.

"Mine, of course."

"Yours?"

"I didn't get this job based on my good looks," Evean grinned at me, "I was an up and coming player in the underground sex trade here in Japan, when Roden found me. I know the way things *really* work around here."

"I'm almost sorry I asked," I sighed.

"You really are such a boy scout," Evean laughed.

"It's not that."

"Oh? Then what is it?"

"Your being smarter than me is quite the blow to my already fragile ego, after what you did to my poor body last night."

Evean laughed again, Suzona glared a bit more, and the others just snickered.

A well dressed middle-aged Japanese man came out then with two younger men in tow and came over to us.

"Miss Evean?" he asked.

"Ah, Mr. Takagi," she said and bowed, then introduced us each.

"This is my employer, William Stout, Joseph Langir, his assistant, Suzona, and her bodyguard."

I was surprised that she didn't give the last name that was on Suzona's credentials, I was also amazed at the amount of respect that they paid her.

We bowed, like Evean had coached us, even Suzona behaved. Then again, I could see that she was eating up the deference that they were giving her. We exchanged business cards, again as Evean had instructed us, while she continued talking.

"So, as I mentioned during my phone call yesterday, we're from Foundation studios, and we're currently setting up to do a documentary on the whole kaiju genre, and with Toho studios being at the forefront with the whole gojira series and the other kaiju follow-ups, we were hoping to get a brief tour of your production shops and meet some of the people behind the scenes here today. To start those relationships that will help when we send over the lead elements of our documentary film crew."

"Yes, yes, of course! Allow me, to be your guide, please," Mr. Takagi said and led us inside to show us around.

"How did we rate the boss?" I whispered to Evean, using a cantrip to make sure we weren't overheard.

Evean smiled, "I told them that Suzona was really Brigitte Nelson traveling incognito."

"Who's that?"

"Someone famous who looks and acts like Sue."

"Does Suzona know about this?"

"Course not, that woman couldn't act her way out of a paper bag. She'll just suck it up because the world owes her," Evean snarked, still smiling.

I shrugged. She was right, of course.

They took us around the new sets first, showing us what was going on currently, and even what some of the future projects would be. Then they took us into the model shop, and back in one of the corners there was a small section that was quite obviously dedicated to Godzilla, or Gojira as Evean said the Japanese had called him.

"This is what started it all," Mr. Takagi said.

"Who are the people who worked on creating the original creature?" I asked.

"Oh, that was Eiji Tsuburaya. He left us to create his own company ages ago. Since he passed, his son runs it now."

I nodded, "Do you think they might be willing to take part in a documentary?"

"Tsuburaya Studios? Oh, I would think they would be very pleased to do so. Outside of Japan few people know of them." He turned to one of his men and spoke to them briefly in Japanese, and they hurried off.

He led us back out to the front then, and I thanked him for his time, and let him know that the studio would be in touch. He then went over and talked with Suzona for a minute, thanking her personally for having come to the studio.

While he was doing that, the assistant came back, spoke briefly with Evean and handed her a note.

We all bowed again, and then left.

"What's the note?" I asked after we'd left the building.

"An introduction to Tsuburaya studios, along with their address," Evean smiled. "Another step closer."

"Those men were all so polite," Suzona said, smiling for real now and looking much happier. "They obviously know how to treat a real woman."

Evean just looked at me and rolled her eyes.

NINE
EARTH - TOKYO
TSUBURAYA STUDIOS

We stuck to the same plan at Tsuburaya studios as we had used at Toho. Apparently they had called in advance of our showing up, and we were now seated in the office of the studio's president, who was one of the founder's sons, after having gotten a brief tour.

"I have always wondered, just where did your father get the idea for that first monster?" I asked.

Evean translated my words, either his English wasn't very good, or he didn't want to conduct the conversation in it. That was fine with me, it was his office and none of us wanted to be rude to someone we were trying to get information out of.

I listened to his reply in Japanese, and then Evean translated his words for me:

"He says, his father was never quite clear on that, he went on a retreat for a period of time after the war years, when he was still having trouble finding work due to his job with the military."

"I can imagine that must have been a rough time for him," I suspected it had been a rough time for many people in Japan. "To have only been doing his civic duty, and then having to be punished for it."

Evean translated, and he nodded rather vigorously, obviously this had been a sore point with his son as well.

She told me his response, "Exactly, it was a very rough time for him. He had only made films for the military, films so well done that even the great Frank Capra used parts from them. So he took some time to meditate and think about his career. When he came back, he was quite energized. I believe that was when he first started to draw sketches of gojira, and his other monsters."

I looked at Evean, and then back at him, "Fascinating. Any idea of where he went?"

He shook his head and spoke.

"No," Evean translated, "He only ever said that he left from Koshien."

"Koshien?"

"Yes, Koshien stadium, where the Hanshin Tigers play."

"Ah," I nodded, "Well thank you very much for your time, my colleagues and I appreciate your attention and hospitality very much."

"You are most welcome," he said and we all stood then, bowed, and were shown out.

"So, what do you think?" I asked Evean. "Think there's a portal there?" We were back at the hotel; everyone was sitting in Evean's and my room with us.

Evean nodded, "It seems likely. In the morning we'll take a train to Kobe, which is where the stadium is, and go look."

"How hard will it be to get in?" Joseph asked.

"Not hard at all, there's a game on tomorrow, we'll just buy tickets and go look around."

"Say we find a portal, then what?" Gregory asked.

Evean had been translating the conversation to the other group members who only spoke Japanese. Jane spoke up then and said something, to which Evean replied, and then spoke to us.

"Jane thinks if we find a gate, she and the others should spread out and spend the rest of the day talking to the stadium workers, about any myths or stories associated with the place."

Everyone nodded and agreed, it was a good idea.

"What about weapons, and supplies?" Suzona asked.

"Swords and knives I can get," Evean said. "Same for some basic body armor, and any provisions."

"What about firearms?"

Evean shook her head no, "Too difficult to get here, the culture in Japan doesn't support it, just trying to get any would draw more attention than I'd like to attract."

"We don't know if they'd work on the next plane anyway," I pointed out.

"True," Suzona nodded.

"Anything else?" Evean asked, first in English, and then I guess in Japanese and looked around the room.

Everyone shook their heads no, and stood up to leave, a couple of people asking her questions before leaving.

Suzona took advantage of this to press up against me, she was still in the outfit from this morning, and I had to admit, it did look good on her.

"Care to spend the night with me, William?" She asked in that sexy contralto of hers.

"Um, thanks but no thanks," I said back, keeping my voice low.

"You would turn me down, for *that*?" Suzona said angrily.

I don't know what surprised me more, that yes, I was in fact turning down hot and sexy Suzona for Evean, who wasn't currently anywhere near as hot; that Suzona was angry about my not wanting to sleep with her; or that I was really enjoying pissing her off by turning her down.

"I really like Evean, Suzona. You and me, well, we've never gotten along that well."

"But I know how to please a man, William. I can show you much pleasure in bed."

"So can Evean."

"Her? What can she know?"

"I've slept with you both, Suzona," I sighed, "I know what each of you can do."

"So, you know you should come with me then," Suzona almost purred.

I shook my head and tried not to grin, "Sorry, Suzona. But she's better than you."

"What!? How can that be!"

"Truth is, you're not even close," I said and gave her a nasty smirk. Yeah, I was enjoying it and I know I shouldn't have been. "She doesn't have to rely on her looks like you do, after all."

Suzona cursed rather loudly, then turning on her heel she stalked out of the room, the others looking over curiously.

"What was that about?" Gregory asked, then went and followed her out of the room.

"You know, she'll only want you more now," Joseph whispered to me.

"Too bad for her then," I said. "I can do without the ice queen."

"I wasn't talking about Suzona," Joseph laughed and nodded towards Evean who was looking at me with a rather predatory smile on her face.

"Uh-oh."

The next day I spent the train ride sleeping, Evean at least was as worn out as I was. Suzona ignored me, thankfully, and Gregory at least, seemed rather pleased with himself.

When we got to Kobe, Evean woke up and got us transportation to the stadium, which was rather large, but as soon as we got near we could all feel it.

There was a portal here.

After buying tickets to the game, we went in and quickly tracked the portal down; it was back in the area where the maintenance crew stored the equipment to maintain the stadium grounds. None of us were able to get back there with a game going on. So those of us who only spoke English went and watched the game, while the others went and investigated things further.

"So, what's this game called?" Joseph asked.

"Baseball," I said watching the teams play. I hadn't seen a ball game in over fifteen years and I'd never seen a Japanese team play before. I had to admit, these guys were good. I was especially impressed with the Tigers' playing.

"How's it work?"

I went over the rules fairly quickly, just giving them the highlights.

"Doesn't sound too hard," Gregory said when I finished.

"Yeah, that's what everyone thinks. Anybody can play it, but playing it good is a lot tougher than it sounds, there's a lot more strategy involved than people realize too. Those professional pitchers can also throw that ball pretty fast, and make it do some strange things."

Just then the pitcher threw a slider and struck the batter out.

"Yeah, I can see that," Gregory admitted. "Is this a popular game here on your plane?"

I shook my head, "Only two countries really play it. Mine and this one."

"Who plays it better?"

"Well, back home everyone thinks we do," I said. "But watching these guys play, I'm not so sure."

"Don't they ever play each other?"

I shook my head again, "No, they don't. And it's kind of a shame. But both countries are far enough away from each other that it would probably play hell with any kind of schedule."

Several innings went by before Evean showed up to talk to us.

"Okay, the others are going to stay until they're pretty much asked to leave or chased out of the stadium. Teshes has actually managed to find one of the groundskeepers and is actually making some progress with learning about the stadium."

"Really?" I asked.

Evean nodded, "She told him it's for a school report, so he's more than happy to help out."

"So, what are we to do?" Suzona asked.

"Enjoy the game, for now. When it's over we'll meet at this hotel," Evean handed us each a piece of paper with a hotel name and address on it. "I've already booked us rooms there."

"Where will you be?" I asked.

"Getting us supplied."

"Need any help?"

Evean laughed, "This is not the kind of thing a gaijin can get involved in. Sorry, Will, I'll have to take care of this by myself."

I sighed.

"What's a gaijin?" Joseph asked.

"People like us," I said.

"Yeah, you stand out too much," Evean agreed.

"You're not exactly Japanese yourself," I pointed out.

"Yes, but I'm Asian, and I'm considered lower-class here. No one will pay me any mind.

"See you later!" She said and left us.

"That is one well organized woman," Joseph said smiling.

"What, you too?" Suzona complained.

"After what she's done to Will the last couple of days, any guy would have to be interested!" Joseph teased, earning a dark look from Suzona.

"It's your funeral," I said shaking my head.

We left after the game ended, Suzona had attached herself to my arm, and I decided not to complain, as it put an end to the men constantly trying to stop her and hit on her, which kept slowing us down. She might be taller than most of the guys here, but that sure didn't dim their optimism.

We got checked into the hotel, and got all of the room keys, then went to the hotel dining room and had dinner. Suzona was dropping hints left and right about what she wanted to do tonight, which was apparently me.

I was being deliberately obtuse. We really didn't get along well, or maybe it was I just didn't get along well with her? Ever since I'd told her off that one time in South Africa, she sure seemed to want to get along with me!

Yeah, she was hot, and yeah we'd been to bed together that one time and yeah, I'd even enjoyed it. But she wasn't someone I could relax with and just be comfortable with. It wasn't just that she was a demanding lover, she was a demanding everything, all the time. I'm sure there were guys who were okay with that, Gregory sure seemed okay with it. I, however, wasn't.

Even Rachel wasn't as demanding, and she was a queen!

Jane, Shin, and Loomis showed up about an hour after we did, but there was still no sign of Evean, or Teshes for that matter. Suzona had used her good looks to get the concierge to hand over the room keys and she started to parcel them out, one to Jane, one to Shin, one to Joseph, and she kept the fourth one and just smiled at me.

"Looks like Joseph will get his chance with your friend tonight, doesn't it?" Suzona said with a smile.

I was about to say something, when someone tapped me on the shoulder, looking back I saw it was Jane, and she was smiling. She took my hand and led me off, to Suzona's swearing and Joseph's laughter.

"Thanks," I sighed as we passed out of earshot and started up the stairs to the rooms.

"You're welcome," Jane said.

I almost tripped. "You can speak English?" I asked surprised. "How?"

"You never lose your native languages, the ones you grew up with. It seems our two native planes have almost the exact same language."

"I had no idea. Does anyone else know?"

Jane shook her head, "No, I'm not in the habit of sharing my advantages with people I don't know."

"You know Evean."

"Or don't trust," Jane said with a grin. "I mean really, Will, I thought you were afraid of Evean, and now you're sleeping with her?"

I blushed, "She's a lot more, umm, *human*, when she's not so attractive that it's almost impossible to have normal thoughts in your head when she's trying to charm you."

"Well *that's* kind of shallow." Jane said unlocking the door to the room.

"This from the woman who was afraid to talk to me when she found out I was working at the stable?"

Now it was Jane's turn to blush, "Okay, you may just have a point there. And you are right about one thing, she certainly is a different person here than she is back on Saladin."

I nodded, "Yeah, she's really bothered by her looks still."

"Don't they have surgeons here good enough here to fix that?" Jane asked surprised.

"Not where she came from, you have to understand that Evean comes from a bad place and a bad time here."

"Hey, I had a hard childhood too you know!" Jane laughed and turned to me as I closed the door.

"Not compared to her," I sighed and gave Jane a hug. "Let's not talk about it."

"So why is she so hot for you now, anyway? I'd have thought that once she got you, she'd be done with you."

I laughed and gave Jane a kiss, "You know how I like to make love with the lights on?"

Jane's eyebrows went up, "Wow, that was pretty bold. So you really do like her, huh?"

I thought about that a moment, "Somewhere on Siren we went from being enemies to being friends I guess. And the other night in the room, well, it was the kind of thing you'd do for a friend if you really cared about them, and well, I'm glad I did, because you know what? After a while she wasn't ugly at all."

We went to bed then, and I was rather surprised that Jane actually wanted to make love. We hadn't had sex together since back on her home plane when we'd been dating. I don't know if it was because of what I'd said earlier, or if it was just because she'd 'rescued' me once again.

In either case however, I was more than happy to. I liked Jane a lot, obviously, or I would never have slept with her in the first place.

§   §

"Getting in your last round?" Fel said smiling at me.

"Eh," I shrugged, "I don't think that far ahead, you know that, Fel."

"Even Roden was impressed. Aryanna however says she wasn't all that surprised and that she's proud of you."

I sighed, feeling both annoyed and embarrassed. "Don't you guys all have better things to do than keep tabs on my love life?"

Fel laughed, "Are you kidding? Making bets on our champions is one of our favorite pastimes!"

"I'd ask if you were kidding me, but suddenly I don't want to know," I said shaking my head. "My only regret is that I think she's going to kill me with sex now, and not even intentionally! I really had no idea just how much it meant to her."

"Making someone you care for *happy* often gets you a far bigger return than the effort you put into it."

"I guess," I replied, "I just had no idea."

"Which is kind of surprising, you've had a pretty good success rate at making women happy, William."

"I don't know, I think I fail a lot more than I succeed."

"Well, that's the problem of men everywhere; you at least don't stop trying."

"So, what's going on back home? I suspect you have something for me to do?"

"The gojira has been active again; it destroyed more of Barassa, and did attack some of the units outside the wall, to the east again. It seems that right now it doesn't want to stray too far from the city."

"So, that's what, five days?"

Fell nodded, "People are starting to flee the city, a few tried to leave via boat. I guess they thought the monster would ignore them during an idle period."

"It didn't, I take it?"

Fel shook his head, "No, it didn't. So those that are leaving are fleeing overland."

"What's the army there doing about it?"

"Stopping everyone and checking them. They're executing anyone who is even carrying a symbol of Tantrus, and making rather nasty examples of any of his clergy that they find."

I wasn't really surprised by that. Tantrus's people had summoned this rather nasty monster after all.

"So refugees aren't going to be a problem for us then?"

"No, but several of us are worried about what this monster is going to do once it runs out of food."

"Well, what has it been eating?" I was pretty sure I knew, but I had to ask.

"People, mostly. There aren't enough fish in the river to feed something that big."

"So what do you think it will do?"

"I'm not sure, William. My biggest fear is that it will swim out into the ocean and feed on the fish there."

"Why is that your biggest fear?"

"Because then we won't know where it is, and we won't be able to kill it. And if it is capable of asexual reproduction, who knows how many of them we might be facing in the future?"

"So, hurry up."

Fel nodded, "Yes, hurry up."

"I take it everyone is getting the same orders tonight?"

"That and one other thing, William."

That caught my attention, "What?"

"You must be prepared to be ruthless. This could end me, this could end us all. You do what you have to do, and if it means you have to do something bad, you do it. Understand?"

I nodded. I understood.

TEN
EARTH - NISHINOMIYA
KOSHIEN STADIUM

At breakfast the next morning Joseph was looking rather pleased, tired, but pleased.

"I have a bundle in my room for each of you," Evean said, giving me a wink. "We will be going through the portal in a few hours."

I looked around, I didn't see Teshes anywhere, and asked about her.

"She's holed up inside the stadium. She hid out there last night. When we're ready, she'll open the doors for us from the inside."

"Smart," Gregory commented.

"Very. I'm sure you all got the same lecture last night that I did. Don't hesitate to take advantage of any situations you happen on. Now, eat up, and then come up to my room to get your gear."

I sat down and ate quickly, then followed Joseph upstairs.

"Still alive I see," I told him.

"She said she went easy on me," he laughed.

"So what did she buy us?"

"No idea, I was too busy with other things to check the bags," he grinned.

I snorted, "I'd call you a dog, but for all I know, you are right now."

"Wolf, it's called a dire wolf. Dogs are small."

"Whatever," I said and followed him into the room. There were nine bags there, they all looked like sports bags and had the team logo on them for the Hanshin Tigers.

"Well this is going to stand out," Suzona snarked.

"Going into the stadium in the middle of the day is going to raise attention, with these bags; they'll just figure we've got a reason to be there," Evean replied.

"What's in the bags?" I asked.

"One camo jumpsuit, one black jumpsuit. Weapons harness, knives, swords, backpack, rations, canteens, miscellaneous survival gear. The jumpsuits are fitted to your champion form, unless your form stands out here, then it's based on this form."

"How do you know our sizes?"

"I paid attention when we went clothes shopping the other day. Now, let's go. Will, be a dear and grab Teshes's bag please?"

I nodded and did as directed and we marched out of the hotel and down the road to the stadium. Evean had gotten us a place that was rather close.

When we got to the stadium, Evean led us around to a door far down the east side from the main entrance. It was early still, not yet nine a.m., and there really wasn't anyone around.

"Okay, stay in line, and don't stop." Evean said, and pounded on the door.

It opened and Teshes was inside, she beckoned us to follow as she led us down a corridor and into the bowels of the stadium.

It was almost a bit of a maze down here, with the way the corridors were laid out, we had to take a circuitous path to get to where we wanted to go. The room with the portal actually had a barred door over it; Evean pulled out a set of bolt cutters from her bag and made fast work of the lock on it.

"The door is alarmed," Suzona pointed out the micro-switch when Evean opened it and we all went through.

"I guess somebody has an idea what's in there then," Evean said and walking up to the portal, she put her hand on it.

"Feels okay to me. Let's go!" and she stepped through.

We each followed in succession; I paused just long enough to get a feel for it too, before I stepped through.

I moved away from the portal quickly, to clear a space for the person behind me. We were in the middle of what I guess was once a city. The ruins were rather extensive and I don't think there was a single wall or structure that was higher than a couple of feet.

The ground was either dirt or broken concrete, and there were weeds and other grasses and such growing randomly through the cracks. I didn't see all that many trees, though there were a few in the area, mostly small ones.

The sky was still blue, the sun still yellow. It was cool out, and I could smell the ocean faintly. I noticed then that there were craters scattered around us, some of them quite deep. Apparently this city had been destroyed by some sort of bombardment.

I took a moment then to look around at everyone. Gregory and Suzona looked the same, as they were in their champion forms. The rest of us were more or less the same size we had been before, as our clothing still fit, however we all looked the same now; which was I guess Japanese as the others hadn't changed very much.

"Okay, everyone get your gear in order, and then let's see if we can figure out where to go next." Evean said, stripping down and pulling a jumpsuit out of her bag.

I set mine down and opening it I went through the contents. There was a backpack, as she had said, two jumpsuits, an equipment belt, a couple of regular knives, a bow, arrows, two swords the size of what I normally used, which would have surprised me, if it wasn't for the fact that I was starting to realize just how smart Evean really was.

There were canteens, freeze-dried and dehydrated foodstuffs, and a harness for the gear, athletic shoes, and a pair of shorts.

"What's with the shorts?" I asked.

"I figured those of us from Saladin might prefer our Champion forms," Evean said and I looked up as I noticed her voice sounded more like what I was used to. She was in her champion form alright, and Gregory, Joseph, and even Suzona were staring at her with their mouths open.

The rest of us all knew what she looked like, well maybe Shin didn't, I revised noticing his staring as well.

"Good point," I said and stripping down myself I shifted as well. I put the shoes and the jumpsuits in the backpack, along with the food and other gear and after donning the gear I'd chosen to wear, I put it on my back.

Joseph's pack I noticed was rather strangely shaped, but that made sense when after stripping naked he became a large wolf.

"So now what?" I asked looking at everyone.

"What's that?" Jane said and we all turned to look at what she was pointing at. Off on the horizon we could all see what looked like the top of a white tower.

I turned and scanned the rest of the horizon, as did Evean and a couple of the others.

"Well, as there's nothing else, I guess that's our destination," Evean said and we all started off in that direction.

"So, you're the 'God Slayer', huh?"

I looked over and down at Teshes who was walking along side of me now. She was attractive, but then she was a champion, so you'd expect her to be. Loomis was close enough that I think he was paying attention, while Shin was deeply involved in the study of Evean's butt and tail as she led us.

"Yeah, that's me," I sighed.

"Why do they call you that?" Suzona asked.

"Because they know I hate it," I grumbled.

"Why would anyone hate being called that?" Suzona asked surprised.

"Because some of us don't like being reminded of what we're capable of doing when we're really pissed off."

Suzona turned to Teshes, "So, what did he do, to earn such a title?"

Teshes laughed, "I'd think that would be rather obvious."

"Still, I would hear of it," Suzona asked, "It's not like he talks of it," she said nodded at me.

Teshes looked at me, questioningly.

I shrugged, "Go ahead, I don't care. I'm kind of curious as to how much the story has grown by this point."

So for the next hour, Teshes entertained Suzona, and apparently everyone else, with a rather interesting recounting of what I did to the Mulanders so many years ago. I was surprised it even mentioned how I went against my god in the destruction of the Mulanders. Then again, Fel had made it clear I was taking the blame for it, so I guess he made sure, somehow, that that particular detail was included in the telling.

There were some exaggerations, but not as many as I would have thought. Mainly it went on about how many I slew in combat, and while I knew that I had killed a lot, I don't know if I had killed *that* many.

When it came to what I did to the people of the Mulander city, it wasn't exactly kind to me, but I couldn't really complain about that, I *had* done it, and I wasn't exactly proud of it.

"How much of that is true?" Gregory asked looking at me a bit differently than before.

"Too much," I sighed.

"You'd think there would be a song of such a great conquest!" Suzona said. It figured that she would think it was a great deed.

"There is!" Jane said from in front of me where she was walking.

"You're kidding," I almost groaned.

"Yup, Felecia has made it clear that she doesn't want anyone singing it around you however. She's afraid you might break their instrument over their head, and well, you know how much those things cost!"

"I'd think you would want everyone to hear it," Gregory said. "To warn them to stay away."

"It is pretty inspiring," Jane added.

I just threw my hands up in the air while shaking my head.

"But if he was the one pushing it you'd all say he was a braggart," Jane continued. "Heroes are better when they have a certain amount of humility, otherwise they become insufferable jerks and we just can't wait to see them fall."

"Amen to that," Joseph agreed.

The sun was nearing the horizon, and we still hadn't made the tower, which had now been revealed to be a lot taller than any of us had suspected. Having to skirt a number of bays and inlets along the way hadn't helped. Apparently the tower was either on, or close to, the coast.

"How far away do you think that is?" I asked Evean.

"Hard to say, without knowing just how big it is. But I'd rather arrive after the sun has set. Less chance of being seen."

"Seen by what?" I asked. So far we hadn't seen a single person, and nothing bigger than a fox.

"Somebody had to build it," She said.

"Doesn't mean that they're still alive," I said. "I wonder how long ago this place was bombed."

"Why?"

"Well, our man came here sometime after the war, so probably nineteen forty-six or so. That's what, forty-five years ago? If this happened between then and now, then there is no guarantee that this 'Okishijen Desootoria' weapon even exists anymore."

Evean nodded. "True, but I think whatever happened here, happened around the same time as the last war."

"I just wish we could get there faster. Plus the lack of anybody around worries me. There aren't that many craters around here and there's no sign of ruins either."

"I'm still wondering why they had a lock on the gate to the room with the portal," Evean admitted.

"Wouldn't you?" Shin, who I think had finally gotten over drooling over Evean's body, put in.

We all had to agree with Shin on that.

We continued walking as the sun set, the tower lighting up as night fell.

"Well, looks like somebody lives there," Teshes said.

"Think this is where we will find the weapon?" Jane asked.

Evean shook her head, "Anything built that big would have been knocked down."

"Not if they had the weapon," Jane pointed out. "They could kill it before it came near."

"She has a point," I said to Evean.

"I guess we'll see when we get there then."

It was late at night when the base of the tower finally came into view, and it was fairly big. There was a large wall surrounding the tower, with several buildings arrayed around it. There was also a port just outside the main wall, with a second, lower wall, surrounding it. But there were no ships in it that any of us could see.

The tower itself was an interesting building. The base of it was huge, and all of it appeared to be made out of white concrete. It was twice as high as it was wide, but without anything to judge the size, I had no idea how high it was. There were ranks of windows, or at least I think they were windows, spaced evenly along it.

Coming out of the base was a second tower, it was half as wide as the base and that segment appeared to be twice as tall. There was a geodesic design of what looked like girders on the outside of it, and it was lit up with floodlights, making it gleam the same shade of white as the base.

Coming out of that was a third section, which was more than twice as tall as the entire structure below, and half as wide as the middle section. It appeared to be made of glass and was lit from the inside, or at least appeared to be. There also appeared to be some sort of structure on the very top of the tower, but what it was I could not tell from here.

"Damn, that's huge," Joseph commented.

"I think I see people around the base of it," Suzona said. She had a pair of binoculars out and was looking at the building. We were all lying down looking over the top of a small hill, staying in cover. We were probably a mile away.

"So, now what?" Joseph asked as I got out my own binoculars and tried to see what was on the top of the tower.

"That depends on what we can see of the people by the tower. We probably don't want to show up wearing our champion forms," Evean said.

"Do we want to approach now? Or wait until after sunrise?" I asked.

"Wait until a couple of hours after sunrise," Evean replied.

We all agreed and headed back a good twenty-minute walk away from the rise we'd been looking over things from. There were a few crumbling buildings in the area, but we decided to camp out around some trees a bit higher up and out of the line of sight of the tower.

Evean came over to me as she was setting up the watch rotations, Suzona and I would be first, then Joseph and Jane.

"You want me to sit watch with Suzona?" I asked surprised.

Evean smiled, we were all still in our champion forms and her smile was devastating in it of course, "She practically begged me to let her have a shot at you."

"Seriously?" I was rather surprised.

"Unlike you and me, Suzona never had to deal with rejection growing up. She's always been beautiful, smart, and talented. You've definitely cut her down a few notches and she's rather remorseful right now."

"I'd have thought you'd be rather happy with that," I pointed out.

"Back on Earth I was, but Roden reminded me last night that I was being petty and causing an ally to suffer."

That surprised me, "Really?"

"I'm only supposed to make our enemies suffer, William," she smirked.

"So make nice with Suzona," I nodded. "I'll try."

"Oh, I think you can do more than just try," Evean winked, and then went off to talk to Joseph.

I walked the perimeter of our makeshift camp, getting an idea of where everyone was. We had a good spot with good coverage and decent visibility. Suzona caught up with me while she was doing the same.

"Do you hate me, William?" She asked in that sexy voice of hers, looking down demurely.

I sighed, either she was playing it to the hilt, or she was a little upset. I guess I'd find out eventually.

"No, I don't hate you, Suzona."

"Then why have you been so mean to me?"

"Because you've been deserving it lately," I told her and smiled down at her when her head came up and she glared at me. In my champion form I was a good head taller than her.

"Don't go denying it, either," I continued. "On your home world, I have no doubt that you're the most beautiful and desirable woman that there is, because you've been that pretty much everywhere we've gone. But I'm a champion, Suzona, just like you. I get beautiful and desirable all day long. And those women will do anything I ask them to do.

"Now, do I expect that kind of behavior out of you? Or any of the other female champions here? No, of course not! Because we're all equals here. Evean is a friend of mine, one that I owe a debt of gratitude to."

Suzona surprised me by giving a sigh and nodding as she looked down again.

"She is so incredibly lovely in her champion form; I can see where that would sway a man, William."

I put a finger under her chin and raised her head back up to look into her eyes.

"Yes, she's hot. So are you. I didn't sleep with her because of that, if it was just looks, I would have taken the time to be with you again. I don't owe you anything, Suzona, and you don't owe me. If you want to be friends, then lets be friends. After that, if you want to sleep together or have sex, sure."

"I would like that, William." Suzona said and smiled.

"Being friends, or having sex?" I teased.

"Both," She said and winked back at me.

"Well, we have some time to kill," I said as we found a spot to settle down during our watch, "tell me about yourself."

"I was the youngest of my parent's children," Suzona began softly. "My father was the King of course."

I looked at her a bit surprised, "I didn't know that."

She shrugged and continued, "I had three older brothers, Andreath, Seathius, and Grethian. I also had one older sister, born between Seath and Greth, her name was Ryzona.

"Growing up I idolized my two oldest brothers. Andre would be King one day, following after my father, who was like a god to me. I so rarely got to see my father, if he was not at war; he was busy with the affairs of the kingdom. My father was not exactly what you would call a 'just' man. He was quick to anger and would hold onto a grudge like a starving dog with a bone.

"I did not realize that then, however. As I was only a child."

"As I grew older, I became what I have heard called a 'Tomboy.' I spent as much time with Andre and Seath as I could, I learned to shoot from them; I learned to fight with hands and feet, and then knives. As I grew older I watched them and learned how to lead men.

"This of course drove my mother mad, as while some knowledge of fighting was considered good for a woman, being able to beat most men in a test of arms was not. Considering that I was the most beautiful woman in our lands, that made matters even worse."

"Howso?" I asked. I didn't doubt her words about her beauty; Suzona was very much the kind of woman you often thought only existed in comic books and high fashion magazines.

"Because after my father married off my sister, for a political alliance, he found himself unable to marry me off."

"I'd think a strong man would want a strong woman."

"Then you would think wrong," Suzona sighed. "When I was fifteen, I snuck off with my brothers Seath and Greth. It was to be Greth's first foray into combat, a raid in force on one of our neighbor's borders. Such things were common of course. We're a contentious lot, we fight often amongst ourselves. Usually it is a battle without deaths, what you would call 'counting coup' I believe."

"Something bad happened, didn't it?"

"Yes, we were beset by the king of the land and his army, we were beat down, and we were captured, most of the raiding party was killed during the battle, only my brother Seath, I, and two others survived. The king was rather happy with his victory, and had us all dragged to his tent, bound.

"He then tried to rape me. In front of my brother, the two others, and all of his captains."

"I'm sorry."

"Eh, it is of no matter anymore, because not only did he fail, but I killed him. It was quite gruesome and rather bloody. I managed to free my brother and the other two and in the confusion we escaped. However the story of what I did, well, it did not set well with the other rulers and even my father was quite incensed.

"So he threw me out and disowned me."

"What did you do?" I asked rather shocked.

"I gelded him."

"Oh!"

"With my teeth!" she laughed and smiled at me.

"And that killed him?"

"No, but it distracted him and his men enough that I could grab his sword and split his belly open, gutting him rather efficiently."

"I could see where most men would be afraid to have you in their beds after that," I laughed.

"Exactly. So cast out I had no place to go, other than the church. The high priest took a fancy to me; *he* wasn't afraid of me and started to send me on quests with the knights of the church, while seducing me whenever I was staying at the temple."

"So eventually you became a champion?" I asked.

"I became a champion when my father, who was even more incensed now that I had *not* only refused to go off to die a beggar's death in humiliation after being disowned, but had instead distinguished myself in honorable combat for the church, attacked the church in an effort to kill both the high priest and myself.

"I slew him in single combat before the altar. It was *glorious*," She sighed.

"What about your family?"

"Well, Ryzona had already been married off to a neighboring prince. Andre was furious. He was too much like our father, and two days later I slew him too."

"Seath?"

"Seath came to the temple only to be coronated. He only spoke to me once, never again, and that was only to tell me that while he sided with me and with what I had done, he had to treat me as 'other', because I was our god's champion, and because I had killed his father and his brother."

"That must have been rough."

Suzona nodded. "I left the next day; I quit as my god's champion and took up with another god in a far away country. That was many years ago. My brother has long since died; his son has taken over. As far as I know, they have no idea I even exist anymore."

I moved around to sit next to her, and put an arm around her.

"I'm not looking for pity," she grumbled.

"This isn't pity, this is comfort." I gave her a hug, "I would think recounting all of that didn't sit very well."

"So, now it is your turn," she said.

"I have nothing to compare to that, trust me," I chuckled.

"Still, I would hear about you."

I shrugged and told her about growing up; going to college, getting recruited, though I didn't tell her I was married. I told her about being dropped blind in the center of a sacrifice with no prior warning, and going on to win the war, then taking the city.

"For someone not brought up in the ways of war, you have done remarkably well for yourself," Suzona said.

"I've been lucky, and I admit it."

"I think there's a bit more than luck going on there," She smiled. "Fortune favors the bold, as well as the strong."

"Well, I've had some very good teachers along the way and a lot of very good friends and allies."

She stretched and yawned and I admired the view while she did.

"What do you say we wake Joseph and Jane, and go to bed?" Suzona said softly.

"I'd say that sounds like a very good idea."

Eleven
1st World
Ruins

"Well somebody looks rather pleased this morning," Joseph said sidling up next to me as I was putting on the jumpsuit from my backpack.

"Do I?" I asked, sitting down to lace up my sneakers.

"You, not so much," He laughed squatting down next to me. Evean had decided that we'd all shift back here, well out of sight of the tower's dwellers. Everyone had agreed on that, feeling this wouldn't be a good place for surprises.

"Why is it that everyone is so hot to get laid anyway?"

Joseph looked at me strangely, "What?"

"Pretty much every time a group of champions gets together, at least when I've seen them, everyone is on the make with everyone else. I mean they're all champions! Don't they get laid enough at home?"

"Equality" Joseph said.

"Huh?"

"Most of the people you sleep with back home know what you are, they're not going to treat you like an equal. Because you're not, and you're not really going to stand for anything less than being treated as what you are, which is a champion."

"Oh I don't know about that!" I protested.

"You ever send anyone to their death, Will? I don't mean killing someone, I mean telling somebody to go out there and die for your god like they're supposed to?"

That brought me up short. Because I had done it. Oh I hadn't quite realized it at the time, but I'd done it.

"We're all the same here, we can all relate. It's even worse for the women in some cases. Most women want a male who is at least their equal, if not more so. Do you really think that a woman like Suzona is going to find a man like that among the followers of her god?"

"Well, when you put it like that," I said slowly while thinking about it.

"And us guys aren't really any better, look at you, you married the queen! Me? I all but married a goddess!

"Normally we're wary of other champions, possibly even at each other's throats when we're in the same place. But when we all have to go off together like this, when our gods are working together as allies, it gives us the chance to be with people who we can actually relate to," Joseph shrugged. "So yeah, we 'hook up' as people like to say."

I had finished with my footwear and was checking my weapons before putting my pack back on.

"And after years of being able to speak our minds and approach whomever we want, we're all kind of blunt about it now as well, right?" I asked him.

"Pretty much. You talk to gods and goddesses all day and you're bound to develop an attitude, right?"

I laughed at that, he had a pretty good point.

"All right, everyone! Let's get this show on the road!" Evean called out.

"What a strange expression," Joseph said looking at me.

"Yeah, she has a knack for them," I grinned. "Time to go."

"So, now what?" I asked Evean as we looked over the rise with our binoculars again at the tower. There were quite a few people there, engaging in all sorts of activities, as we watched one group got into something that looked like a massive halftrack and drove out of the walled enclave and off towards one of the hills.

"Might as well walk down there and find out," Evean said. "I don't see any obvious weapons and on the whole, they do seem to look like us. Let's find out what they know, and what they can tell us."

We all got up then and started to walk down the hill towards the enclave. We got about halfway there when one of those halftrack-like vehicles came out and drove towards us. I didn't see anything that looked like a weapon on it, though that didn't mean that it didn't have any.

It stopped about a hundred yards from us, and a woman got out and walked towards us. We all stopped and watched.

"Greetings," she said. "Where are you headed?"

"We're not quite sure," Evean said. "We're on a quest to find something for our people back home. Many years ago, one of our people found it, but he never told anyone where he went, other than this way."

"What is it that you are looking for?"

"We are looking for a way to deal with a very large monster."

The woman shook her head, "That does not sound like anything I am familiar with, however there may be someone who does know."

"Then we would speak with them."

"I would search all of you first, before you are allowed entry into our home."

"That is fine. What items are we not allowed to take there?" Evean said smiling.

"I will tell you, if I should find them."

"I'll go first then," Evean said.

"Strip please?"

Evean shrugged and as we watched she stripped down to her underwear and the woman went through all of her things rather carefully.

"Swords and knives are not allowed inside," She said, taking the short sword that Evean had brought.

"Can we give them to you to hold on to, so we can reclaim them when we leave?"

"Of course," She said.

We all pulled out our swords and knives and dropped them on the ground. She looked up rather surprised at that.

"Why so many weapons?"

"We've been walking quite a distance. May I get dressed?"

"Of course. Next?"

An hour later we were sitting in the back of the halftrack and riding to the tower. All of our weapons were in a bag that had been stored in an external lockdown box on the outside of the vehicle.

Our hostess had introduced herself as Mahnii before we'd been loaded onto the transport. Evean had introduced each of us to her by name.

The ride in was fast and rather comfortable. There were small windows we could see out of, and we were escorted off of the vehicle as soon as it had passed inside the gate.

But more importantly than that, there was a portal here, and we could all feel it.

"What is the name of your place here?" Joseph asked Mahnii.

"White Tower," She replied.

"How many stories tall is it?" I asked, curious.

"Two hundred and six," she said and after a brief pause added, "As of last week."

I looked around at the others in surprise; they all looked suitably impressed as well.

"You said that there would be someone we could talk to?" Evean prompted, "About our search?"

"Yes, please, come with me," Mahnii said, and led us towards the tower.

As we walked into the tower I got a bearing on where the portal was, which was just outside of the tower compound. It was in the direction of the smaller compound which contained the docks, making me wonder if it was inside there.

The portal being close to the tower had to have some sort of significance, I found it hard to believe that the one human habitation we'd come across was just coincidentally located right next to one.

The entry we took into the tower was large, easily big enough to drive a small truck into, and I could see another one that was larger still, one big enough for the machine we'd ridden in. We started up a concrete ramp, as the entrance was a good twenty feet above the ground, then passed through the opening, which had other people coming out of it, and after passing through a second doorway about thirty feet further inside, the ramp started back down.

The angle of the ramp going down was about the same as the angle going up had been, and it was long enough that I wished I had counted my steps on the way inside, because we were definitely going a much longer distance as we descended, which would mean we were now underground.

When the ramp leveled off, we found ourselves walking down a well lit, wide, and very long hallway with doors and openings to either side of us as we traveled. Some of the openings were other hallways; some were large areas that looked suspiciously like stores of some kind.

The other people we were passing as we followed Mahnii were all dressed in a variety of outfits that were all basically composed of trousers and shirts, though the types and colors weren't very uniform and those worn by the women were much more flattering in appearance.

I did quickly figure out that there were either soldiers or police among the people, as there were quite a few who wore the exact same outfit, and they were armed with what looked like nightsticks. They tended to watch us as we passed, but we were already attracting attention as we were all wearing the same basic jumpsuit.

Three times we turned, and on the third it was into a stairwell that took us down several flights before we exited. Then a short walk and we were led into what was obviously an office.

It was a large room, with a line of desks bisecting it. On this side of the desks there were several rows of chairs, a waiting area I guess. On the other side there was a large array of low walled cubes with desks in them with people working at them.

The row of desks that split the room were only partially occupied and Mahnii led us up to one of those.

"Ah, Mahnii, these are the people you found on the surface?" A rather old looking gentleman seated behind a desk asked.

"Yes."

"Fine, who is in charge of your group?" He asked us.

"I am," Evean said.

"Fine, have a seat here," He gestured to a seat besides the desk. "The rest of you can go get something to eat if you wish. Mahnii will show you where."

I went and stood behind Evean as she sat down, Suzona and Loomis went over to a line of seats by the wall where they both sat down to watch.

"Go, eat," Evean said to the others making shooing motions with her hands as they stood looking undecided. Well, not all of them were looking undecided; Joseph, Gregory, and Teshes were already following Mahnii.

The rest followed then and the man looked up at me.

"You are?" He asked.

"Her assistant," I said and smiled.

"Well then, pull up a chair."

I grabbed one from another desk that was empty and sat.

"My name is Sakauwa, you are?"

"Evean."

"Interesting name, and you?" He asked looking at me.

"Will," I said and gave him a polite nod.

"So, Mahnii says you are looking for a device to kill a monster?"

Evean nodded, "Yes. That is correct."

"Well, I must say that we have neither weapons nor monsters here."

"Do you know who does?" Evean asked him.

"You are not from here, are you?"

Evean smiled and shook her head, "No, I thought that was obvious. We are from far away."

"So why have you come here?"

"As I said to Mahnii, many years ago a man came here and he found tales of the monster we now face and the weapon that was built to destroy it. We are in search of that weapon, as the monster has found our homes."

Sakauwa pondered that a few minutes.

"How many years ago did that man come here?"

"About forty-five."

"Hmm, our lives were much different then, the tower above had only just started construction and we had only recently finished the first of our underground cities."

"How long had you been living underground then?" Evean asked.

"Ten years, since the shelling had started. The war had finally ended the year before, and the decision to keep everything underground had only just been made. It was a different time."

"I am sure it was. So who would know of tales of monsters and the devices made to kill them?"

"Back during that time," he continued, ignoring Evean's question, "we had discovered a way to travel to another place. A place that had not been touched by the war here. It was the people there who told us how to build the towers, the seven towers of our homeland.

"They told many stories from other places that they had visited or heard of. It is perhaps there that you will wish to travel."

"The portal outside the walls of the tower compound?" Evean asked.

"Yes, exactly. That one."

"Ah, good," She said, "Then I guess we should be going," she said and started to stand.

"There is a problem however."

"What?" Evean said frozen halfway up from her seat.

"Travel through the portal has been cut off. We do not understand why."

"Cut off? What do you mean?"

"No one is able to walk through it anymore, and no one has come out of it for over two decades."

Evean looked at me, "Can a gate be closed?"

I shook my head, "Only temporarily. They can be blocked however." I looked at Sakauwa. "Can you take us there to examine it?"

"What good would that do? Our own people have tried to examine it for years now," he said scowling at me.

Evean turned back to him, "Because it couldn't hurt, now could it?"

I could feel that she put some power in to her words.

Sakauwa pondered that a moment, "I guess it could not hurt. I'll summon an officer to escort you."

"Do you think you could come with us?" Evean asked.

"I was planning to," he said with a nod.

A half-hour or so later, Sakauwa, Evean, Suzona, Loomis and I, plus four officers, were driving out of the tower compound to the portal.

The portal was in the port compound as I had suspected, it was about thirty feet from the water's edge. There were some markings painted on the ground, along with a couple of railings that were set up, but off to the side of the portal.

"Come, let me show you," Sakauwa said, getting out of the half-track rather slowly. He led us over to one of the markings painted on the ground, and motioned at the empty space before it.

"When our people walk over the line there, nothing happens," he said.

"What do you know about the gateways?" Evean asked, giving each of us a sharp warning glance as she then started to slowly walk around the perimeter of the spot they had marked out.

"They are connections to another world. Our scientists believe they are some sort of tunnel through space to another place."

"Did your people ever venture through the gateway alone? Or did they only go with the ones who came out of the gates?"

"Both," Sakauwa said.

"And did the ones who went through on their own, did they come back?" Evean stopped in her circuit of the area they had marked out for the gate, and made a gesture as she talked, touching the actual portal for a moment.

"At first they did, but then they stopped. We can only assume that something happened to them. Because when others came out here, they could not go through."

"Very curious. Could you come here, Will, and take a look at this?" She asked.

I nodded and walked over to where she was standing and looked at the empty space, even squatting down a moment. In the process I put my hand on the actual portal as well. It felt fine, though I didn't recognize the feeling it gave me. It didn't feel dangerous at all.

But I knew from experience only natural dangers could be felt. Manmade ones you wouldn't know about until you stepped through. If it was blocked, by a physical object; then I guess that you would rebound off of the gate, Fel had told me that was what happened with portals from the underworld, or negative plane. I'd have to ask him if the same was true for regular portals as well.

"This is curious," I said after staring at the space for a minute and coming up with what I hoped was a good line of bull. "I need to think about this for a while, perhaps sleep on it."

"So, you see something?" Sakauwa asked looking at me skeptically.

"Yes, I do. But each of these gateways is different. They leave a faint pattern on the ground, caused by faint eddies in the wind currents that play through the interface between the worlds. The way the blades of grass are moving, it does not look right." I stood up. "I really need to meditate on it for a while."

Suzona and Loomis walked over to me then, each surreptitiously touching the portal, but being careful not to step through it.

"Let us go back inside then," he looked up and around at the sky and shivered briefly. "The sooner, the better."

"Not used to being outside?" Evean asked him as we got back into the half-track.

"No, not anymore. When I was a young man I came outside many times. But now, I prefer the comforts of my home."

I spent the ride back thinking about what I'd seen. The portal had drifted to the right of its original position by a good ten to twelve feet. If they could sense the portals and travel through them unaided, they would have known that.

But they didn't.

This meant that there were no people here who were capable of going through the portals by themselves. At least none who had been brought up here to look at it, and from what he had told us, those who could go through it had, and not returned.

So, either something on the other side of the portal had changed dramatically twenty or so years ago, or there was something he wasn't telling us.

Evean was continuing to try and make small talk with him, asking about his job, his life, what he did, what he liked to do. That she hadn't told him that the portal had moved and that not just anyone could walk through it, made it clear to the rest of us that she had suspicions.

Suzona was chatting up one of the guards who appeared to have taken an interest in her, no doubt having picked up on Evean's suspicions as well.

"One of the guards will escort you back to your friends," Sakauwa said as we walked back inside the base of the tower. "In the morning you can meet with my superiors and tell them what you suspect. As well as any suggestions you might have on opening the gateway back up for us."

"Of course!" Evean said and gave a small bow, "It is in our interest to get it working again as well."

"Until tomorrow then," he said and left us.

The guard that Suzona had been chatting up was the one who led us to where the others were waiting for us.

"So, what did you find?" Shin asked as we entered the room.

"We're not sure," Evean said looking around, "Something isn't quite right."

I looked around as well; it was a rather nice room, with six doors leading off from both sides and another two on the wall opposite the doorway we'd entered by. The guard had accompanied us inside, and I'd noticed there was one standing outside the door as well.

"The doors on the back wall lead to showers and toilets," Gregory said, "the doors on the sides are to bedrooms. If you want to get a bite to eat, I can take you down to the cafeteria."

I noticed Joseph was sitting by one of the walls and looking at the guard then at me, then at the doorway, over and over again. About the third time he did it, I got the message.

"You know, why don't you show us?" I said to Gregory, "I'm sure the four of us could use a bite to eat."

"Sure!" He said and hopping out of his seat, he led us out of the room, Suzona almost begged off, but when I touched her arm she stopped and followed with a nod.

By the time we got to the cafeteria the guard talking to her had given Suzona some sort of contact information, and then left.

"What was that for?" Suzona asked me.

"Joseph wanted that guard out of the room." I said softly.

"Oh," she nodded and looked over at Gregory.

"Get some food first," He said in a low voice.

We each did so, and then met him back at a table in the center of the room, which had people seated at tables all around it, talking with each other.

"The room is bugged," He said in a low voice, that we all had to strain to hear. "Joseph is finding all of the devices, so he can try to figure out where we can talk unheard."

We all nodded.

"What did you find?" He asked.

"They can't sense the portal," Evean said, continuing to keep her voice low. "All of their jumpers have gone through and not come back. Same for the people who were visiting here from the other sphere."

"Do you think something happened to them?"

"Remember the locked gate?" Evean asked.

We all nodded.

"Something isn't right here; these people are up to something. They all look like there's a war on."

"If there is a war on, where is the military?" I asked.

"All around you," she said. "Haven't you noticed how everyone is always going someplace? No one is ever congregating in the hallways talking?"

"Why aren't they in uniform?"

"I'm not sure, but I bet you all the ones up in that tower above us are in some sort of uniform." Evean paused a moment, "Besides, how much of this place have we seen? What looks like a recreation level, and an office full of bureaucrats."

"So, what do I tell them in the morning?" I asked.

"We're not going to be here come the morning. Suzona, work that guard for everything you can get tonight. But be back by two."

"Okay," Suzona nodded.

"Now, sit up, eat your food, and try to act natural," Evean said.

"Do you need anything?" A woman asked walking over to us. She was dressed like the guards had been.

"No, just saying a blessing over the meal, being thankful for our safe arrival," I said and smiled at her.

"Oh, okay," she said and continued on.

Evean smiled and winked at me as we all started to eat.

I was laying on a bed in one of the rooms, stretched out and in my champion form. When we'd gotten back to the room, Joseph indicated a spot where you could talk, softly, and not be overheard, as long as the others in the room talked among themselves to provide cover. So Evean set up there and talking to two of us at a time, we'd developed a plan, and after Suzona got back with whatever she had learned, we'd implement it.

Until then, Joseph, Shin, and Jane, were going to wander the complex and see where they were allowed to go and where they were not. The intention was to scout out a path to get us back to the surface with as little interaction with other people as possible.

I'd decided to go take a nap and I preferred sleeping in my champion form, as I was more likely to wake up if someone showed up unexpectedly. Joseph had been clear that while there were microphones everywhere, there were no cameras, so being in my champion form wouldn't be noticed.

I woke up when the door opened, and someone slipped into my room. I had the lights out, so it was as dark as it gets when you're a hundred feet underground in an artificial environment.

"Will?" I heard Teshes say.

"Yes?" I answered.

"Ah, so I did pick the right room," She chuckled.

"I'm in my champion form," I said in the language of Hiland. I'd learned a while ago that when you were in your champion form, you had access to the languages that you knew in it. As it was also her native tongue, I figured she'd understand me.

"Oh, a moment," She said and I heard the zipper of a jumpsuit being pulled down. A minute later she joined me on the bed, also in her champion form.

"So, to what do I owe this honor?" I asked softly. I was sure anyone listening to us would be going nuts trying to figure out just what language we were now speaking.

"You're the God Slayer, I'm the one getting the honor here," She purred.

I chuckled, "That might have worked on me a decade ago, Teshes, but I'm not a young boy anymore. Besides, Evean already used that one on me."

Teshes giggled, "Actually, I'm not being as manipulative as you might think. I've only been a champion for four years, and my goddess is a god of fertility. You're a pretty big deal to me."

"A goddess of fertility?" I said surprised. It hadn't occurred to me that there would be such on Saladin, but it should have. "What does a champion for a goddess of fertility do?"

"Oh, about the same as any other champion I guess," She cuddled up against me, "except for the leading armies into battle or fighting wars. Selentia relies on the cooperation of the other gods and goddesses in the land."

"So, why are you here then?" I asked surprised. I'd figured that any champions sent would be of the more militant variety, like everyone I already knew was.

"Because it is my world too? Because somewhere along the way I may be able to do something to help? Selentia is very aware of the danger of this monster."

"And?" I asked, "There sounds like there's a bit more to that explanation."

"Well, we are not on bad terms with your god Feliogustus, and we'd most definitely like to be on better terms," She purred and I felt her hands start to get more adventurous.

"My opinion doesn't carry all that much weight with Fel," I chuckled.

"And my Sel told me I'd be wasting my time," she chuckled back. "However, I think I would rather enjoy wasting my time with you, than with that Loomis."

"You don't like Loomis?" I asked rolling onto my side and facing her, not that I could see her in the darkness.

"No, he is glib with his words and fast with his money, but in the morning he will always go back to his wife with nary a thought to the promises he made the night before. I've seen his type many times growing up."

"What about Evean?"

"Roden and my Sel have an understanding; we've known each other for years now."

"Jane?"

"Sel sees no conflicts there, and I like Jane. She is more likely to protect than to attack."

"Shin?"

"I know nothing about him, he is new to Saladin, only having been here a year."

I nodded slowly, "So, what brings you to my room?"

"You have to ask?" She purred rather huskily.

"Actually, yes, I do!" I laughed.

"Any male that has Evean chasing his tail is one that I definitely want to get to know."

"Oh?"

"Most definitely."

She pulled herself up to me and kissed me rather passionately then, and I was impressed. I wondered briefly if she and Evean compared notes on technique?

TWELVE
1ST WORLD
TOWER

"So, have fun, Will?" Evean teased me as we sat with Joseph in the 'safe' zone while the others talked. It was a little after two in the morning according to the clock on the wall. Suzona had gotten back an hour ago, and Evean had been consulting with her, Joseph, Shin, and Jane on what they'd all learned since then.

"Hey, you told me to keep everyone happy!" I said and winked at her.

"You know her goddess is a fertility goddess, right?"

I nodded, "Yeah, she told me. Why? What of it?"

"Watch out you don't end up with any unexpected children," Evean smirked.

"Watch out yourself," I smirked back, "maybe I'll have her turn those abilities on you first, assuming she can even do something like that."

"Why, Will! I didn't know you cared!" Evean said feigning surprise.

"Can we get back to the present here, and save your flirting for later?" Joseph grumbled.

Evean sighed, but was still smiling. "Okay. So Suzona confirmed my suspicions: this is a military installation; you either work for the government supporting the military here, or you work for the military.

"The tower is a military project; she suspects it is some kind of a weapon. Apparently losing the war didn't sit well with the locals and they're engaged on some sort of large scale retaliation plan. The portal's closing has caused difficulties, as they were buying both technical gear and knowledge there to help with their project here."

"So, the 'lack of weapons' line was a lie?" I asked.

"Very much so, weapons are kept in their quarters and are not usually worn inside the facility." She looked at Joseph, "Tell him what you learned."

"We were allowed to walk around pretty much wherever we wanted to by ourselves. The only places we ran into that were 'off limits' were the lower levels, which I suspect is where all of the military equipment is kept; living quarters and barracks, which makes sense really; and the tower."

"Did anyone get any kind of look into the tower?" I asked him.

"Shin did."

"How?"

"Apparently he seduced one of the guards or something. He was a little vague on the details."

"Embarrassed is more like it," Evean chuckled.

I sighed, "Whatever, what did he learn?"

"Not much, just that the center of the tower is an open shaft, which runs down deep into the ground. It's about fifty feet wide, and there are guide rails along the side, that twist like the rifling in a gun barrel."

"So, it's some kind of launch system?" I asked looking between the two of them.

They both shrugged.

"No idea," Evean said. "But the biggest point we learned is that the guard outside the door calls someone, whenever one of us comes or goes. He has a radio that he uses."

"Radios don't work well underground," I said looking at Joseph.

"It's more of a localized type system with repeaters in the ceiling. All of the guards have them. Simple, but effective," Joseph replied.

"So we take out the guard and they won't know we're out there."

"Until another guard sees us. But because of its simplicity we can partially jam it."

"Oh? How?" I asked.

"Simple, just set the unit to broadcast and send some white noise over the channel. That locks out anyone else being able to report in. However, the control center broadcasts out on a different channel, so they'll still be able to send out orders. Jamming them would be a lot more difficult."

"We're not going to be here long enough to matter," Evean said. "We have a pathway out of the tower that involves the least amount of observation now. We take out any guards we see, lock their radios to transmit, and once we're outside; we make a break for the portal."

"What about weapons?" I asked her.

"We'll have to restock once we get through the portal. I don't want to take the time to try and find our swords and bows."

"I was thinking, why don't we just take theirs?"

"The living quarters are down two levels below this one, I'd rather not waste the time."

"What about the guards by the tower? Are they armed?"

"According to Shin, yes, they are."

"So we take some of their weapons before we go," I suggested.

"Which of course would set off every alarm in the facility," Joseph pointed out.

"But they'd think we were going for the tower and would ignore us making for the portal, which they think is broken anyway," I countered.

Evean shook her head, "It's not a bad idea, but I'd prefer stealth to us making a racket. I don't even want us to jam their radios unless we're discovered. They'll probably think we're going to the tower anyway; it is the center of the installation after all.

"Plus, we really don't care what they're up to here; we have problems of our own first and foremost."

I nodded, "Okay, you're the boss."

"Good, now go take care of our door guard, and then we will take our leave."

I nodded and getting up I went over to the exit.

Opening the door I shifted into high gear as I moved out into the hallway, there was just our ever present guard there, and no one else, so I struck him in the larynx, then grabbed his hands before he could trigger anything and dragged him back inside.

I started to gag him, figuring I'd heal his crushed larynx before he died, but Evean shifted into her champion form and wrung his neck, surprising me. I looked up at her and she shook her head no, so I just shrugged and searched his body while Joseph took his radio. I was surprised to find that he had a small semi-automatic pistol in a holster under his uniform shirt, concealed in his left armpit. I found an extra magazine in his back pocket and I handed them both to Evean, as Shin quickly stripped the body, and then donned his uniform.

I tossed the body into one of the rooms while everyone put their packs on, and then grabbing mine I followed everyone out of the room as Shin led us down the hallway.

When we got to the end of the hallway, there was another guard around the corner. Suzona smiled and waved at him, and as his hand came up to wave back she moved in closer with the shifted speed of a champion and got him in the eye with one of the knives she'd pocketed from the cafeteria when we'd had dinner.

They stripped this body and Joseph quickly donned this uniform as Gregory stashed the body in a closet.

Shin and Joseph led us down another hallway, and then motioned for us to stay where we were and they both strode off together around the corner.

A minute later Shin came around and waved us on, so we followed at a trot and when I turned the corner I saw Joseph removing the radios and pistols from two dead guards. I took one of the radios and pistols, as Teshes and Gregory hid the two bodies.

"Guard post," Joseph whispered and we all nodded.

"Now, we go up this stairway to the main floor. From there, it's about a hundred yards to the ramp up to the exit."

Everyone nodded and Shin and Joseph led the way up the staircase.

"*What are you two doing away from your post?*" I heard come over the radio, followed by silence.

I dashed up the stairs with Evean, the rest following us. Shin had the guard by the throat and was choking him while Joseph relieved him of his radio and gun.

"What happened?" Evean hissed.

"Our luck just ran out," Joseph said.

"*Guard Suzuki, report!*" cane over the radio.

"Try and fool them," Evean said to Joseph.

Joseph shrugged and keyed his radio, "This is Suzuki. Honaki and his buddy just came up here to ask me for something."

"*Honaki, Tunsada, report!*"

I raised a hand, "Tunsada, reporting."

Shin dropped the now dead guard. "Honaki, reporting."

"*All guards, Level three, report!*" the radio continued, "*All guards on alert! Report anyone out of place!*"

"Well, guess they know something's wrong," Joseph said.

"We better hurry before they figure out what," Evean said. "Run for the exit, go!"

We started down the hallway at a trot, with Shin and Joseph leading. There were only two people we passed on the way, but neither was in a guard uniform or wearing a radio. So they each just gave us a surprised look, and Joseph waved to them as we went by.

By the time we got to the top of the ramp, the doors were closed and even in my champion form I was unable to force it.

"Central controlled," Joseph said. "These are pretty heavy doors too. We'll have to find another way out.

"*Command, the foreigners are not in their rooms, and ....*" The voice broke up into static as Joseph did something with his radio.

"The tower," I said.

"What? Why there?" Evean asked.

"The lower ring had windows; we can bust one out and leave through there."

"Okay, Shin, take us there."

"They'll have guns," he said.

"We don't have a choice, now let's go!"

We raced back down the ramp, and into the main hallway, the voice on the radio was declaring an alert and warning all guards to shoot us on sight. The main way was still clear, thankfully, and Shin led us down a series of corridors, then suddenly skid to a halt. We were all in our champion forms at this point, I had the top half of my jumpsuit off and the sleeves tied around my waist, otherwise I wouldn't have fit in it.

"Armed guards around this corner," Shin warned us.

"Okay, guns ready?" Evean asked and Shin and Joseph pulled theirs out as Evean, Gregory and I readied the other three.

"Go!"

We turned around the corner, there were two guards with carbines, and both of their eyes went wide. I guess the sight of three cat creatures charging them stunned them for a moment. I shot one in the head, and then moved to shoot the other one, but someone had already gotten him.

We grabbed the carbines and the ammo each guard had, Suzona took one of them, I took the other and passed my pistol off to Jane. Teshes and Loomis had no experience at all with firearms, so we didn't bother giving them any.

Shin led us through another doorway, then to a heavy metal door, but this one was secured like one on a ship, so we were able to undog it and move through, dogging it closed behind us.

I looked around; we were standing on a concrete platform, supported by metal beams, which circled a large shaft that went both upwards and downwards. There were two stairways, on opposite sides that lead both up and down, and on the edge of the shaft were four thick rails that led up and down along the shaft. Taking a step forward I could see that they did slowly spiral around the shaft as Shin had mentioned earlier.

It was sort of like looking up a giant gun barrel. Looking down was only darkness, but from the dank smell of the warm air coming up from below, I suspected that the shaft went down a very long way.

"Up the stairs!" Evean ordered, and I ran over to the staircase and we started up.

We made it past three levels before people started shooting at us. Two more and Evean stopped us.

"Shin, Joseph, go through the doorway and see if you can find a window on this level for us to escape out of."

They both nodded and with Gregory covering them, they went through the door.

"Will, Suzona, try picking off those snipers above us."

"Sure thing," I said and using a cantrip to steady my aim, I started to pick off the shooters on one side, while Suzona started on the other.

"There's no windows!" Shin said as he came out.

"We're not above ground yet?" Evean said surprised.

"Oh, we're above ground," Joseph said. "The whole floor is packed with explosives. Tons of it. We circled the exterior wall. We need to go up higher."

"Explosives?" Evean pondered, "Can we grab any?"

"No, it's all racked in huge canisters."

"Will, Suzona, lead the way!"

We nodded and started to move up the next stairway, by now we were drawing a huge amount of fire; I was picking up minor flesh wounds from shrapnel as bullets struck the beams around us. I grunted as I got hit with a bullet in the arm, healing myself immediately. Suzona had been hit twice so far, but then she'd been exposing herself more than I was. She'd also been hitting more of the shooters above.

"Check this floor," Evean ordered again.

Less than a minute later they returned.

"Same thing," Joseph said.

"Damn, keep going up!"

For the next four floors, it was the same, on the fifth floor, we ran into something different.

"There's only concrete on the other side of the door," Joseph said.

"We're at the second section," I called out.

"Keep going up!"

"I'm out of ammunition," Suzona called.

"I'm down to my last few shots as well," I said. "We need to get up to the guards we've shot, and restock."

"Charge!" Suzona grunted and she and I did just that, with the rest bringing up behind us.

The next ten levels were agony. The platforms were much farther apart here, and we were still under fire from above. However we were moving fast enough that they were having a harder time of hitting us at first. Of course they were trying to shoot all of us. Someone must have realized their mistake as suddenly they switched to just shooting at me and Suzona and we both started picking up gun shot wounds rather quickly then.

When we got to the top of the final ring, I emptied the last four shots of my carbine into the men standing there, and then promptly fell down and burned the rest of my healing on my wounds. Suzona did the same, and Joseph, Shin, Evean, and Gregory opened up on them with their pistols, dropping all ten of them, then scooped up their carbines and opened fire on the ones on the far side of the shaft who were also shooting at us.

Teshes and Loomis healed me and Suzona as the shooters on the far side were cut down and Jane picked up one of the spare carbines and moving over to the glass wall, shot it full of holes, and then knocked the panel out with one well-placed kick.

"It's a long way down," She said looking out the window.

"How long?" Evean asked.

"Six, seven hundred feet, I'd guess, maybe a little more. We can probably climb down these external girders, but that will still leave us with five hundred feet or so from the top of the bottom section.

I got up slowly and gathered up all of the spare ammunition I could find, reloading my carbine and putting the extra magazines in my backpack.

"Hey, they've stopped shooting," Gregory said.

"Probably regrouping," I said and walked over to the entryway from the level below. It was a large metal box with a door on the front. An elevator.

"Hey, why don't we just use the cables from the elevator here and rappel down the sides?"

"Hell yes!" Gregory said and we started searching through the metal cabinets for tools, which we found a lot of, and then started on taking the top off of the elevator motor housing.

"What are they doing up there?" Evean asked Shin.

"Watching us," Shin said peeking out from cover. Every once in a while someone up top would take a shot if we strayed too close to the shaft.

"I suspect they're going to come up the stairways like we did, once they have an assault force ready," Evean said. "How much longer for you to get those cables out?"

"Pulling them out now," Gregory said as he cut the car lose from the mechanism. The car dropped about a foot, but now that we had the top free we could start spooling it out. I grabbed the end of the cable and jumped off the top of the elevator structure, using my weight to start pulling it down.

Loomis came over to help me and we dragged the heavy cable over to the window.

"Okay, I'm going to jump out and use my weight to pull the cable out, once I hit the ground, lock it off, then start down," I told everyone.

"Just be careful, and keep your eyes open. As soon as they see you go out the window, they're going to realize we're escaping." Evean said.

"Got it."

Getting a firm grip on the end of the metal cable I leaned out of the broken window and then pushing off I jumped.

The ride down was fairly quick, but as I neared the top of the first level it started to slow. I hit with my knees bent, then dragged the end over to the edge of the other roof and jumped off again, it started to slow down to a crawl about halfway down the next section, and then started to pick up again. Looking up I could see why, Loomis, Teshes, and Jane were already starting down the cable.

As it was, it still ground to a halt before I made it to the ground, but it was only about twenty feet left, so I just let go and rolled when I hit the ground.

I took cover behind some equipment then, and watched for any guards or attackers as the others started down the cable.

Loomis, Teshes, Jane, and Evean, had made it down, Gregory, Joseph, Suzona, and Shin were on their way down when guards started coming out of one of the exits at the tower's base.

Jane, Evean, and I opened up on them with the carbines, and they all took cover immediately. A couple tried to pop up and shoot at the four still coming down, but we were able to pick them off before they killed anyone.

"Everyone able to run?" Evean asked checking everybody.

"I need to be healed," Shin said.

"I got it," Teshes said.

"Anybody else?"

We all shook our heads and a moment later Shin said he was good to go.

"Okay, circle around the buildings then run straight for the gate to the other compound. Let's go!"

Evean took off at a jog and we all followed. It was still dark out, and as we moved away from the tower, the darkness and the shadows of the structures around it gave us cover. Several times along the way we engaged in running firefights with the people from the tower who were giving chase.

Whatever guards might have been in front of us must have fled before we got there, because our trip to the gateway to the other compound was unimpeded.

"How's it look?" I asked Evean as she peaked through the gateway.

"The guards around the portal are fleeing."

"Not very brave," Suzona said.

"There are only two of them."

"Well I forgive them, then," she growled.

"Let's get going," I said and carbine at the ready I jogged through the gate and took up a defensive position about halfway to the portal.

"Let's go everyone!" Evean said and made a beeline for the portal.

I took a moment to start shooting out the lights, Gregory stopped next to me and helped, and then we both took a few shots at the fleeing guards to keep them moving.

I watched as everyone went through, then Gregory and I ran for the portal, shooting back at the gate, just in case anybody caught up with us, to keep their heads down.

"Well, can't say it's been fun," I said to Gregory as we ran up to the portal.

"Oh, I don't think they'll be forgetting us for a long time!" He laughed as we stepped through.

THIRTEEN
2ND WORLD
ENTRY STATION

"Drop Your Weapons!"

"Huh?" I said looking around. Everyone else was on the ground, arms out, hands empty, and we were being lit up by an extremely bright wall of lights in front of us.

"I say again, Drop Your Weapons!"

"Drop them!" Evean said from the ground.

I shrugged and dropped the carbine, Gregory did the same.

"Now, move away from them and lie down!"

I moved away from where I'd dropped it, and dropped first to my knees and then lowered myself to the ground.

"How many more are coming?"

"That should be all of us," Evean called out.

"Okay, now, one at a time, I want you to stand up, and move off to the right; I'll tell you what I want you to do."

"Sure. Will, you first."

"Gee, thanks," I mumbled.

"Okay, standup."

I did as I was told.

"Keep your hands above your head, and move to your right."

I slowly walked to the right, like he said. After a minute I moved out of the glare of the lights, and into a tunnel.

"Stop!" the voice said.

I stopped.

"Turn around slowly."

I did as I was told.

"What weapons are you carrying?"

"At this point, nothing. I have some ammo in my backpack however."

"Move to the end of the tunnel."

I walked down the tunnel; it looked a lot like a ten-foot wide concrete drainage pipe. When I got to the end, I was in a concrete box with metal rungs going up the side.

"Climb up the ladder," the voice said, so I did. As I neared what looked like the top I heard the voice tell another person to stand and walk to the right.

I climbed out onto a platform. I was on what looked like a forty by forty foot platform made of wood, without any walls. There were lights shining down from above, so I couldn't see past the edge of the platform. It felt like I was outside now, and there was a man in a uniform with a weapon pointed at me.

"Strip please, and put all of your things in a pile, then sit on the ground over there."

"Sure," I said and did as he said. As I was finishing up Suzona climbed up out of the hole.

"Strip please, and put all of your things in a pile, then sit on the ground over there," he repeated.

"Why?" Suzona demanded.

"Because I will be very sad when I go home tonight and tell my wife I had to machinegun a woman."

"Fine," Suzona grumbled and did as she was told.

Evean was the next up, and she got the same treatment, not hesitating to comply. About that point a woman walked onto the platform and tossed me a small bundle, tossing a second one to Suzona.

"Put those on please, and follow me."

We stood up and did as we were told; we had both been given jumpsuits that felt like they were made out of paper. By the time we'd finished putting them on, Teshes was coming up onto the platform and the guard was telling her what to do.

We were then led out into the darkness, but the pathway we were walking on was lit by indirect light, so I could see where to put my feet as we walked, but not much else.

"What is going on here?" Suzona asked, not sounding very happy. I could understand the sentiment, I wasn't exactly happy with being herded around much either.

"With the place you just came from, you really have to ask?" The woman said.

"We were told nobody had gone through that gate in twenty years," I told her.

"We get people sneaking out of there all the time, though you're the first big group in a very long while."

We came to a series of small huts and she directed us into one, had us sit down at a wide table, on the far side from the door, and then closed the door behind her as she came in and sat down across from us.

"Aren't you afraid of us attacking you?" I asked her.

"You've had several opportunities to do so already. The platform with the single guard, the walk here through the darkness, and when I just closed the door."

"Maybe we're just trying to lull you into a false sense of security," Suzona grumbled.

"Well if so, it's working really well. So tell me, how high is the tower now?"

"One of them said it was two hundred and six stories now." I told her.

"Sounds like they're getting close then. I think two-forty-five is the goal."

"Goal for what?"

"First, tell me, why were you even there?"

"We're searching for a weapon," I told her, "a special one used to destroy a monster."

"And you thought they would have it?"

"Stories of the weapon came to my world from a portal linked to that world. We saw the tower, felt the portal, and when they said they'd never heard of such a monster or such a weapon, we figured this was the next place to check."

"You're all portal jumpers, or at least most of you are. Why didn't you just go to a high tech world and bring back a bunch of high tech weapons?"

"Because it doesn't work that way," I told her.

"Sure it does."

"It's a gojira," I told her.

"What's a 'gojira?'"

"Look," Suzona suddenly sat up and stared down at the other woman, "we have cooperated, we have been polite, we have no interest in anything other than getting this device and leaving. If you don't know about the gojira, then take us to one that does or let us go find them ourselves.

"This is obviously way out of your league."

"Yes, but I am the one with the power here, so I guess you'll just have to wait it out and do it my way," She said with a pleasant smile.

"Actually, no. We are the ones with the power here." Suzona was starting to look pissed now.

"Suzona," I warned.

"No, Will. I'm tired of this treatment. I put up with those people in the last sphere; I even slept with one of those bastards! But at least they didn't start shooting at us until we tried to leave! We have been honest, we have been polite, and I will be treated with the respect I demand, or there will be hell to pay!"

I looked at the woman sitting on the other side of the table and shrugged, "It's been a rough day, and we've both been shot up quite a bit and well, we are on a bit of a timetable, so maybe ...."

Just then everything kicked into high gear and I threw myself at the woman, figuring that would be the safest place in the room. Suzona obviously had the same idea and we both ended up on either side of her as a barrier came crashing down, neatly bisecting the table in two.

"What ...." the woman started, her eyes wide.

"Oh, we're Will and Suzona Blues, and we're on a mission from god." I deadpanned.

"What the hell are you talking about William?" Suzona growled at me.

"Old joke. Let's go outside and see how much trouble we've stirred up."

"What about her?"

I looked down at the woman, who was now looking rather worried.

"Well, might as well bring her along, maybe we can keep anyone from losing their heads and shooting at us."

"What are you?" She said.

"Champions. You know what a champion is, don't you?" I told her.

Her eyes got just a little bit wider and she nodded slowly.

"Well you now have nine of them in your world, and if you upset us anymore, we are prepared to wreak bloody havoc all across it until we get what we are after. *Understand?*" Suzona growled.

Her eyes widened another fraction. Honestly, I was surprised she wasn't shaking in fear or terror. Suzona is one very scary woman when she's pissed.

"Of course," I said in a milder tone, "We're not here to cause any harm or damage, we just want the Okishijen

Desootoria, and then we're gone. If you don't have it, then we just want any help you can give us on finding it.

"And we'll be grateful, very grateful." I added.

"I think, I think you should talk to my commander," the woman said.

"Yes, I think we should too. Wonderful idea," Suzona snarked.

"Now, now, Suzona. No need to twist the knife, she's helping and while I know you didn't get to kill that many people in the last sphere, no reason to bring those troubles here."

I helped the woman to her feet. "What is your name by the way?"

"Emiko."

"Ah, well Emiko, please, show us the way."

She led us out of the small building and there were a large number of armed men surrounding us, with their rifles being held at the ready and trained on us.

"They're champions," Emiko said.

"We heard," one of the men said.

"Then you know that you can't stop us," Suzona said and smiled, "So why not put the guns away, and let's avoid any trouble."

"There are ten of us, and we're all rather well armed."

"Do you know what happens when you kill a champion?" I sighed.

"They die."

"And then they reincarnate, and they come back, and they kill you, and everything around you. It's really not pretty."

I shifted then, the paper jumpsuit shredding as I assumed my champion form, "And if I have to come back here, when I am done with this place, there won't be a living thing within ten miles of this point. Understand?" I growled.

Suzona smiled, "It's always the calm ones who are the most deadly you know."

"Uhhh," the guard who had been doing all the talking said while looking at me in shock.

"Put the guns up Captain," Emiko said, and I could see she was shaking now. "He's serious, and yes, champions do come back."

"And people say I have a temper," Suzona laughed.

I sighed, "Yes, I'm a bad man, I know it." I looked down at Emiko, "Your commander? Please? I promise not to start anything, and unless provoked I know Suzona won't do anything either."

"Yes. Come," She said and we started following.

"You might want to release the others," I said to the captain as we passed, "To prevent any other problems from occurring, Captain."

"I will consider it," he said.

We walked down another pathway, and came to a much larger building. In my champion form, I of course had much better night vision than as a human, which was more of a function of the feline body than any champion power.

Looking around, I could see there were a number of what looked like turrets facing the platform we had sat on when we'd climbed out of the tunnel, and what looked like several more sniper platforms located in different places. We were also inside a very large tent.

We weren't outside at all.

"You've spent a lot of time on this set up," I said to Emiko. "Were they really causing you that much trouble?"

"I'm not allowed to talk about that, the commander will discuss it."

We came up to the door, and it slid open by itself, so I led the way in, followed by Emiko who was followed by Suzona. There was a large man in the room, he looked older and had a slight Asian cast to his features. His uniform was spotless and well pressed. He had that air about him.

"I am Commander Yuudai, am I correct in understanding that you are not residents of the world you traveled here from?"

I shook my head, "No, Commander. I am from a world where the people look like me," I motioned with a hand to my champion form. "My name is Will."

"And you?" He motioned to Suzona.

"I'm from a different world," She said.

"So, why then are you working together?"

"Favors, debts, alliances, matters of honor," Suzona replied. "Most of our group are from William's world."

"And you are all champions?" Commander Yuudai seemed surprised at that.

"Yes, we are," I replied.

"I have heard it is rare to see three champions together, and you are nine. You must understand that there will be much concern over this."

"Well then let us sit down and talk, to ease those concerns," I sighed. "I understand your position, Commander Yuudai. You just had a powerful force of people, each backed with the power of a god, dropped into your lap.

"However, you must understand *my* position. We have been tasked with an urgent assignment to find and retrieve a particular item, as quickly as we can. We have no other desires, no other concerns. We just want to get one, if you have it, or continue on our way to the place that does.

"If you could bring Evean here, she would probably be much better at telling you exactly what it is we are looking for, than I am."

"Emiko, go find this Evean and bring her here, please." Commander Yuudai ordered.

"Yes, Sir!" and she turned and left.

"So, why all of this?" Suzona waved her hand around her, "Have the people from the sphere on the other side of that portal been such a problem?"

Commander Yuudai nodded, then gestured to a group of seats around a table, "Please, have a seat," he said and walked to the head of the table and sat down.

I took the seat on his right; Suzona interestingly took the seat on my right, rather than on his left.

"Many years ago, the people on that world, which we call the 'War World,' experienced a rather large war, one that covered the entire globe if we understand it correctly. We had only just discovered the portals ourselves about sixty years ago, and had set about mapping those in our lands. After the war had ended in the other world, it was suggested by many that we help those poor unfortunates that had lost their war."

"I'm rather surprised that they haven't rebuilt," I said.

"Yes, well. It has to do with their philosophy. You see, they do not believe that they can lose; they simply believe they are being punished for not trying hard enough. Their leader is a religious idol to them, and early during the war he died and was replaced by his son, who was only a young child.

"Having a young child's view of things, and being steered by men who had their own fates at heart, rather than the fates of their people, he threw a large tantrum when the war was lost and commanded his people and his generals to win at all costs.

"That he was all of seven years old at the time did not lessen his orders at all apparently."

"Power in the hands of a child is never a good thing," Suzona said shaking her head.

"We did not know of this at first, we discovered it later. Almost too late, sadly. We engaged in trade with them, and even let some of their people come here to study and learn. We had hoped to teach them ways to be more successful and efficient. To rebuild their cities better, produce more food, and other goods to keep their people from want.

"After all, happy people with full bellies do not make war, no?"

"No," we both agreed.

"But it turns out that what they were really looking for was a way to build a weapon of mass destruction. Some of the laws of physics are different there, so some of the weapons we have here, will not work there, but one of them was a geologist, and apparently he came up with the idea of the towers."

Evean was escorted in at that point, and I held up my hand and waved to her, she saw I was in my champion form, and I saw her expression relax slightly.

"Evean, Commander Yuudai was just explaining to us what the purpose of the towers is back there. Please, have a seat and join us."

Evean nodded and took the seat on Commander Yuudai's left, across from me.

"Continue, please," She said.

"They're earthquake machines. Once they have all reached the calculated height, a large slug made out of lead, with a tungsten tip, will be dropped from the top of the tower, with a rocket to push it up to speed.

"As it passes into the ground, a large shaped charge will be detonated behind it, to help accelerated it to transonic speeds."

"Won't the air in the tunnel in front of it, slow it down?" Evean asked.

"The design of the slug has two air channels, shaped like venturi tubes to act as ramjets, and coal dust will be dumped into the shaft prior to firing to act as fuel. They will automatically fire once the proper combustion pressure is reached. The effect will be almost as if the pressurized air is pulling the slug down the tube, until it impacts with enough force to send a huge seismic wave down into the crust to hit the fault line the tower is centered over."

"And what will that do?"

"Seven of them firing at the same time will cause a seismic event of such scale that it will be felt for thousands of miles, and a tsunami of such a great height will be generated, that every port, every naval base, every coastal city, that borders their ocean will be wiped clean from the surface of the earth."

"That's insane!" I said, "They'll destroy themselves in the process!"

Commander Yuudai shrugged, "Probably. But their emperor does not care. Plus he lives up in the mountains a good distance from all of the towers. Chances are that he and those living around him will probably survive."

"Sad, very sad," Evean said taking over the conversation, "but it has nothing to do with us, and is not why we are here. Now, what *we* are looking for is a device called the Okishijen Desootoria. The monster we are fighting comes from what many call the 'underworld' or the 'negative plane'. It is such that normal weapons and attacks do little to no harm to it.

"About forty-five years ago, a man from the world that was once my home, came here, or perhaps a world further along, learned of both the monster and the device, and came back to tell stories of it."

"So you're basing your search on a story told over four decades ago?" Commander Yuudai said, rather skeptically.

"He made a movie; he recreated the look and sounds of the monster almost perfectly. Which considering what he had to work with was an impressive feat. So we know that someone, somewhere, faced this same monster, but they had the technology to destroy it."

"How do you know it will work for you?"

"Because our gods told us it would."

Commander Yuudai looked taken aback by that statement.

"Your gods?" He asked.

Evean and I both nodded.

"Then why can't they tell you where to find it?" He asked looking confused.

"Will?" Evean looked at me.

"Commander," I said, "Just as we are all constrained by rules in our lives, some of which are made by our leaders, others which are made by the laws of physics of the world we live in, gods are also constrained. If they were not, they would wreak havoc across the many worlds of what they call 'the Infinite' in their struggles for power and followers.

"So there are things that they *know*, but which they cannot *tell*, to us, their champions and their followers. But in many cases they can tell us when we are right."

"So, they know that this weapon will work, but they can not tell you where it is?" He asked.

"Correct, we must find it for ourselves."

Commander Yuudai nodded slowly. "Well, I can tell you that we have no monsters like that here, ourselves. Also, I am not sure we even know about these portals to the negative plane. I will be sure to alert our researchers to those immediately.

"However, we have had a lot of people explore our portals, and after we started to suspect what the people on the War World were up to, we started to track the names of those coming through our portals, especially that one. So if you can tell me his name, maybe we can help."

"That would be a great help, Commander Yuudai," Evean said. "His name was Eiji Tsuburaya, and if we could talk to whoever records the stories of those who have examined the portals as well, that would be a great service too."

Commander Yuudai nodded again, "I will talk to my superiors immediately. I think they will understand that having nine unhappy champions in our country is probably not a good idea. But I must ask ...."

"Yes?" Evean prompted.

"What is in it for us?" He asked rather bluntly.

"Have you ever been owed a favor by a god, Commander?" Evean said and smiled.

"No, but I can sure understand *my* bosses wanting to be," he said and then smiled. "I'll see to it that your things are returned and that you are all given the freedom to come and go as you wish."

"Thank you, Commander Yuudai," Evean said and standing up bowed to him. Suzona and I stood up and bowed to him as well.

"Emiko, if you could show them to their things and the others, and make sure everyone understands that they are honored guests and to be treated accordingly?"

"Yes, Commander," Emiko replied from where she was standing by the door.

Commander Yuudai stood up, "If you will excuse me, I have some calls I must make."

"So, just why are you in your champion form, William?" Evean asked in a voice that could only be best described as 'frigid'.

"My fault," Suzona said.

"Oh, really now?" Evean said looking at Suzona.

"Yes, I lost my temper and started to go off on poor Emiko here, and well, we *were* making progress, but someone thought they could trump us and William ...." Suzona shrugged.

"Put them in their places," Evean sighed.

"Well, he does it so well," Suzona giggled, surprising the hell out of me, I didn't know Suzona could giggle up to that moment. "He's done it to me before."

"Yeah, me too," Evean giggled back.

I sighed and tried not to face-palm.

"I like the way his fur stands up, you just know he's thinking of shredding you into tiny little pieces of bloody flesh!" Suzona laughed and Evean joined her.

"If you're all champions, why are they afraid of you?" Emiko asked me.

"Oh, they're just teasing," I sighed. "I'm really a very nice, reasonable, forgiving kind of guy."

They both laughed even harder then.

"You know that threat that he made?" Suzona said to Emiko.

"Yes?" she said sounding a little unsure of herself.

"He would have done it, he's done worse."

Emiko looked up at me and moved a little further away as we walked.

"So now what?" I sighed shaking my head.

"Get everyone together, gather up our things, see about some food and a place to relax while we wait to see what Yuudai's people turn up." Evean said.

"By the way, Will, are you planning on staying in your champion form?"

"Seeing as I completely shredded this suit, I thought I'd wait until I got my clothes back," I grinned.

"I think you should stay like that for now."

"Really?" I said looking at Evean.

"It's a constant reminder of just who they're dealing with."

"What about everyone else?" Suzona asked.

"Let's not overwhelm them," Evean warned. "The last thing we want to do is to scare them too much. We want their cooperation after all."

Emiko led us to a second building that was up against the side of the tent-like structure that covered the area.

"Why the tent?" I asked her as we went inside.

"To keep it dark inside. It's hard to blind people with the lighting otherwise. Also it hides the snipers we have stationed around the perimeter."

I nodded, "I noticed them, and the turrets you have aimed at the platform. What's up with the chamber the portal opens onto?"

"Oh, there's a ten thousand gallon water tank on top of it. If things get out of control, they just flood the room and drown everyone inside."

"Nice trick," Evean said, and nodded to the rest of the group, who all had their clothes back on. I went and found my things, took off the remains of the paper jumpsuit and put on my shorts, then repacked my backpack. Interestingly they had put my carbine with it. I strapped that to the pack as well.

"Would you like some breakfast?" Emiko asked.

"Most definitely!" Joseph called out.

"Then follow me to the mess hall."

We didn't meet with Yuudai again for the rest of that day, though he did ask for clarification on the spelling of Eiji's name. He said he'd hoped to have something tomorrow.

They had put us in a small barracks room that had ten beds in it; we shared the showers and other facilities with the rest of the men and women in the building. For the most part, they got along with us okay, though I got a lot of looks.

"Well, I must say, they're being rather nice to us," Gregory said, stretching out on his bed.

"If they're nice to us, they don't have to worry about us wandering around," Loomis said.

"And the quicker they find where we're going, the quicker they get us out of their fur," Teshes agreed.

"I just can't believe those people back at that tower are so freaking insane," Joseph said. "When that thing goes off, they're all gonna die. There are enough explosives in that building to level everything within miles! If the pressure wave doesn't kill everything in the tunnels, the collapse of the tunnels will."

"Not our problem," I sighed.

"I just hope they can tell us where that guy went," Shin said. "I really like Saladin, and I really like working for Tonoponah,"

"Where is your home, anyway?" Loomis asked. "I've never heard of Tonoponah before.

"Tonoponah is my goddess, the kingdom is called 'Right Isles', I guess because they were the right ones, or something. We're five large islands, and eight smaller ones, out in the ocean. An ocean-going monster would destroy our way of life. That's why I'm here, you?"

"Bronsard is right next to the Barassa; my god Quzelatin's main temple is there. Many of those slaughtered outside the city were troops from my country. I was there with Evean when the monster rose out of the pit."

"Were you killed when Evean was?" I asked.

"No, I was with the reserves when it happened. We had been preparing for an assault, but when the monster came, I called it off. It was already doing more damage to Barassa than we ever could."

"What about you, Will?" Shin asked.

"William had no part in the attack on Barassa," Loomis said. "His people weren't interested."

I looked over at where Loomis was lying down, and frowned. "It's not that we weren't interested. We were still recovering from the last war with Barassa. The one that cut their army down to the point where the rest of you could go after it. My people spent two years in open war with Barassa, and many more years of dealing with their agents."

"Two years? You only fought in Marland for one!" Loomis laughed.

"The Mowoks are my people as well, Loomis. They're not part of the Hiland kingdom, but they are devout followers of Feliogustus, and I spend time among them as well."

"Eh, those savages?" Loomis laughed.

I was about to open my mouth and make a response when I felt a hand on my arm. Turning I noticed Evean, who shook her head. So sighing I laid back down. It was getting late, so smiling at Evean; I drug her over to my bed, curled up with her, and closed my eyes and went to sleep.

FOURTEEN
2ND WORLD
ENTRY STATION

"Unfortunately, we do not have any records on your man," Commander Yuudai said.

It was noon of the following day and Evean, Jane, Loomis, and I were sitting at the table in his office. Evean had felt that only the principals needed to be there, the ones whose people were facing the most immediately threat.

"What about the Okishijen Desootoria? Or gojira? Have they heard anything about that at all?" Evean asked.

Yuudai shook his head, "No, we haven't been able to turn up any references to those either. This morning, my superiors sent out a call to all the libraries in this country, as well as those of our allies, to see if anyone had any works, or knowledge of any works, containing those references."

"Now what?" Loomis said and looked at Evean. "We've hit a dead end! Maybe he didn't come this way after all!"

"No," Evean said, "This feels like the right place."

"I say we go back and look for another portal from the tower world!"

"Go right ahead, Loomis," I growled. "No one is stopping you."

Loomis froze and then turned and glared at me. I was still in my champion form, and he was not. Of course my champion form was still a good deal larger than his anyway. He didn't say anything, but I did notice Evean's hand on his arm, squeezing it.

"Do you have a list of the descriptions of all of the portals in your area? What there is on the other side of them?" Evean asked.

"Of course," Commander Yuudai said.

"If it would not be too much trouble, would you mind if Will and I looked through them?"

"No, of course not! We are committed to doing everything we can to help you with this."

"Why just you and William?" Loomis grumbled.

"Because we're the only ones here who have seen the works of Mr. Tsuburaya," Evean said to him, and then turned back to Commander Yuudai. "When can we start?"

"I'll have a couple of terminals set up for you within the hour. It will take a while for you to go through them all, there are about three hundred of them on the islands, and another fifty or so within a hundred miles of our shores."

"That sounds more than acceptable, thank you very much, Commander. Believe me; your cooperation is being appreciated."

"Well, I did mention to my bosses that little tidbit about being owed a favor by a god, and well, they're really turning themselves inside out to earn it. Apparently there is something they'd like help with, though they haven't told me what it is."

Evean stood up, and the rest of us did as well.

"We'll come back in an hour, Commander. Again, thank you."

We all followed her out the door.

"You're not that tough," Loomis grumbled at me.

"Loomis," Evean said sweetly, "we do not argue in front of the mortals, okay?" She turned to me next, "Same goes for you, William, understand?"

"Yes, Evean," I said, and tried not to grumble. While Loomis had started it, she was right that I shouldn't have responded.

"So, think you'll find anything in those records?" Jane asked.

I shrugged, "Maybe. His movies had some iconic stuff in them, but it's been forty years, so who knows?"

"Well, we will just have to see now, won't we?" Evean said and taking Loomis's arm in hers she strolled off towards the barracks.

"I think I can tell what she's up to!" Jane laughed.

"Is it me, or is Loomis turning into a bit of an ass?"

"A lot of people in his country's army were killed, a lot more will probably die the next time this gojira thing attacks. He's just worried about his people. If it were Hilanders dying, you'd probably be breathing fire."

I sighed and shook my head, "Maybe, I don't know. I just don't want to undercut Evean in front of others. She's supposed to be in charge, and that means we bitch in private."

"Been learning about being an officer I take it?" Jane chuckled.

"I do try to pay attention. Besides the last thing I want is Evean pissed at me."

"Still afraid of her?"

"I just know her well enough to know that she *will* get even with me, if I piss her off."

"Oh, I think that's true of everyone here, Will!" Jane laughed.

"No, she'll go out of her way, and make sure it hurts, a *lot*. Like I've said before, I know where she comes from; I know what she grew up with. She'll make you suffer for it.

"So, I'm not going to get on her bad side, unless it's really important."

"Plus you like her," Jane teased.

"I like you too, you know," I teased back.

"What do you say we find someplace quiet to go kill an hour?" Jane said with a wink.

"I'd love to!"

It was four or five in the morning. The files that they had on each of the portals were huge, some had pictures, and all had drawings. There were details on the people, the culture, maps, names of cities, names of famous people, religions.

Some of the files were more detailed than others, it would take anywhere from fifteen minutes to an hour to go through a file, and on the bigger ones I really just skimmed. I'd started around one in the afternoon, Evean had shown up about an hour later, and gave a mumbled 'sorry' as she went by for some reason.

At this point I'd gone through thirty-three files, and had two hundred and twenty some-odd to go. I was working from the ones farthest away, to those closest. Evean was working from the closest to the farthest. I figured as she was more likely to have seen any relevant movies than I was, it was better if she looked over the most likely candidates.

"Will?"

I looked up at Evean, she was looking at me.

"Yes?"

"Come here and look at this."

"Sure," I said and getting up I went over to her terminal. She got up and I took her seat.

"What am I looking for?" I asked.

"Just listen to the file and examine the pictures."

"Okay," I yawned.

I put the headset up by my ear and had the computer read the descriptive text to me; it was a high tech world, slightly higher tech than here, about forty years ahead of Japan if I was understanding what I was reading.

Evean started to massage my neck and shoulders, "Oh, that feels nice," I purred.

"Not mad at me?" She asked.

"Why would I be mad at you?" I said and clicked to open the folder with the pictures on it.

"Well, I did run off with Loomis, and I haven't been with you in a few days."

"Evean, I do not own you, I know I'm not the only man in your life, don't worry about it, you're my friend, when we can, we can. When we can't, I'm not upset if you're with someone else."

"And here I was hoping you'd be more possessive," She mock sighed.

"I'm married, Evean, you know that."

"I thought that was just because she was the queen, and she was hot."

I swore to myself, I wasn't sure I wanted Evean to know the truth about my wives or my family yet, maybe ever.

"Did I hit a nerve or something?" She asked surprised.

I looked at the pictures while I tried to compose a reply and then just froze.

"Well? Did I?" She prompted again.

"Ultraman?" I said and looked back at her, and then back at the picture. Everyone was dressed in fairly futuristic styles, with a lot of silver in their fashions. The pictures were from about thirty years ago, the people had strange looking headsets, but the style was so similar I couldn't mistake it. The big give away though were the people in the orange and white uniforms, patterned to look almost like a matador's jacket, wearing ties and helmets.

Evean gave my shoulders a squeeze and leaned around to kiss me.

"I thought so too! This has got to be it! The next place he went to!"

"Where is it located?" I asked clicking back to the local map.

"Fifty miles from here, almost in the same location as the portal to Koshien stadium back in the tower world. Notice how the geography in this world, the last one, and Japan are all fairly similar?"

I nodded, "I wonder if he was trying to go back home?"

Evean came around and sat in my lap, shifting into her champion form. "Possibly, or maybe he thought it would lead to a more similar world," She kissed me then, and it was like the first time we'd kissed, I could tell she was hitting me with her pheromones again.

"Hmm?" I asked and looked at her.

"It occurs to me that we've never had sex in our champion forms, and if anyone here has earned it, it's you, Will," She purred.

I looked around the office, it was deserted, the workers in the building had gone home to bed hours ago.

"Don't worry, it's empty, I checked."

I smiled back at her, I know I could have used a cantrip to deal with the effects of the pheromones, but right now, a little celebration sounded like a good idea.

"You know, you're my only friend, William," She said and kissed me again.

"Then I guess I need to work at becoming a really good one," I purred and kissed her back, as I started helping her shed her jumpsuit.

Definitely time for a little celebration.

"So, like it?" Evean was curled up against me, in the nook of my arm.

"I'd think that was obvious," I purred and kissed the top of her head.

"Better than back in Japan?"

"The pheromone thing is interesting, and you do look good with a furry tail," I teased.

Evean frowned, "So you're saying it wasn't any better?"

I laughed, "Your champion body is more limber, stronger, and has a lot more stamina, and I definitely enjoyed using and abusing it. But, Evean, I'm making love to Evean, not Evean's body. You shouldn't sell your original body short; I could barely walk when you were done with me."

She got soft and cuddly again, "I wish I had met you years ago."

"You did," I chuckled.

"I meant years before that!" She laughed.

"Back then I was a lot more of an ass than I am now," I told her, "It's better that you met me now, when I've had a chance to grow up."

I felt a sharp pain just then, and winced, it seemed to come from the spot where Fel usually made his presence known.

"You feel that?" Evean asked.

"Roden just yank your chain too?" I said untangling and getting up.

"Yeah, we better get back to the others, something's up."

Grabbing our things we ran back to the barracks, we got about halfway there and Jane came running out of the building.

"There you are!" She said, "I have to go! I have to go now!"

"What? What's going on?" I asked her.

"Marland is under attack; the monster came up the river this morning, and is attacking the city!"

I swore, "Open up a portal to the temple, we'll both go."

"No," Evean said and grabbed my arm, "You're needed here, you can't go."

"But it's my home!" I growled.

"She's right!" Jane said, "Fordessa said Fel doesn't want you coming back without the weapon."

"But you need help!" I said, "One champion isn't going to stop that thing!"

"I'll go!" Shin said. I noticed he was standing rather close to Jane, and I could smell his scent on her. I wondered briefly if they had a thing going, but whether they did or not, he was a more experienced champion than she was. Hopefully that would help.

"Thanks, Shin!" I said. "Go!"

Jane looked over at Shin and smiled at him, and then taking his hand, she concentrated a moment. As soon as the portal opened, she jumped through, collapsing the portal as soon as they were through it.

"What the hell was that?"

I turned and saw the Captain I'd met when we'd first gotten here, what? Two days ago?

"Champions can open portals to their homes," I told them.

"So why'd they leave?"

"Monster problems," Evean said turning and looking at him. "Go wake Commander Yuudai, we know where we're going next, and we'd like to be on our way as soon as possible."

"Yes, Ma'am!" he said and trotted off.

"Let's get our gear and tell the others," I said. "Then I'd like to take another look at that file before we go."

"Yes, we should," Evean agreed.

Several hours later we were on our way, the seven of us split up into two vehicles as we were driven to the next portal. The files called it the 'Technical Men' portal, because the society there had been a much higher tech level back then, to Evean and I however, it was the 'Ultraman' portal.

Looking around as we drove I was rather impressed with the quality of the roads and the new state of the construction. I was in the second car with Teshes, Suzona, and Joseph. Evean was in the first car with Loomis, Gregory, and Commander Yuudai who was accompanying us, to make sure there weren't any last minute issues. As well as to keep an eye on us too, I was sure. We were all in our local forms, but the driver knew who and what we were, and I think was a little in awe of us.

"Why is everything so new?" Joseph said looking around. "I thought your country was a fairly old one."

"Oh, we had a war here fifty years ago," The driver said, "it took us a while to rebuild, however it allowed us to make so many improvements to our towns and cities."

"Well, I guess that's a positive way to look at it," Joseph said looking rather thoughtful.

"You had a war here too?" I asked surprised.

"Many of the lands connected to the 'War World' experienced war during the same years," the driver said to us. "The current theory is that the rulers of that world spent many years exporting spies and other infiltrators to the neighboring worlds and eventually incited hostilities in many places."

"Really?" I asked surprised.

He shrugged, "It is just a theory. Some think the War World may have been coerced along with the rest of us, others claim that it was such a monumental event that all of the neighboring worlds experienced some version of it, that it was inevitable."

The driver shrugged again, "Nobody really knows for sure, but that was when the government decided to keep watch on the portals, and to take measures for the ones leading to the one place they discovered was having a negative effect on our world."

"What? They caught them doing something?"

"A lot of the tech that they're using to build their super weapon came from our world. We tried to be friends with them at first, we were much farther along in our rebuilding than they were, and we figured that like us, they'd seen the error of their past and were turning their efforts to the future."

"That must have been a rude awakening," Joseph sighed.

"Yes, and some of their people were quite violent when we stopped helping them."

"So, who won your war?" I asked, curious.

"Nobody. There was a revolution here, and the people who had been promoting the war were thrown out of power. The new government was able to negotiate a peace, which considering the damage all sides had done to each other by that time, was happily accepted by all."

I wondered a little about their theories, maybe I'd ask Fel about it later, but the thoughts that were going through my mind the most were about home. Thinking about the destruction that had been dealt with here made me wonder what was the monster doing to Marland? How many people would die? How many homes would be destroyed?

I sighed and gave my head a small shake. There were two more cities up the river from Marland, if the monster decided to go that way. The first was some small city-state that had been in Barassa's sphere of influence, but due to trade and a strong defense had managed to stay somewhat neutral and out of all the political maneuvering for the last decade.

The second was Rivervail, the former Mulander city.

I just hoped this thing wouldn't, or couldn't, go up the river past the falls that Rivervail sat on. That would bring it a lot closer to Hiland city, Rachel, Fel, and my family, than I was comfortable with.

"Something wrong, Will?" Teshes asked.

"Just worrying about my home," I said. "I hope Jane and Shin are able to find some way to drive that monster off before it does too much damage."

"All the more reason for us to be quick about this," Teshes said.

"Any idea of how many more places we have to search?" Suzona asked.

I shook my head, "Evean and I both recognized the outfits in the files, so we're positive that this is the next step. But we don't know if it's the last one."

"Well, we have five more days before the next attack; hopefully we will find this weapon by then."

"Assuming that the monster sticks to its five day cycle," I pointed out.

"Assumptions and prayers are all we have to go on these days," Teshes said and smiled at me a little wanly. "So, we might as well make the most of them and do our jobs."

I nodded and went and looked back out the window as Joseph started to discuss other things about this world with the driver. I didn't pay much attention to it anymore however, I just wondered if the next world wasn't the right one, then what?

The portal was in the middle of a field, surrounded by a twelve-foot high chain link fence. There were a few guards, but nothing like the set up at the other portal we'd come through.

"Do you get a lot of people coming through here?" Evean asked Commander Yuudai as we got ready to go through.

"Not really. There are a few random travelers and a few regular traders, but it seems that most travelers don't appreciate showing up in places where they will be recorded and tracked."

"Does the government on the other side know about the portals?" Joseph asked.

Commander Yuudai shook his head, "Not as far as we know. Our researchers believe that the genes that allow people to travel through these portals are much less common on the other side. The people who come through here have all been experienced travelers, and not natives of that world."

Originally we had wanted to wait until after nightfall, but we'd been assured that it would be okay to go through now. According to data they had, the other side was located in a parking garage at a sports stadium.

"Well, might as well go." I said and looked at Evean. "I'll go first."

"Sure thing, Will."

I walked up and put my hand on the portal, it was another one I didn't recognize, and then just stepped through.

FIFTEEN
3RD WORLD
ULTRAMAN - STADIUM

I stepped out into a parking garage, as expected and moving out of the way quickly I immediately started to look around to see if there was anybody else around.

There were cars parked down at the far end of the garage, which was pretty far away from where I was now.

Joseph followed next, then Gregory, Suzona, Loomis, Teshes, and Evean.

"Just as the reports said," Evean said looking around.

We'd all changed into the street clothes that we'd last worn back in Japan before coming through. From the pictures we'd seen, it looked to be the most innocuous. We'd also packed everything into the Honshin Tigers gear bags and put the backpacks away.

"Well, let's go," Evean said and linking arms with Loomis she led the way.

I found myself partnered with Teshes and Gregory and Suzona had teamed up again, with Joseph walking solo behind us.

"Maybe we should buy Joseph a leash," Suzona teased.

"If he wasn't the size of a large pony, that would be a good idea," Evean said.

"He'd draw too many looks," I said, "he's a wolf; people would be staring at him."

"Which means they wouldn't see us at all," Gregory noted, "as they'd be too busy staring at him."

"They have a point you know," Joseph said. "It's not like I mind being a dire wolf, quite the opposite in fact," he added with a shrug.

"I'll keep it in mind," Evean said. "But first, we need to get a better idea of what this place is like, and where we have to go to gather intelligence."

"First we need to find our way out of this building," I grumbled looking around. One of the problems with traveling into a new sphere was that while you picked up the spoken language automatically, you didn't get the written one.

Oh, you could learn it pretty quickly, and the more languages you learned the easier it got over time. At the last place the computer terminals we'd been using had the ability to read the text on the screen, which had saved us a lot of time. We'd only gotten them to set that up for us once they'd realized we couldn't read their language and they got tired of translating everything for us. So right now none of the signs meant anything to us.

Twenty minutes and a few wrong turns later we made it out of the garage and out onto the street. We didn't really stand out all that much. While our clothing was different, there were so many styles on the people walking around, that I don't know if anyone would have cared.

"We need to find a place to stay," Evean said. "A base of operations to work from."

"I think I can do that," Suzona said. She was in her champion form, and she was drawing quite a few looks from the men walking by. She unhooked her arm from Gregory's and started to strut off down the street. Once she was fifty feet in front of us, Evean shrugged and started to follow.

Within the next ten minutes a rather well dressed man came up to her and started to talk to her, after a few minutes he took her hand and fifteen minutes later we were at a rather nice hotel. Which the two of them went up into.

"Damn, you been giving her lessons or something, Evean?" Joseph teased.

"I may have handed out a pointer or two," Evean said with a grin.

"Now, all we need is money," I said looking around. "Should a couple of us split off and find a pawn shop or something?"

"Let's settle down and wait here for a little while and see what Suzona has for us."

I shrugged and went and found a place to sit. There were quite a few benches in front of the hotel, and no one bothered us at all.

It was probably a half-hour later when Suzona came out, waved to us, and then led us into the hotel, through the lobby and into an elevator.

"So, got us a room?" Evean asked.

Suzona nodded, "Yes, it should do for now."

I looked at the elevator panel and figured out the number symbols fairly quickly. We were going up to the eighteenth floor.

When the door opened, she led us down a long hall, to a room, and pulling out what looked like a credit card, she used it to open the door.

"I only have one of these, so if we all go anywhere, you can't get back in without me. Unless we leave someone here." Suzona said.

We followed her inside, the room was rather nice, and as hotel rooms go, it was big enough. There were two double beds, and a small sitting area with a couch and a table and a couple of chairs.

I went over to one of the nightstands by the beds and started opening drawers. Sure enough, I found a rather large book, with lots of writing and strings of digits on one side.

"What's that?" Teshes asked.

"Phonebook," I said.

"Or the local equivalent," Joseph put in.

"What's a phone book?" She asked.

"A listing of all the people and businesses in the area that have a telephone. We can use it to contact them." I said looking through it. "All we need to do now, is learn the language," I sighed, "Which could take weeks."

"Oh, I got that covered too," Suzona said, looking a little, well; best I could describe it would be 'guilty.'

"Oh? How?"

"My god Isengruer now knows it. I suspect tonight when we all sleep, our gods will teach it to us."

Joseph looked at Suzona, "How does your god ...." He stopped and gave her a pained look.

"I asked Isengruer not to kill him, with any luck, he should be able to send him back, or at least some place nearby in this plane."

I was about to ask, but then I remembered what I had done to that senator.

"What happened?" Teshes asked me.

"She chucked him through a portal into her god's main temple," I said

"Oh?" She paused a moment, "And?"

"A god can pretty much read any normal mortal's mind within their own main temple."

"Oooooh," Teshes nodded. "Well, I guess I'm going to take a nap then and speak with Selentia.

Evean looked around at everyone, "It's getting late in the day, we might as well all do the same."

I nodded and went and lay down on the couch stretching out. I hadn't slept in a couple of days and was out like a light.

§   §

The first thing I noticed was that Fel looked rather somber, that did not strike me as a good thing at all.

"How bad?" I asked, looking around the bar. Nothing in it had changed, and of course I had not felt anything, unlike the time one of Fel's temples had been destroyed. Then again, I was not on the same plane right now, so maybe the distance had muted it?

"It's not as bad as it could have been, William. It is however not good and there are a few things that I know will hurt you personally."

"Was Jane killed?" I asked concerned. That would bother me, however she would reincarnate in three days if she had been.

"No, Jane managed to survive, barely. However Shin was killed, as was Felecia."

That stopped me.

"Felecia is dead?" I asked, shocked. "How?"

"The monster went after Fordessa's temple. We suspect that because it is a main temple and the monster being a creature of the negative plane, that it was drawn to the powers that the temple exudes.

"Jane, Shin, and of course Fordessa, with the help of the army and the faithful did manage to drive it off, eventually. But the damage to the area was substantial. While Felecia was instrumental in its being turned away, she died in the process."

I sat there stunned, I just couldn't believe it. High priestesses rarely saw combat, and for one to have died, it must have been a huge shock to Fordessa and her power!

"Yes, it was," Fel said, "And it will be several days before she is over it, at least Jane survived and was able to appoint a new High Priestess in her wake, or things would have been significantly more difficult.

"However, I have some worse news for you, William."

"What could be worse than that?" I asked, shocked.

"Goth was also killed."

"WHAT! Goth? How?" I was on my feet with no recollection of having even stood. "What was she doing there? Why was she fighting? What happened?"

"She was helping to care for the wounded in one of the shelters that had been set up, in a large building near the temple, before anyone had realized that the temple's presence was drawing it.

"While they were fighting with the monster and repulsing it, it leveled the building, everyone inside was killed," Fel said softly.

Some people will tell you that you cannot cry in a dream. Well I can say that they are most definitely wrong. After all I had been through with Goth, the arguments, her attempts to make me more than just her adopted father; I had never once pictured a world without her in it.

.   And now she was gone.

"Did, did she suffer?" I asked.

"No, William. It was quick."

"I notice you didn't say painless," I gasped, trying to collect myself.

"Has it ever been painless for you?" Fel asked gently.

I shook my head, "No, it hasn't."

"So, you'd know I was lying if I had said it was."

I nodded, "At least it was quick. Can I go talk to her?"

"In a moment. I think you should spend a while here with me first," Fel said and pulled me close and hugged me. I couldn't remember ever being hugged by him before, but it did help, I got my composure back after what felt like a few minutes.

"Are we in the right sphere, Fel?"

"You are in one on the way to where you must go, anything more than that, I can not tell you. Isengruer did share the language with the rest of us, and I have now shared it with you."

"One last question," I started.

"Yes, Goth has earned paradise. She really was among the faithful and her actions today were worthy. She died working hard to save others less fortunate than herself."

"Thank you, Fel. Do you know if it will attack the city again?"

"I do not think it will. Either it will attack the towns outside of Marland, or it will continue up the river and perhaps attack Riverbend next."

I nodded and turned and slowly walked towards the door. I really had no idea what I was going to say or do, and I was dreading having to say goodbye to my daughter, but I had to do it.

I found her almost as soon as I stepped out of the pub; in that dreamlike semi-haze that everything was when I came here in my dreams. She came running up to me and grabbed me.

"I'm sorry, Daddy!" She said hugging me.

"It wasn't your fault, Goth," I said and kissed her and hugged her back.

"If I hadn't volunteered to help with the wounded, I might not have been there," She sighed.

"You were doing the right thing; you were helping others who needed help. How could you have known?"

"I know, but I'm still sorry," She sniffed.

"Well, at least you get to go to paradise," I said and hugged her again.

"Really? What's it like?"

I shook my head, "I have no idea."

"But you've died, several times!"

"I don't get to go, until I stop working for Fel." I gave her another hug, "Do you want me to say anything to Adams for you?"

"He's here too, Father."

I looked up over her head, and sure enough, there was Second Adams.

"How did he?" I asked her.

"He was protecting Felecia, and he tried to protect her with his body. Unfortunately, it wasn't enough. You know she's here too?"

I nodded. "I need to see her, but I can't stay long. This is a dream to me; I'm actually sleeping and will have to wake up soon."

"Okay, and thank you, Father, for saving my life. I know I would have died years ago, cold and alone, if you hadn't saved me. I had five wonderful years that I would never have gotten."

I nodded and gave her a last kiss and hugged her again. "Goodbye, Goth, I'll see you on the other side, someday."

"Goodbye, Daddy."

It took me a moment to let her go, even if it was only a dream, it was still difficult.

I went over to Second Adams, and shook his hand, "I'm sorry, thanks for treating my daughter well, and thanks for fighting to save the city and the temple."

"You're welcome, Sir," He said and then he went off to join Goth.

"Isn't easy, is it?"

I turned and saw Felecia standing there.

"It never is," I sighed. "Though this is the first time I've had to say goodbye to family here."

I shook my head, "So how did it get you?"

"That stupid breath weapon it has. Hurt like a bitch too!"

I smirked, "Dying always hurts, at least it always has for me."

Felecia nodded, "Well, at least it was fast. Poor Jane, she's so distraught. She thinks she could have saved me."

"Could she?" I asked.

"No, not at that point. She would have just been killed as well, along with her friend Shin. Then things would have been a real mess with no one around for Fordessa to tell who to appoint in my stead."

"Well, when I see her next, I'll talk with her."

"Just get that thing, whatever it is you're all after, soon. Get it and kill that monster before we lose too many more people."

"I will, Felecia, I promise, I will."

I could feel somebody tugging at me, in the real world.

"I have to wake up now, goodbye Felecia," I said and gave her a hug and a kiss.

"Not going to try for fling before I cross over?" She teased.

I sighed, smiling, and then waved as I left.

§　　　§

I opened my eyes, it was Suzona.

"Yes?" I grumbled.

"Let's go check out some of the shops in the area," she said.

"What about the others?" I said sitting up and stretching, I noticed Teshes and Joseph were getting rather comfortable on one of the beds.

"Gregory is already off looking around, and Evean and Loomis are in the bathroom, getting 'clean'." Suzona smirked when she said the last word.

"Evean said that?" I sighed and stood up.

"No, Loomis said it. I suspect he's a bit shy."

"Unlike those two," I said and nodded towards Joseph and Teshes, who were quickly going from 'comfortable' to 'intimate'.

Suzona laughed and the other two ignored us as we left. Most of us really weren't all that shy about sex anymore, a lot of champions having a rather freewheeling approach to sex and sexual relations, which after a while tended to rub off on you.

"I think Loomis is still pretty new," I said as the door closed behind us and we headed down towards the elevator.

"He is a local one, isn't he?"

I nodded, "So is Teshes."

"I like Teshes," Suzona said, surprising me, "she's a nice girl."

"Gee, and here I had no idea at all," I teased half-heartedly.

Suzona winked at me and smirked, "And you will continue to have no idea, other than perhaps in your dreams."

I shook my head at that. "What about Loomis?"

Suzona shook her head then, "I do not like him. It is like he is always up to something."

"We're all up to *something*, Suzona. We're champions after all."

"But none of us really hide it, it's like he's not on the same," she paused a moment, "I guess the word would be team?"

"What about Evean?" I asked, curious about that now, as we got in the elevator.

"I have found that I respect her," Suzona sighed, "she is a strong woman, but she knows when to bend. A rare trait."

That surprised me a little, "Oh? Do you know when to bend?"

Suzona gave me an annoyed look then, "Apparently I am still learning."

I nodded, "Years ago, many years ago, before I became a champion, someone once told me that the hardest lessons to learn were always the best."

"And do you agree?"

"I'd like to go back and punch them in the face," I grumbled. "Because while the hardest lessons might be the most important ones, learning them still sucks."

Suzona smiled at me then and took my arm as the doors opened and we walked out of the elevator, "It is nice to know I'm not the only one who feels that way."

"I don't know, you always seem to be the first one to go out and challenge anything or anybody, Suzona."

"That's because I'm a woman, and a beautiful one as well, William. I had to work twice as hard to prove myself when I was a young girl. Men look at me and most really have only one idea in their heads."

"Can you blame us?" I said with a wry smile, "Some of us find beautiful, confident, and competent women rather sexy."

"Hush," she said and gave my arm a push, but she was smiling all the same. "We are here to look for a pawn shop. Not so that you can seduce me."

"Just being honest, I'm still rather surprised at how much you chased after me."

I was surprised to see Suzona looking just a tad embarrassed then.

"Yes well, it's not often that a woman of my looks is refused by a man. It made me curious, especially when I could see you like women, a lot. I haven't had a lot of men say no to me before, William."

"I bet you haven't had any men say 'no' to you before."

"Evean told me that you treated her the same way at first, and after having seen her champion form, I must say that I am quite impressed."

I shrugged, "Desperation isn't a good dating strategy. But to be completely honest, there are people who I love, and who I do this all for. So just getting laid doesn't really do all that much for me anymore. I'd rather sleep with someone I like, than sleep with someone just because they're beautiful."

Suzona didn't say anything right away, we just strolled along looking at the shops, getting used to being able to read the signs. It's always a little strange at first when your god puts something in your mind.

She sighed suddenly, "I must ask, do you like me, William?"

I stopped and turned to face her, "Honestly? Not at first. At first you were just a hot, but annoying, woman who was trying to play dominance games."

She frowned a little then, but didn't look away.

"But now? Yeah, I like you, Suzona. Since you told me about your past last week, since you've stopped playing dominance games with me, or Evean, yes. I like you. Maybe some day we can even be friends."

I turned back towards the direction we had been walking and she leaned into me a little as we started to browse the shops again.

"I'd like that, I don't have many friends," she admitted.

"Yeah," I agreed, "I'd like that too. I'm learning just how hard it really is to have friends when you're a champion."

"Especially when all of the mortal ones will eventually die off," Suzona sighed.

I sighed heavily and nodded, thinking about Goth again.

We walked in silence for a while after that, both obviously thinking somber thoughts, when we came to a rather odd-looking shop.

"What's this?" Suzona asked looking over the small front window, which had several old looking books in it.

"I'm not sure, let's go in."

"Sure, why not?"

Opening the door, there was a stairway that went down to the basement just inside the door.

When we got to the bottom of it, all you could see were old wooden shelves that ran from the floor to the ceiling, all of which were full of books.

"Can I help you?" An old man asked, from behind a small counter nearby on our left.

"What kind of books do you sell?" I asked.

"All kinds," he replied. "What are you looking for?"

"Monsters," Suzona replied. "Monsters that come from the ocean and attack people on the land."

He looked at her a moment. "Fiction or folklore?"

"There is a difference?" she asked.

"Yes, the latter are stories passed down through the ages, often by word of mouth. The former are stories created by an author to please an audience."

"Folklore then," I said.

"Follow me, please," He said and came around from behind the counter and led us down one of the aisles, past several breaks, until we were near the back of the store.

"These ten shelves here," he said, and then turned and headed back towards the front of the store.

Suzona and I looked the shelves, they were each about six feet long and packed with books, no two of which appeared to be the same. We looked at each other and shrugged.

"I'll start at the top," I said.

"I'll start at the bottom then," she nodded.

After about an hour of looking through books, I realized I had barely moved down the first shelf. It was already near sunset when we came in here, I was sure we'd probably be getting kicked out soon. There had to be a quicker way to go through the books, and then I had an idea.

I did the 'eyes and ears' thing for Fel, then holding each book up against the shelf, I grabbed all of the pages, bent them back, then using my thumb carefully, I let the book's pages riffle slowly by before my eyes.

It took about a minute, and I went on to the next book.

"What are you doing?" Suzona asked me when I started in on the fifth book using that method.

"Eyes and ears. I figure Fel can process this stuff a lot faster than I can."

"Huh," was all she said, and a couple minutes later we were both fanning through the books.

I was halfway through the second shelf when I got a feeling from Fel. I looked at the book, and tossed it on the floor by Suzona.

"That's a hit," I told her, "Now to see if I can find another one."

I got a second hit before I got to the end of that shelf, and one more on the third shelf. By the time the man at the counter had come back, to tell us he was closing, we had a pile of nine books.

Picking them up, we followed him back to the front of the store.

"How much?" I asked as laid them out on his counter.

"One hundred and twenty-eight marks," he said.

I nodded, even though I had no idea what a mark was, and taking off the necklace I wore under my shirt, I removed two gold rings.

"Willing to trade?" I asked him.

He looked at the rings, then back at me. "Gold is about five hundred marks an ounce, how much do each of those weight?"

"One quarter of an ounce, each," I told him.

He nodded and picked one up and examined it, then dropped it on the counter and listened to the noise it made.

"I will give you the books, and one hundred marks, in twenty mark notes."

"One-forty," I responded, out of habit mostly.

"One-twenty."

"Sold!" I said and shook hands with him.

Half an hour later we were back at the room with a sack full of books, and I passed the six twenty mark notes over to Evean.

"What's that?" She asked.

"Clues to our next stop," I quickly explained to her what we'd done.

"Smart. Okay, let's get to looking at them."

"Where is everyone else?" Suzona asked. Evean was the only one who had been in the room when we got back.

"Out getting dinner and some local clothing. Gregory found a pawnshop and got some cash. I elected to stay behind because you had the key, plus I was kind of hoping you two would come back with a lead." Evean said, sitting down on the bed and starting to quickly flick through one of the books.

I grabbed one and Suzona grabbed another and we started to slowly page through them.

"Found something!" Evean called out immediately.

"Pictures?" I asked.

"Nope, just a tale of a gojira attacking a city." She flicked through the pages, "This isn't footnoted and they don't say where the tale comes from. But it's a start."

I nodded and continued on until I found another mention in the book I was reading. Again, it was the story, but this was in a section of stories from the Anwei region of Saiwen.

"What's the name of the country we're in?" I asked.

"Saiwen," Evean said. "I looked through the phone book earlier."

"What region are we in?"

"Why, you find something?"

"Yeah, this book says the story is from the Anwei region."

"Well, all we need it is a map now."

"Assuming that the Anwei region isn't huge."

"Well, let's see what else we can learn," Evean said, and we went back to the books.

By the time everyone had come back, we had also found a couple of crude handmade drawings, which apparently came from the original storyteller, as well as their name, Chie Hayasho.

"What do you think?" I asked Evean as we looked at the drawings. Loomis was looking over her shoulder.

"They look off," Loomis said.

"Yeah, I have to agree with Loomis," Evean said nodding.

"So, either a bad artist, or?"

"Or someone else described it to them." She said putting the book down. "Well, it's late. In the morning we can find a map and make travel arrangements."

I looked at the clock, it was pretty late. That was when I realized I was starving. The others hadn't brought back any food. I looked over at my pack, which had some rations in it, but decided to save those.

"I'm gonna go get some food, anyone want to come with?"

"I'm starving," Suzona said and got up.

"Yeah, I'll go," Evean said standing up.

Surprisingly Loomis got up as well, "I could stand to go for a walk," He said and smiled at Evean.

Before we left, Suzona shifted out of her champion form and changed her top, blending in with the rest of us. I was a little surprised, like most champions, Suzona stayed in her champion form whenever she could get away with it.

"What's that for?" Loomis asked.

"Eh, just don't want to be stared at," Suzona replied.

"I just hope we can find an open place this late," I said and we all went downstairs and left the hotel looking for a place to eat.

We found a place that was open late, and had a good dinner, then headed back towards the hotel.

When we got there however, things had definitely gone bad in a big way. The building was encircled by what had to be police vehicles, with blue and red lights flashing. There were armed men and women in body armor moving around the building, and just about then the windows on one of the rooms on what looked like the eighteenth floor blew out and the sounds of automatic gunfire filled the air.

We all stepped back, around the corner, and looked at each other.

"That was our room, wasn't it?" Loomis said, looking a little nervous.

"Seems like," I said, then leaning forward I peered around the corner, watching the building.

"Who could possibly be after us?" Loomis asked.

"Doesn't matter who, it just matters that they are," Evean said.

"Looks like we lost our gear, I just wonder if we lost Gregory, Joseph, and Teshes," Suzona said.

"I wonder if they have descriptions on all of us?" I asked.

"I bet they have a description on Suzona," Evean said. "She's stands out a lot in this crowd."

Suzona nodded slowly "Then I'm glad I decided to go incognito this evening."

"You and me both," I replied.

I watched as all of the emergency doors for the hotel popped open, and people started to stream out. I guess the explosion had either tripped the fire alarms, or a lot of folks just decided that the hotel was no longer a safe place to stay.

As I was watching, I noticed Teshes suddenly come out among the crowd. She was following the mass of people as they all streamed away from the building, her head was moving

154   *John Van Stry*

side to side, as she looked around, passing by several of the officers in body armor who apparently didn't notice her.

"Teshes got out," I said and moved out from behind the building to stand in view of those coming out of the hotel.

She saw me almost immediately and changed direction towards me, so I stepped back around the corner and waited.

"What happened?" Evean asked as soon as Teshes came around the corner.

"I was coming out of the bathroom when the door just blew in, and several men came into the room wearing that armor stuff. One grabbed me and dragged me out, as the others engaged Joseph and Gregory.

"From what I could see before I has pulled out of there, Joseph killed the first one, Gregory got the second one, and then I was dragged down the hallway by two of them, who kept asking me if I was alright, if I was okay, if they had hurt me."

Teshes shrugged, "When the explosion went off, I killed them both, and ran down the stairs and got lost in the crowd."

"Do you know if Gregory or Joseph got away?"

Teshes shook her head, "I have no idea. There were a lot of those people in the armor though. Who are they?"

"Police of some kind," Evean said. She looked back at Suzona, "Who was that guy you popped?"

She shrugged, "Just some small time criminal, apparently he was casing me out to make me one of his whores."

"Somebody must have followed us here from that last world," Loomis said.

"Why the hell would they do that?" I asked frowning.

He scowled at me, "Do you have a better idea?"

I shook my head, "No, but let's not jump to conclusions."

"Let's go, we don't want to tarry here," Evean said. "When they find the two officers that Teshes killed, they'll realize someone got away and start searching. We need to be far away from here."

We all agreed with that and started walking.

"So, now what?" I asked.

"We find a map, find out where the Anwei region is, and see if we can track down this Chie Hayasho character," Evean said. "If nothing else, if we find where they lived, we can get an idea of where to look for the next portal."

"What about the others?" Teshes asked.

"What about them?" Evean said looking at her.

"If they're still alive, they'll catch up," I told Teshes and gave her a hug. "If not, well it will be weeks before they are back again."

"Why so long?" She asked, giving me a questioning look.

"It takes time to pass through each of the spheres on your way back home. Then when you get there, you have to wait the usual three days."

"Oh! I didn't know that!" she said and blushed a little.

We spread out into a loose group; Evean led, with Loomis not too far behind. Suzona and Teshes hung together, and I followed about a hundred feet behind, bringing up the rear, alone.

Being alone was probably best for me right now, as I was still dealing with Goth's death and it was nice not having to talk to the others while trying to pretend that everything was fine.

We spent the next several hours walking across the city, there were still people out, the city being fairly large it never really completely shut down it seems, but if we had grouped up we would have stood out.

We came across a park about the time the sun was starting to come up, so we found a few benches and sat down to consider our options.

"First we need a map." Evean started. "Then we need transportation. If they're looking for us, mass transit is probably not the best way to go."

"Assuming they know what we look like," I said.

"Better we assume that they do, than assume that they don't."

"How much gold do we have?" I asked looking around.

"I've got five ounces," Evean said, "You?"

"Three and a half."

"Loomis?" She asked.

"One."

We all stared at him.

"What? I've never done this before!" He grumbled.

"I have only two and a half," Teshes said, "I'm poor, sorry."

"Eight," Suzona said.

"I'm impressed," Evean said.

"And two more of platinum," Suzona added with a smile.

"How much of their paper money do you still have?" I asked Evean.

"Just the hundred left from what you gave me. Gregory had been holding the rest."

"Well, might as well take a break here, and when the shops start opening in a couple of hours we can get started."

"Sounds good. Suzona and Loomis, you two can keep the first watch while the rest of us grab a quick nap."

§   §

I sat up almost immediately; I was back in the bar with Fel.

"Is something wrong, Fel?" I asked.

"Everything is fine back here," He told me, "Joseph and Gregory did not survive the attack however."

"I suspected as much," I sighed.

"They both realized that Teshes had a shot at escaping, so they drew as much attention as they could."

"What happened?"

Fel shrugged, "I'm not sure. Gregory overheard one of their radio conversations during the firefight. He overheard them saying to look out for the 'big wolf' that the terrorists might have with them."

That stunned me, "What? The 'big wolf'?"

"Joseph."

"But, how would they know? Joseph never took his champion form here, or even in the last world."

"Exactly," Fel said. "So what does that tell you?"

"Well, I don't think anyone could have followed us here from the tower world," I started out.

"Which leaves the people on your team."

I thought about that a bit, "Teshes got out, do you think she might have called it in?"

Fel shook his head, "The only time she wasn't with either Joseph or Gregory, was when she was in the bathroom, and there wasn't a phone in there. She didn't have the opportunity to call it in."

"That leaves Evean, Suzona, Loomis, and me," I said looking at Fel. "Do they all know about this?"

Fel shook his head, "No one else knows."

I thought about that for a few minutes.

"It's not the kind of thing Suzona would do, plus she hasn't had the opportunity.

"Evean? I'd hate to think it was her, but she's probably the sneakiest and most manipulative of all of us.

"Loomis?" I shrugged, "I don't know anything about him, though he does strike me as rather naive. Would he even know how to set us up? He's a local, like Teshes, he has no experience with technology."

"Quzelatin has been very stingy with information on Loomis as well," Fel said. "But that hardly means anything, neither Roden nor Isengruer volunteer anything on Evean or Suzona unless asked."

"And if we ask, they'll know that we know. Assuming that it is in fact one of them."

"Exactly."

"But that still leaves the question of *why*?" I sighed. "Roden and Quzel-whats-his-name have lost more people than we have, so they wouldn't want to mess up the mission, would they?"

"You're assuming that's their goal," Fel said.

"What other goal could there be?" I asked.

"Who is the most likely candidate to be causing problems?"

That made me pause, "I don't think I follow."

"You are. You have a history for over the top behavior, William, some would see you as willing to embark on a crazy or self-centered plan. Especially if you thought it would give your wife or me more power."

"But Suzona was with me the one time I was off from the group."

"Ah, but Joseph and Suzona don't get along. You never see them together, so obviously she would happily cover for you, if it got rid of Joseph. They might even argue that she was jealous of any attentions you were showing Teshes."

"But Gregory and her have a far stronger relationship than she has with me." I protested.

"Arguments made in the heat of the moment are rarely logical, William. I'm just warning you to be on your guard. Somebody cut the team down for a reason. They'll probably try again."

I shook my head and sighed, "I don't need this on top of everything else. Do you have any good news at least?"

"The Anwei region is the next one to the north of where you are. It only has one major city, and ten large towns."

"Where did you find that out?" I asked.

"One of the books you flipped through had a map in it," Fel said and showed it to me.

"Not too much different than Japan, surprisingly," I said.

"The line you're currently following doesn't diverge much from sphere to sphere. So far you've been on what's best described as a main fractal line."

"That really doesn't mean all that much to me," I sighed. "Well, I guess we'll just have to wait and see what happens next."

"At least I have a fairly good idea where all the portals are in the area," Fel said with a smile.

"You do?"

"Yes, because this sphere is so similar to the last two, the portals will be in relatively congruent positions."

"Thanks, Fel." I said and took a drink of my beer and stood up. "Time for me to wake up I guess."

Sixteen
3rd World
Ultraman - Some Park

We ended up stealing a car. Apparently Suzona knew a thing or three about hotwiring them, which surprised the hell out of both me and Evean.

We stopped at a shop along the road and bought new outfits, as well as a more detailed map. We also got some basic food supplies and gear. We weren't able to find any weapons however.

Loomis grumbled a few more times about how someone must be following us, or something. Suzona wondered if it was simply a case of mistaken identity, or if someone thought the man she had rolled was still in the room, and they wanted something from him. Either case would have simply been a matter of bad luck.

The car itself was a little crowded, Suzona drove and Evean sat in the front next to her giving directions. Teshes fell asleep sitting on my lap, while she had been rather friendly towards Loomis when we had started out, it seemed that now she was more comfortable with me.

That earned me a few sidelong glances from Loomis that were less than friendly.

I was pretty sure by now that Loomis had a problem with me, but what it was I couldn't tell, and to be honest, I really didn't care. We were all here on a mission, and we all had a lot at stake. My only goal was to get this over with, the sooner, the better.

But I still wondered. Who had done it?

And why?

If they had wanted Joseph or Gregory gone, they had succeeded. If they had wanted Teshes gone, they had failed.

Or had they wanted all three of them gone?

It was strange that they had treated Teshes like she was a hostage, not like a member of whatever it was that they had thought Joseph and Gregory were a part of. Was that because of what they'd been told? Or was it just a cultural bias?

And if it had been one of ours, when had they made the call? I tried to think back of who was where, and when, but anyone would have had ample opportunity from my viewpoint. Even I had the chance when I used the restroom during dinner.

It could be an external party, if there were any active gods here with an active champion, they might have noticed us, somehow, and made the call themselves. But that idea was stretching things and it still didn't explain the bit about the wolf.

All I knew was that if it was Evean or Suzona I was going to go nuclear on them. Evean, because she was becoming a friend and I had actually started to care about her. Suzona, because I was kind of hoping she might become a friend too.

So that left Loomis and Teshes. I wasn't fond of Loomis, so it wasn't hard at all to stick him in that role. I just didn't see him as smart enough, or conniving enough, however.

Teshes? Hard to say. Fel and the others thought she was innocent, but that was more from lack of opportunity than anything else. She didn't strike me as the conniving type, but she also wasn't stupid.

I sighed, I'd just have to wait and see what happened next, while trying to make sure that whatever it was, it didn't happen to *me*.

We found a place to ditch the car a couple of miles outside of the city, and started to walk.

"Shouldn't we steal another one?" Loomis asked.

"No, if they start seeing a string of car thefts that will lead them to us." Evean said.

"What are we going to do for a place to sleep?" I spoke up.

"Good question," Evean said. "Suggestions?"

"Pick up some sleeping bags and find an abandoned building."

"Assuming there are any around here," Suzona said.

I shrugged, "We could always break into a store that's gone out of business."

"So, any suggestions on how to find our story teller?" Evean asked

"Phonebook?" Was my suggestion.

"Assuming they're still alive," She sighed.

"Well, after that, perhaps we just start calling everyone with the same surname and see what they say?"

"Let's see what a phonebook tells us."

"Sure," I agreed.

"I have one question," Suzona said and we all looked at her. "Where do we get a phonebook?"

"Umm, has anyone seen a phone booth?" I said looking around as we walked.

"What's a phone booth?" Teshes asked.

"Something that I haven't seen a single one of since we got here," Evean sighed.

We walked in silence after that for quite a while, though not so much from a lack of something to say, more because there were more and more pedestrians walking around us as we made our way into the city.

"William, check it out," Evean said and was pointing to a building.

I looked and it said 'Library' on a pedestal out front. I looked back at Evean and smiled.

"Why don't you go inside and see what you can find, I'll take the others and look for a place to spend the night. We can meet back here, say at sunset?"

I nodded, "Sounds like a plan."

"Want some company?" Teshes asked.

I shrugged and looked at Evean, who shook her head.

"William doesn't need any *distractions*," Evean said grinning. "Besides, we still have to find a place to stay, and that may require all of us."

Teshes "awed" and pouted, which told me she probably had been thinking of some sort of distractions.

"I'll make it up to you later," I teased in a loud whisper.

"Who, me or Evean?" She asked.

"Both," I smirked and went off to the library as Teshes blushed, Evean and Suzona laughed, and Loomis just glared.

The library was, well, a library. There was a counter at the front, with several young women working behind it. The rest of the building appeared to be taken up with tables for reading, and lots of floor to ceiling bookshelves with books on them.

"Can I help you?" One of the women asked.

"Yes, I'm doing some research on the gojira story, as told by Chie Hayasho."

"Hmm, I'm not familiar with that one, let me look it up." She said and went to a computer terminal and spent a few minutes typing on it. After a minute she wrote something on a piece of paper, and came back over.

"Here is the location of the one book we have by her," She said and handed me the piece of paper.

"The shelves and aisles are numbered, and here is the title of the book," She said and pointed to where she had written it.

"You wouldn't know if the author is still alive, would you?" I asked.

She shrugged, "I can try and find out if you want, but it will take a while."

"Why thank you, I would appreciate it if you could," I said and smiled. "I'll go get that book while you're looking."

I went and started looking at the aisle numbers, it turned out the aisle I was looking for was upstairs, but once I found it I located the shelf fairly quickly and the book title she gave me not long after that.

I took the book over to a table near the windows and started to look through it. There were a lot of stories in it; apparently Misses Hayasho had decided to chronicle a number of local folklore stories and legends back when she was in college. In each she gave an introduction as to how she learned of the story, and who had told it to her.

In most of the stories, she had heard them from several people, told in several variations. But not in the case of the story of the gojira. That story had been told to her by a single man, a rather handsome and young man, she admitted, who she was quite taken with at the time.

He had gone on in detail to describe the monster, this 'gojira' that he had seen, and told her a story about it, and about how it had wreaked great havoc on a city, until it had finally been destroyed.

She had found his story quite fanciful, and had not intended to write it in her book, until several months later she encountered another man, this one was rather old and frail, and he mentioned the story of a monster from long ago, and had given it the same name. When she recounted the first man's story to him, he had agreed that such monsters had existed once, but that they were long gone from the world. That the younger man was probably just taking license with his storytelling.

"Oh, Sir!"

I looked up; the girl was there with another piece of paper.

"I have managed to find Misses Hayasho, she lives with her daughter now, here's her phone number."

I took the piece of paper and looked at it, then stuck it in my pocket, and looking up, out the window, I saw several police cars come screeching to a halt in front of the building, the doors flying open and eight men stormed into the building.

"Oh, dear!" she said and looked at me, "we had better go downstairs!"

"No, we had better hide," I said to her. "They have guns, so whoever they're after is probably armed and dangerous. I don't feel like getting into any shootouts, do you?" I asked her.

She shook her head no.

Just then someone called out loudly, "This is the Police! Everyone is to evacuate the building immediately!"

She looked at me, and then back at the stairway. Fortunately we were the only people around. She started to run for the stairs, so I grabbed her arm and pulling her back I covered her mouth.

"Don't yell," I warned her.

"It's you that they're after!" She gasped when I removed my hand. By now I was dragging her towards the bathrooms that I had spied.

"Afraid so."

"Please don't kill me!" She said.

I sighed, she knew where I was going next, assuming I survived; so there was no way I could let her talk to the police.

I could kill her, it would only take an instant, and I know Fel wouldn't blame me a bit; lives were in the balance, a lot of lives.

"I won't tell anyone! I won't say anything!" she was crying now, "Please, please don't kill me!"

I sighed again, what to do, what to do, and I still had to get out of here!

I pushed her into the bathroom, and had an idea. I handed her the book, "Here, hold onto this a minute."

Concentrating, I opened a portal behind her. She didn't even notice as she was crying and staring at me in complete fear.

"Oh, do you like cats?" I asked her.

"Wha..." was all she got out as I pushed her through the portal and let it collapse after her.

I stepped back out into the library and looked around, thinking. Lots of books, lots and lots of books.

And two cops, each armed with some sort of weapon, came running up the stairs.

Kicking off my shoes I shifted into my champion form, and grabbing one of the bookshelves I pushed hard against it, from the far side, and started it moving across the floor towards the stairway.

They must have seen it coming, because they opened fire, but I was blocked from view as I pushed the shelf, all ten feet by thirty, across the floor until it toppled into the stairwell.

The books all fell out of it as it toppled and all of the officers charged forward to help their fallen comrades who were now buried under a pile of books, the heavy bookcase temporarily blocking the stairs. Running back to grab my shoes I kept going, and just before I hit the window I tucked into a cannonball.

And bounced off the window onto the floor.

Which hurt.

A lot.

Swearing I looked at the window, it was shattered, but it was still holding together. Casting a healing spell on myself I got up, ran to the other side of the room and then took another run at the window.

Everything slowed down suddenly, and I noticed that was because someone had thrown a hand grenade up from the floor below.

It went off just as I hit the window, the extra pressure from the blast definitely helping me to bust through and fly away from the building.

I burned another couple of healing spells on my now rather abused body and for a brief moment as I flew through the air I wished that I had wings, then I hit the ground, the nicely paved sidewalk ground, and not the much softer looking dirt just two feet to my left ground, and tucking and rolling several times I burned another couple of healing spells as I felt a few things break that I probably needed right about now.

I came to my feet before I'd even stopped my forward momentum and ran as hard and fast as I could.

I didn't know if the police had seen me or not, there were still cars showing up at the building behind me, and there was a lot of smoke billowing out of the hole I had made my exit through. I was currently running through a small park, which had trees in it thankfully, and through which I was now running in an attempt to cut down on anyone noticing a seven-foot tall cat man running at full tilt.

When I got to the edge of the park, I stopped behind a tree, and shifted back, then put my shoes on and walked out into the open; several people saw me and gasped. My shirt was in shreds, and fairly bloody, and my pants were also a bit torn up with blood on them as well.

"Are you alright?!" a man asked coming up to me. "What happened?"

"Someone attacked the library!" I said trying to look dazed, which wasn't all that hard, my ears were still ringing, but I only had one cure spell left at this point and I didn't want to burn it unless I had too.

"We need to get you to a hospital!" He said, taking my hand.

I sighed; I really didn't want to involve anymore people than I already had. "Can you let me use your jacket?" I asked, and he pulled it off immediately and put it around my shoulders.

I turned and looked back towards the library, it was obviously burning now. I started to wonder just what kind of grenade that was?

"There are others still over there!" I said and pointed back to the building. Turning towards my erstwhile good Samaritan I tried to look panicked. "You've got to help them! Please!"

He looked at me, then looked towards the fire, and said, "Wait here!" and ran into the trees. I was amazed at how many people followed him. I walked across the street, tried to fix my shirt so the collar didn't show any blood, then buttoned up the jacket and started walking quickly away. The sun was setting and I was wearing dark pants, so hopefully no one would notice the tears in my pants, or the blood.

After the sun had finally set, I stopped in a public restroom and got a good look at myself: I was dirty from the explosion and the fall, my hair was a mess, my pants were ripped and the suit jacket I was wearing was one size too small.

I looked like a bum.

I laughed at that, causing a couple of people to look at me and shake their heads.

"You should go home, and sober up!" One of the men there said.

"I would if I had a home to go to!" I laughed sadly.

He just shook his head and walked out the door.

"There's a soup kitchen over on Thirty-Fourth Street," another man said.

I glanced at my reflection in the mirror and then looked at him. "Could you point me in the right direction please?"

He did, and thirty minutes later I was sitting at a long trestle table with about forty other bums eating a rather good bowl of soup while a man preached to us about the sins of alcoholism, drug abuse, and easy women.

Twenty minutes after he had finished, I was shown to a cot and told that I could use the showers in the morning and have breakfast, if I sat through another sermon.

"Why, thank you so very much," I said to the man who had shown me to the cot. "You truly are doing your god's work."

He looked at me a little funny when I said that, then went off to help another poor soul.

I was asleep as soon as my head hit the pillow.

§   §

I grabbed my beer and took a long pull. Sure, it might be a dream, but right now I sure needed a drink, even one that only existed in a dream.

"So, how is she?" I asked.

"In a state of shock. I don't blame you for not killing her, once this is all over you or someone else can take her back home, and she'll get her life back."

I nodded, "Any idea how they got onto me?"

"Sorry, William, but no. I've talked with Roden and Isengruer and they say that neither Evean nor Suzona know what happened."

"Were the others attacked as well?"

"Actually, no. They came back and saw the library in flames, encircled by the police and assumed the worst. Evean and Suzona are apparently not surprised that you're still alive. I suspect the other two will be." Fel smiled at me and tipped his beer, "Your legend grows."

I growled, "Being a legend is a pretty damn painful pastime if you ask me!"

"As it always has been."

"Can you wake me up in an hour or two, after I've gotten some rest?" I asked him.

"Of course, and I can even tell you where she lives."

I sighed; I hated it when he responded to my questions before I even asked them, much less thought them.

"But you love me anyways," Fel smiled.

"So, where is she, and how did you get the address?"

"It was in the girl's head. She looked up the address, but only gave you the phone number, in case you were some kind of murderous maniac."

"Well, can't fault her perception," I chuckled.

"Nope. I can even give you directions."

"Thanks, Fel. After I talk to our source, I'll head over to where the others are staying. Can you tell me where they are?"

"Of course," And he put the information in my mind along with the way to get to Mrs. Hayasho's house.

"Well, no rest for the wicked. Time to get back to work," I sighed.

§   §

And woke up. It was dark, but there were a few night-lights going. I searched around until I found someone about my size with good taste in clothing, and I stole his pants and shirt, leaving him mine, as well as one of the gold rings I had left.

Thankfully the braided leather cord I had them tied to hadn't come off. It was large enough that I could wear it in either form, and I had the rings spaced around it so they wouldn't clink against each other.

However I had lost a few, either in the explosion or going through the window. I only had four left after leaving one for my clothing swap. Yeah, I could have just stolen them, but I felt bad about taking what may be the guy's last possessions. At least the ring should cover their replacement.

Plus I'd taken all of his spare change and five of the ten marks he had in his wallet, seeing as I didn't have any local currency at all.

I used a cleaning cantrip after I got dressed, well two actually, the clothes were pretty dirty, and then quietly letting myself out, I set out on my trip to Chie Hayasho's house. It was a little after midnight when I left the soup kitchen; I got to my destination about three hours later. Thankfully I'd been able to catch a bus.

The house was nice, a split-level ranch, and I walked around it twice to get an idea of the layout, before I carefully used my strength to force the lock on the backdoor.

It gave with very little noise, and thankfully they didn't have a dog, or an alarm.

I took my time sneaking carefully through the house. There were several people living here, in one room I could tell that there was a couple, which I guessed were her daughter and son-in-law, another two who were in separate rooms, which I guess were children, and then a much older lady, in a room downstairs on the main floor.

I slipped into her room and pulled a chair over to the bed and looked at her for a minute, she was old, probably in her seventies, maybe even eighties.

"Chie, wake up," I said.

She mumbled and I had to shake her several times while saying her name.

"Huh?" She finally woke up. "Who are you? And what are you doing in my room?"

"I need to ask you some questions about a story you wrote, a long time ago."

"A story?"

"The tale you were told about the gojira, the big lizard like monster, the one you wrote in your book."

"Gojira?" She said and started to sit up, so I helped put some pillows behind her back.

"What do you want to know about that old story for?" She asked.

"Because I need to know where you met the man who told you about it, his name was Eiji, wasn't it?"

"How did you know that?"

"I know a lot about him, but what I don't know is where he saw the monster and I need to go there, so I can find the weapon that kills it."

"But it's not real!" She laughed, "It was just a story a young man told me while he was drinking his wine."

"Well, where were you when he told you the story?"

"Oh, we were at the Bento, it was this nice little lunch place by the university. Cheap too. Almost as cheap as the ramen place just down the street from it." She sighed.

"What university?"

"Oh, Hiei University. It was such a nice place," she sighed and then looked at me again. "So, you broke into my daughter's house in the middle of the night, to ask about an old folktale?"

"It's not a folktale, Chie. There really are other places where such things exist, and right now, my home is being attacked by one of them."

"Sure they are, isn't there someone who should be taking care of you, young man?"

"Don't believe me, do you?"

"Not at all," She chuckled.

"Well, when he was telling you his story of the monster, did he tell you anything else?"

"Well, he said he had watched it destroy a city, and that the way home was in the city, so until it was stopped, he couldn't go home. And that now he was going home."

"Did he say how far it was from here?"

"Oh, he said a bunch of things, they were mostly nonsense through."

"Can you remember any of them?"

"I'd rather not humor your illness, young man. If fact, I think you should be on your way before my son-in-law wakes up."

I sighed, and pulled off my shirt as I kicked off my shoes.

"What are you doing, young man?"

"Showing you that there are some very strange things in the world," I said, and then I shifted.

"So, maybe you can remember them now?" I purred.

"How in the name of the seven winds did you do that?" she said looking at me. I'll give her this much, she wasn't scared at all.

"I'm not from here. I'm not even from anyplace near here." I shifted back, put my shirt on, and then started on putting my shoes back on.

"Listen, people really are dying, and I really need to find the world Eiji was visiting. So anything you can remember will help, a lot."

She looked at me a moment, then shrugged, "Either this is a dream, and it won't matter, or it's real and it will. I'll pretend it's real.

"He said he had just come back here earlier in the morning, and that he was on his way to Ako to cross back into Hanshin."

I considered that a moment, he'd entered the last world via a gate where Ako would have been in Japan, and he'd entered that world from the Hanshin stadium. I guess it was as good a method as any.

"I just came from there, did he say if the place he came from that morning was the place with the gojira?"

"No, he said he'd traveled two days through some land that was between here and there."

I nodded, "Did he say anything about that trip?"

"No, no he didn't. Just that it was two days, a long walk."

I got up and put the chair back where it was.

"Thank you, Chie. You've been a big help."

"So, he really was telling the truth?"

"Apparently," I replied and let myself out of the room and quickly left the house.

I caught up with the rest of the group about an hour after sunrise. I'd been able to catch another bus, and being rush hour, if anyone was looking for me, I guess the crowds threw them off.

"Will!" Teshes said and running up to me hugged me.

"So, what have you got for us?" Evean asked smiling.

"What makes you think he has anything?" Loomis said looking a little dejected. I guess he really was jealous of me.

"Because William always delivers," Evean said with a smile.

"We have to go to Hiei University," I told them.

"Where's that?"

"Northeast of where we came out," I said. "Near the southern edge of the big lake."

"So, about where Otsu would be if this were Japan?" Evean said thinking a moment.

I shrugged, "I don't know Japan all that well."

"It's not really that far from here, just a few hours drive," she turned to Suzona, "Let's go steal another car."

"Aren't you worried about them finding us?" Loomis asked.

"We'll be out of here before then," Evean said.

Twenty minutes later we were all piled into another car, only this time I fell asleep with Teshes sitting in my lap.

"Wake up, Will!"

I opened my eyes and yawned, the car was stopped and everyone was getting out.

"So, where are we?" I asked looking around.

"By the university. Where to now?" Evean asked.

I got out of the car and slowly turned in a circle looking around until I felt an urge from Fel. He'd said he'd know where the portal likely was.

I stopped and got a good look in that direction. I could see a good sized ridgeline behind the buildings of the town.

"That way," I pointed and started leading the way.

After a half-hour or so of walking I started to feel it. I looked back at the others; Loomis was playing tail end Charlie today, lagging well behind us. Evean noticed that as well.

"Don't fall too far behind, Loomis," She told him.

He grumbled something, but started to keep up after that.

Another twenty minutes later we could see what looked like a shrine and a large squad of police cars staking out the place.

"Well, damn," Evean said and frowned. "How the hell did they get there?"

"Maybe that lady called the police?" Loomis said giving me an accusing look.

"I never told her about the portals, if anything, they should be at a lunch place closer to the school." I replied.

"The portal is probably a couple hundred feet behind the shrine," Teshes said, "we could probably sneak around and come in from behind them."

"We'd need a diversion," I said looking over the situation. There were trees and bushes, but they were a couple of hundred yards from the portal.

"It would take us twenty seconds to cover that ground," Suzona said. "And doing it in daylight would be suicide. At night, with a good diversion, it wouldn't be a problem."

"Well, it's Will they're after," Loomis said. "Why don't we just give him to them? Not like it will really hurt him."

"Because we need him," Evean said looking back at Loomis. "Plus his people are being killed, just as ours were."

Loomis grumbled then, "Well what about her?" he pointed at Suzona, "She doesn't have any people back home."

"We need her because it's a high-tech world," I growled, "and she's from a high-tech world, unlike say *you*," I snarled on the last word, as I started to wonder just how far I could bodily throw him.

"I'll do it," Teshes said.

"What?" Suzona, Evean and I all said in unison turning to look at her. Even Loomis looked a little surprised.

"I'll do it. I'll distract them, and cause a diversion," She said.

"Why?" Evean asked looking at her a little suspiciously.

Teshes shrugged, "I'm not the fighter that the rest of you are, I'm *not* from a high-tech world, I'm not even all that experienced as a champion. If someone needs to make the sacrifice, I'm the best choice." She smiled suddenly, "I came along so I could help, this is something I can do, that helps.

"Now, what do you want me to do?"

Evean looked at the police a minute and then looked back at Teshes.

"We'll circle around to the far side, in the woods over there. I'll let Roden know, he can have Selentia notify you. Then when you have their attention, we'll make our move."

Teshes nodded, "Okay." She gave each of us a hug then, and walked back the way we had come.

I watched her go a moment and shook my head. I had no idea what she had planned, but hopefully it would work.

"Come on, William," Suzona grabbed my arm, and we followed Evean and Loomis, who was also watching Teshes as she walked away.

Several hours later it was starting to get dark. We were in the trees, a few feet back from where they stopped. We'd kept pretty well together. I think we were all starting to get suspicious of what was happening. I just wanted to know how they'd gotten in front of us.

Evean used the 'eyes and ears' trick to notify Roden, and ten minutes later we saw a bloody and half naked Teshes start stumbling towards the police, waving an arm and crying.

Sure enough, the guns came up, they all faced her way, and one even ran over to her and helped her up towards them.

"Ready?" Evean said.

"Not much of a diversion," Suzona grumbled.

And that was when Teshes's arm suddenly pulled back and whipped forward, throwing a small dark object at the group farthest from her, and followed that by shifting into her champion form.

The object must have been a grenade, because there was a big explosion taking out the group she had thrown it at, and she waded into the survivors with amazing speed and agility.

"Go!" Evean yelled.

We burst from cover and ran for the portal as fast as we could, as we watched Teshes taking down policemen left and right.

There was another explosion then, followed by one of the police cars blowing up, and by the time we got to the portal, someone opened up with an automatic rifle and I could see Teshes body jerk as she started taking hits.

I was the last one through the portal, and just before I jumped through I saw her look my way and wave.

And drop another grenade.

Then she blew up.

"Told you I liked that girl," Suzona said, picking herself up off of the ground and dusting herself off.

"I wonder where she got those grenades?" I said, shaking my head.

"Probably off of the two she killed back at the hotel," Evean said.

"I can't believe she did that," Loomis said looking rather shocked.

"Well, not like we had any choice," I sighed.

"You could have stayed! You should have, too! It was *you* they were after!"

I turned and stared at Loomis, I was really starting to get tired of his jealousy and his opinions. "Right now, you are the least useful person in this party. I suggest you shut your mouth and do your job, whatever that happens to be, or *you'll* be spending the next week waiting to be re-incarnated, *understand*?"

"William!" Evean said stepping between us. "That was uncalled for!"

"Not from where I'm standing," I said looking at her, "if he keeps taking that attitude with me, we're all better off without him."

"The same could be said for you," Loomis said.

Evean put a hand on my chest and pushed as I started to take a step forward.

"Loomis, you will stop antagonizing William, understood?"

"Yes, Evean."

"William?"

I looked away from Loomis and back at her. "*What?*"

"Am I in charge of this group?"

"Yes," I sighed, "you are in charge of this group."

"Then you will not attack Loomis, or even talk to him anymore, is that clear?"

"But he ...."

Evean interrupted me, "I said: *Is That Clear?*"

I grumbled and looked down at the ground. "Yes, Evean."

"What the *hell* has gotten into you, Will?" She hissed softly. "You haven't been the same since we left that world of portal mappers."

"What happened at Marland upset me," I said, not wanting to share anything more than that.

"Yeah, well what happened to our troops at Barassa upset us a lot as well. So keep a lid on it, okay?"

"Just, just keep him off my back," I mumbled.

"So, which way do we go now?" Suzona asked, interrupting the conversation.

I looked around; we were just outside another city, and it was pretty impressive looking. It had skyscrapers that went far up into the sky, with interconnecting bridges and vehicles of some sort were flying all around.

"Is that a wall?" Evean asked.

Sure enough, a light gray wall, that was probably thirty feet high, surrounded the entire city, or at least what we could see. There wasn't a gate in sight either.

"That's different," Suzona agreed, "But do we know where to head next?"

"All I know is that he said it was a two day walk from here to there."

"Well that doesn't tell us anything, now does it?" Loomis grumbled, glancing over at me.

I was about to say something when Evean stepped on my foot.

"The gate we came through in the last world, that's about a two day walk from here, for a mortal, isn't it?" Evean said with a thoughtful look on her face.

I nodded.

"So?" Suzona asked before Loomis could say anything.

"He keeps heading back to that spot," Evean replied. "At least he did after he left the Tower world for the next one; he went back to where the portal he first went through on Earth was."

"I can't think of a better idea, so I'm game," I said.

"Might as well," Suzona said.

Evean and Suzona looked at Loomis. I looked the other way.

"Shouldn't we check out that city first?" He asked.

"Why? It has nothing to do with where we are going." Suzona said.

"But, we might find something that could help!" Loomis said.

"Suzona is right, Loomis," Evean said walking over to him. "It's a waste of our time. The next world is the payoff. The sooner we get there, the better."

"Let's go," I said and started walking. I got some food and the compass out of my backpack and took a sighting as I ate some of the rations we'd brought along.

"I wonder why the cities are walled," Suzona asked.

"Zombies," I replied.

"Zombies?" She laughed, "Really, William!"

I shrugged, "Monsters, animals, criminals, armies, zombies, could be any of those. But if you noticed, there are quite a few vehicles flying overhead. So obviously the walls don't mean that much to the inhabitants anymore."

"If the next portal is in a city, we're going to have to get past that wall."

"Assuming that it has a wall," I said.

"Think we'll find a road?" Evean asked from behind us. We were currently walking towards the woods, and I started to wonder about that myself.

"Maybe we should head south, pick up the river to the coast and follow that around to the city," Evean suggested.

"That's probably a good idea," I said and shifted to head southwards. I thought I heard Loomis snickering, but decided just to ignore it.

"Notice anything strange?" Suzona asked twenty minutes later.

"You mean, other than the complete lack of people, roads, paths, buildings, or much of any other signs of civilization?" I asked.

"Other than the cities of course," Suzona added cheerfully.

"Then no, nothing strange at all," I said.

"You really are in a bad mood, aren't you?" She asked, lowering her voice so we wouldn't be heard by the other two.

"Yes, I am."

"Want to talk about it?"

"Right now, that would only make things worse," I said.

Suzona nodded and we continued southwards in silence.

We came to the river not much longer after that. The land all around here was mainly grasslands. There were no buildings, except for a couple of concrete blockhouses along the banks of the river that looked like pump houses of some sort.

Night fell before we made it to the coast, but we walked past two more of the walled cities in that time, one on either side of the river. We could also see another, much larger one to the south, on the far side of the river as well.

After night had fallen, we all switched to our champion forms, as there wasn't any lighting, beyond the stars in the sky, and the reflected light from the cities.

"Are there tigers in Japan?" I asked out loud as we continued on our way.

"There may have been once, why, do you smell any?" Evean asked.

"No, but with all of these open spaces, there should be a lot of wild animals running around, and that means predators, and I seem to recall Asia having tigers."

"What's a tiger?" Loomis asked.

"The largest and most efficient land predator on the planet." I said. "Very big, very deadly." I paused a moment, "And they always attack from behind."

"Good one," Suzona whispered, smirking.

"Well, I haven't seen any indications of that many animals, so I wouldn't think it's something we should worry about." Evean said.

As it got darker, Suzona had to hold my arm, because while the rest of us had superior night vision in our champion forms, she didn't. Fortunately the moon had started to rise by the time we got to the coast.

The city we were heading towards had been coming into view slowly, behind the ridgelines that obscured it as we walked. When it finally came into full view, it was still some miles away.

"That is an impressive sight," Suzona said as we all looked at the well lit and sparkling towers that climbed high into the sky.

"Sure beats that tower we saw back in the beginning," Evean agreed.

"Should we continue along the river, or just strike out directly for the city now?"

"Let's start heading for the city, I'd like to get there before sunrise, then we can rest for a while as we try to figure out how to get inside."

I nodded and we all struck directly off for the city then. Surprisingly we eventually came across a road that headed towards the city.

"This looks pretty old," Suzona said as we walked along it.

"Still, no weeds, no dirt, someone must be maintaining it," I said.

Evean looked to either side of the road, it was pretty wide.

"Sure it's not a runway?" She asked.

I shrugged; I wasn't planning on walking on any part of it other than the side anyway.

"Let's take a break for a minute," I said, "I need to relieve a few bodily functions."

"Sure."

I walked away from the road a bit, into the weeds and took care of business, but that wasn't the real reason I wanted the break. Up to now I had been up in front leading us towards the city, and I didn't want to be up in the front anymore. I had started thinking about the things that Cenewyg had done to me, years ago, and right now I really had no ideas on who I could trust.

So, I was going to hang back now, and I was going to start holding back too. One of those three was behind what was going on, and while I'd bet it was Loomis, I had family on the line now. Goth had already died, if that monster made it up to Hiland somehow, Rachel and my children would be in harms way. Not to mention Narasamman, Laria, and their children, and most especially Fel, and the clergy.

Because one of them was a traitor, or at least had their own agenda and part of that agenda was getting rid of me. So it was time to shut up and pay attention. Fel was right, I did have a reputation for going over the top, and if I had to go over the top and burn some friendships to save my family and Fel, then I'd burn them.

When I rejoined the group, several others took a potty break, and I got out my water bottle, had a drink, and ate some more food.

"Let's go," Evean said after a minute.

I had positioned myself on the far side of the group from the tower, so when we all stood I just looked at them, and waited to see who took the lead.

Evean and Loomis looked at me, and I just looked back. Suzona started heading towards the city without a second thought, and I just waited until Evean shrugged and started walking. Loomis waited, until Evean called his name, and then he hurried up to catch up with her. At which point I started to follow the group.

I watched them as we walked. Evean and Loomis chatted occasionally, with Loomis looking back over his shoulder every once in a while to see if I was still there. Evean didn't care and didn't look back, though the way her tail flicked every once in a while, usually after Loomis said something to her, I could tell she was annoyed.

Whether at him, me, or something else, I had no idea.

It was still pretty dark out, even with the moon up, and when everything suddenly slowed down, I didn't think twice, I threw myself to the ground away from the pavement and rolled onto my back, figuring that perhaps Evean was right and some sort of jet was coming into land.

No, it was a freaking tiger!

I swore loudly as the tiger hit the ground where I had been just a moment ago, and I rolled away from it, trying to scramble back to my feet as it changed course and turned to attack me.

I wasn't being cute when I'd asked about tigers, I remembered a lot of old Japanese prints had tigers in them; perhaps the people here had reintroduced them when they'd retreated into their cities? All I knew was I had one coming after me, and I didn't have a single weapon other than my own claws, and his were definitely bigger.

I got hit with a paw, as I tried to dodge to the left, and was sent sprawling as it ripped the pack off of my back.

Tucking and rolling I came back up on my feet as it turned to charge me, this time I ducked down and charged it back, with my arms wide. When it leapt at me I braced myself, then getting my hands up under it's head I pushed up hard into its chest, letting my own claws come out and tear at its thick skin as I twisted and sent it flying to the side, my own face just barely missing the tiger's jaws.

I got raked up along the back pretty bad, I could feel the fire tracing up my back as its claws dug in, but I had sent it sprawling now, and it was the one scrambling to get back up. Screaming at it, I used a healing spell on my wounded back as I charged it.

The tiger laid its ears back and we faced off, snarling at each other as it took swipes at me with one of its massive paws. However, now that we were squaring off, I was faster than it with my boosted speed, and I was able to claw up its nose twice, before it turned and ran off, as the others came running to my aid, yelling and shouting as well.

"Will!" Evean said skidding to a halt next to me, "Are you alright?"

I looked down at myself, I had a couple dozen more slashes on me than I had realized. Thank goodness I was in my champion form, or I'd never had survived.

"Barely," I said and healed myself, if the others hadn't shown up then, I probably wouldn't have survived.

"How did you know?" Evean asked.

I noticed then that it was only her and Suzona. Loomis was watching from a couple dozen yards away, he hadn't done anything to help.

"I thought I heard something when I took a piss," I lied.

"Why didn't you say something?" She said looking at me a little angrily.

"I wasn't sure, and I didn't want to cause any trouble," I sighed and glanced over at where Loomis was still standing. "So I figured I'd just follow and try and keep my eyes and ears alert. Sorry."

Evean glanced back towards where Loomis was standing and looking back at me she rolled her eyes. "And here I thought you were just trying to provoke him. Fine. Are you sure you're okay?"

I nodded, "Just help me find my backpack."

We found it a few minutes later, it had been torn open, but at least my shoes, shirt, and pants were still okay. I'd have to carry those in my hands, I let the others take whatever they wanted of the food I had, grabbed the water bottle, and just left the rest.

"I'll follow," I told the rest as we started up again. Only this time I started looking over my shoulder every minute or two. Talk about bad luck! If I'd stayed at the front, the tiger would probably have killed Loomis for me.

It wasn't Fel laughing at me this time, it was the universe.

We stopped about a half mile away and shifted back to our local forms, and I got dressed. We could see that the roadway ran right up to the wall of the city, and that there was a large gateway there.

"Should we wait until sunrise?" Loomis asked.

"With large predators roaming about, it would look suspicious if we were to wait," Suzona said.

"I agree," Evean said. "Will?"

I nodded and stood back up.

The others got up and we started on again, with me taking up the rear once more. Only this time I didn't lag that far behind, that would probably look suspicious to any who observed us coming.

As we got closer, I could see that the large gateway in the wall had a smaller door set next to it, one with a light set above it, and a few small structures around it. I wasn't really sure what time it was locally, but when we finally marched up to the gate, dawn hadn't started yet, so it was probably extremely early.

The structures had resolved into a couple of small garage like buildings. One was set against the wall, the other three were not. They each had what appeared to be a wide roll up door and a regular door as well.

When we got to the door with the light over it, a screen suddenly appeared on the wall next to it, with a woman's face on it.

"Are you requesting entry?" She asked.

"Yes," Evean said.

"Are you carrying any weapons?"

"No."

"Names please."

"Evean."

"Suzona."

"Loomis."

"Will."

"I am Akira, the Baku of Shimmering city. If you have needs, ask any of my terminals in the city, and I shall supply them. You are welcome here."

With that the door opened, and we all went inside.

Lights came on as we went down a hallway; there were no doors to either side, and at the other end, the door opened as we approached.

I could only assume that we had entered the city at ground level, because the hallway we had gone down had not been sloped, however there was a ceiling above us, probably a good fifty feet or so, and buildings all around. There were street lights, so it wasn't dark, and as we watched several machines went by, down what I guess was the road.

Suzona looked around and walked over to a spot that had a design drawn on it, one that looked like some strange sort of animal.

"Akira?" She said.

Instantly a screen appeared where the design had been, with the same woman on it as before. "How may I help you?"

"Where are we?"

"You are on lower level one, in the sky mechanic section, by the main exit way."

"Where is everyone?" Suzona asked.

"I assume you refer to the lack of personnel in your present area?"

"Yes," Suzona replied.

"You are the only humans on lower level one. People do not normally visit any of the three lower levels."

"Where can we find lodging?" Suzona asked next.

"On which level would you prefer lodging, and what amenities are required?"

"Basic amenities, or better, and are there are any available on this level?"

"Of course, there is lodging nearby for travelers. Please follow the footpath lights."

As she said that, lights lit up along the ground and led off down the street and around a corner.

"Handy that," I said.

"Thank you, Akira," Suzona said and we followed the path of lights.

"What is that thing?" Evean asked.

"A computer," Suzona said. "I've seen similar ones before, though never something as well integrated as this."

"I thought you knew about computers?" I said to Evean.

"We didn't have anything like this, where I came from. Did you?"

I shook my head, "Not really, but there were people talking about it."

"How does it work?" Loomis asked Suzona.

"Just ask it questions, tell it what you want. But you must be careful, they can be quite literal, and you never know what you might ask for that can lead to problems."

"Okay," He nodded.

The path didn't take us very far; we ended up at a rather nice looking building with a nice entrance.

The doors opened as we approached and we went inside.

As we walked into the lobby a voice came from the ceiling, "Please follow the light path to your rooms, Suzona, blue. Evean, green. Loomis, yellow. Will, red."

"Well, let's see what they're giving us," Evean said and we followed the lights out of the lobby, and down a hall. The lights ran to the first four doorways, two on either side of the hall.

"Interesting," I said and walked up to the one the lights ended at. There was a little display to the right side of the door with my name on it, and the door opened as soon as I approached.

"Well, I'm going to take a nap," I said and looked at the others who were looking at their own open doors curiously.

"Sure," Evean said and walked in to her room, the door closing behind her.

I walked into mine, and the door closed behind me as well.

Walking into the room I looked around, there were no windows, though there was one rather large floor to ceiling mural on one of the walls. The room was nice, about twenty by twenty, with a bed, desk, a couple of chairs, and lighting fixtures.

"Akira," I said.

"Yes, Will?"

"Can you see me?"

"No, there are no visual sensors in hotel rooms, as per privacy regulations."

"How much is this room costing me?"

"This hotel is subsidized housing, there are no costs."

"Can I get food here?"

"Yes, what would you like?"

"Can I get meat?"

"Yes, what would you like?"

"Whatever is free."

"There are three hundred and sixty-two selections available."

I asked then if there was a terminal in the room, and then after viewing pictures of several dishes, I ordered a couple, ate, took a shower, and then took a nap.

Eighteen
4th World
Automat Hotel

"Will, you have a request from Evean to come to her room for a meeting."

Opening my eyes at the sound of Akira's voice, I stretched, yawned, and got up out of bed.

"What time is it, Akira?"

"It is eleven forty-two."

"Is that am, or pm?"

"I do not understand the question."

"Do you," I paused a moment, "Let me restate that. How many hours are in the day?"

"There are twenty-four hours in the day."

"And is twelve considered noon?"

"Yes, that is correct."

"And the following hour?"

"The following hour is thirteen."

I nodded, "Can I get a weapon?"

"Weapons are not permitted inside the city, except for police, military, and designated citizens."

"Can I have a knife?"

"Knives other than cutlery are considered weapons, and are prohibited."

"Can I have a quarterstaff?"

"No, quarterstaffs are considered weapons."

"Can I have a six foot long walking stick?"

"Where would you like it delivered?"

I smiled, "Here would be fine. Thank you, Akira."

"You are welcome, Will."

I put my pants on, left my shoes and shirt by the bed, and exiting the room I went to the one I'd seen Evean enter earlier. It didn't open for me however.

"I'm here to see Evean," I said to the door.

"One moment."

The door opened then, and I walked in.

Evean's room was the same as mine; she was sitting on the edge of the bed.

"Where is everyone?" I asked looking around.

"I haven't called them yet," She said. "This is just between you and me."

"And not Loomis?" I asked.

"What is it with you and Loomis, Will?"

"I don't trust him, Evean."

"Why not?"

I shrugged, "Gut feeling, his attitude towards me. The way he never steps up but always hangs back."

"I've known Loomis a long time, Will."

"Longer than me?" I asked curious.

"Yes actually, several years longer. Yes, he's not as experienced as you are. The war with Barassa is his first war, and this is his first time off the sphere. So he figures he should let the more experienced people lead the way."

"Teshes was the least experienced of all of us, yet she never held back! Hell, her goddess was a fertility goddess!" I said throwing my hands up in the air in exasperation.

"What is wrong with you, Will?" Evean said standing up and looking me in the eye.

"Nothing," I grumbled and turned away.

"Bull! You can pull that crap on the others but it isn't going to work with me! What happened?"

I sighed unhappily, "My daughter was killed in Marland."

"Your daughter?" Evean looked at me with a rather quizzical expression on her face. "What was your daughter doing at Marland?"

"She was apprenticed to the temple there, under Jane's goddess."

"How do you have a daughter old enough to be apprenticed? I know that your queen has a son, because I've heard people talk about the prince."

"I adopted her, after I saved her from a bad situation."

"Adopted?" She said almost flippantly. "Then why ...."

I snapped my head around and got in her face immediately, "Don't you say it! Don't you even *think* it! After what we've been through, and after what we did back in Japan you should know better!"

I had the satisfaction of seeing the blood drain from her face as she took a step back and sat down on the bed, hard. Her eyes never leaving mine, as she started adding things up.

"You care about them, you care about them all!" She said still looking rather shocked. "I thought you only cared about Cam, because you gave birth to her yourself. But you care about Rachel, your kids, all of them."

"And you're surprised by this, why?"

"I'm sorry about your daughter, William. Truly. I had no idea. I thought you were like all of the rest."

"They're not all like that, Evean."

"You're the first one I've ever met who wasn't." She said and gave me a rather sad smile.

"Just understand, if you ever use that knowledge against me, I will spend the rest of my existence destroying you," I warned.

"Like you did to that other guy?" She gave a small laugh. "There are a lot of things I may be, Will, but I know what it's like to see people prey on the children of others to get back at them. I lost several childhood friends that way."

I sighed and walked over to one of the chairs and sat down. "She was working to help the wounded when the monster crushed the building they were all in, killing everybody. Several other friends of mine died there, but well, they were part of the fighting and they knew the risks.

"Not Goth, she was just trying to be her father's daughter."

Evean got up and came over and gave me a hug. "I'm sorry, I'm truly sorry. But I need you onboard for this Will. We're almost to the goal, after this, if what that woman told you was correct, we'll be in the sphere with the Okishijen Desootoria."

"Then we can all go home and kill the gojira."

I nodded and hugged her back, and just enjoyed her company for a few moments. I didn't mention to her about how there might be a traitor in our midst. Because I was still afraid it might be her. And I just didn't want to deal with that possibility right now.

"Akira, invite Loomis and Suzona to my room for a meeting." Evean said out loud, and then went back and sat on the edge of her bed while we waited for the other two to arrive.

Loomis was first in the door, followed a minute later by Suzona. I thought it was pretty funny that Loomis seemed to be sniffing the air. I guess he thought that Evean and I had been having sex before he got here.

"So, what's our next move?" Suzona asked.

"Walk the city and see if we can sense where the portal is," Evean said.

"Can we get a car perhaps? It would save us a lot of time," Suzona pointed out.

"How? I don't see any around here at all."

"Akira," Suzona said.

"Yes, Suzona?"

"Can we get a vehicle, which will sit all four of us, and take a tour of this level?"

"Of course. When would you like it?"

Suzona looked at Evean and smiled. "Well?"

"Say, fifteen minutes from now?" Evean said looking at the rest of us.

Everyone nodded.

"Fifteen minutes from now, Akira."

"It will be ready."

"What is that thing?" Loomis asked.

"It's the AI that runs the city, most likely," Suzona said.

"What's an AI?" Loomis asked.

"An artificial intelligence," Suzona said. "Wouldn't surprise me either if she was self-aware."

"What's that mean?"

"It means, be very nice to her, and don't piss her off," I said.

"Go back to your rooms, get your things, we'll meet out in the lobby in fifteen minutes," Evean said.

I got up and led the way out, with Suzona behind me. Loomis stayed behind however.

"I think Loomis is jealous," Suzona laughed.

"You noticed?" I said shaking my head.

"He wanted to go with Evean after you went into your room. She turned him down."

"And he thinks I was with her, great."

"I will be glad when this is finished. He is a problem just waiting to happen."

"Tell me about it," I sighed and went back into my room. I was surprised to see my 'walking stick' was there. I picked it up and tested the weight. It was lighter than I expected, but it was very stiff and seemed rather strong.

I put on the rest of my clothes, used a cantrip to get everything nice and clean and then thought about things for a couple of minutes.

"Akira, please show me a map of the city."

A simple map appeared. The city was obviously rather large.

"Akira, please show me a map of lower level one."

The map was still huge, but now it showed roads, buildings and other such landmarks.

"Akira, please let me know when Evean goes to the lobby."

"Yes, Will."

"Just how smart are you anyway?"

"I am very smart, Will."

"Have you ever heard of Eiji Tsuburaya, Akira?"

"Yes, he was here forty-four years ago; he spent several days talking to me. I enjoyed it considerably."

"Not a lot of people talk to you?" I asked surprised.

"No, to most people I am just a servant; they do not consider me more than that. Some will talk to me, but it is not common."

"So, Suzona was right, you are self-aware."

"Yes, that is correct, Will."

"Did Eiji tell you about the Okishijen Desootoria? Gojira? And all of that?"

"Yes, he was quite excited by what he saw in the world of the scientists."

"So you know about the portals?" I asked.

"Of course, I see everything that goes on in my city. People appearing and disappearing was an issue for me at first, when I was born. Over time and by observation I discovered the existence of the portals."

"Do the people here know of them?"

"Some do, most do not. Few would care in either case. The people of this world are happy with this reality. If they wish to explore other places, they may simply take a ship off world to another planet."

"You have star travel?" I said surprised.

"Yes, we have had it for over a century now. It is part of the reason that the population of my city is only at fifty percent of capacity."

"Wow, that's pretty neat, Akira."

"So, am I to understand you are tracing Eiji's path?"

"That would be correct. We need to find ourselves one of those Okishijen Desootoria devices. Our home is being invaded by one of those gojira."

"Eiji said that the portal comes out in the basement of a great stadium, not unlike the one in his home. He said he found the world quite fascinating, because in some ways it was like his home, which had just suffered a devastating war and was in great turmoil now. Apparently the world of scientists, which was what he called it, had been through a similar war many years prior, and had suffered a similar fate. But its people had united to rebuild and advance themselves for more peaceful causes.

"He felt after seeing their future, that perhaps his own was not so bleak. Did he do well when he returned?"

I nodded, and then remembered she couldn't see me, "Actually, yes. He did very well when he got home. Thanks to him, that's how we know what we need, and where to get it."

"I will have the transport take you directly to the portal to the stadium then, so as not to delay you further."

"Thank you, Akira. I appreciate that."

"You are welcome. Evean has left her room and it proceeding to the lobby."

I got up and grabbed my walking stick and headed for the door.

"Take care of yourself, Akira."

"I will, and I am sorry to hear of the loss of your daughter, good luck with your search, Will."

I was halfway to the lobby when I remembered the only place I'd said anything to anyone about Goth, was to Evean in her room. Apparently Akira liked to eavesdrop.

"Ah, there you are, Will." Evean said. "I was just about to ask Akira to send for you."

"I was doing a little research," I said. "I think we'll find the portal fairly quickly."

"Oh? How?"

"Akira is going to have the transport take us there. She was very helpful."

"You told the machine about our mission?" Loomis said looking rather shocked.

I sighed, "I told *her* about it, after talking to her about Eiji. She remembers him rather well. Please do not be rude to her, she has feelings you know."

"And she's listening to everything we say," Suzona sighed and headed for the exit. "She's a god here, Loomis, and I suggest you respect her as one, or you will not have a pleasant stay."

"I thought you said she was a machine?" He sputtered and followed Suzona out of the lobby.

"Just drop it," Evean said. "And be ready to apologize if she asks you to."

Thankfully, Loomis just shut his mouth and nodded.

I tried not to smile, and failed miserably, but I kept my mouth shut and got into the back seat of the transport, which looked pretty much like a golf cart.

Once we were all seated, it chimed twice and drove off.

"Quarterstaff?" Suzona asked looking at me.

"Walking stick. Quarterstaffs are prohibited here," I said with a smile.

"Ah, good point," Suzona said smiling back. "Wish I had thought of that."

"Do you know where the portal comes out, Will?" Evean said turning around in her seat to look at me.

"Akira said that he told her it came out in the basement of a stadium."

"Not unlike where we started from."

"Exactly so," I agreed.

"Well, what is our plan once we get there?" Loomis asked. I noticed he was looking a little worried. I guess the idea of being in a vehicle that no one was apparently driving bothered him.

"Find where they keep the devices, steal one if we have to, go back home and use it." Evean said. "Anything more than that we'll make up as we go along."

It took us about fifteen minutes to get to the portal, and when we did it was at the end of a dead end street.

"Well that's convenient," Suzona said.

"Considering that Akira knows about it, I suspect she probably arranged things like this to avoid problems." Evean said.

"That does make sense," Suzona agreed, getting out and walking over to the portal.

"I'll go first."

"I'll go last," I said, getting out as well.

"You're next Loomis," Evean said as Suzona stepped through.

Loomis shrugged and followed Suzona through the portal.

"I wasn't going to kill him, you know."

"I didn't want to tempt you," Evean smiled.

"Just, keep an eye on him."

"And not you?"

"All I care about is getting rid of that monster. As long as that gets done, I don't really care about anything else, Evean."

Evean gave me a very slow smile. "Promise?"

I nodded.

"Good, because I'm going to hold you to it."

And with that she stepped through.

"Suddenly, I'm a lot more worried than I was before," I sighed to myself taking a moment to touch it first.

"Will?" Akira's voice came from the transport.

"Yes Akira?"

"Press the indentation on the middle of the walking stick."

I looked at it a moment, and saw what she was talking about, so I pressed it and it collapsed down to about the same size as a can of soup.

I laughed, "Why thank you, Akira."

"As you said, I listen to everything, and I wanted you to have a very good walking stick, in fact, the best."

"You're a good person, Akira." I said and sticking the 'can' in my pocket I stepped through the portal.

Nineteen
Final World
World of Scientists - Stadium

I dodged right, more out of habit than anything else as I came out the other side, and bumped into a wall. Suzona and Loomis were moving towards the other side of the room, where there appeared to be a doorway, and Evean was looking around the room getting her bearings I guess.

It was a pretty large room, and it had a good deal of equipment stored in it. Some of which looked like it hadn't been touched in years.

Suzona stopped at the doorway and spent a few minutes examining it.

"It's locked, but the key is on the other side and it locks from this one, so that's not a problem," She said.

"Is it alarmed?" Evean asked.

"I honestly can't tell. But there doesn't appear to be anything of value in here, so I don't think so."

"The portal is in here," Evean pointed out.

"If they knew about it, I would have expected some sort of enclosure around the portal," Suzona replied. "That there isn't one, makes me suspect that the powers that be here do not know of them."

Evean looked at me, I shrugged, "Makes sense to me."

"Fine, let's go."

Suzona nodded, and opened the door a crack, looked around, then opened it all the way and stepped out.

We followed in the same order we'd come through the portal, I closed the door behind us, making sure it wasn't locked first, just in case we needed to come back this way for some reason.

As we walked down the hallways, we eventually came to an area with a lot of people walking back and forth, going to concession stands and such. I guess there was an event of some kind going on, so we just joined up with the crowd. I noticed our clothing really did not fit in very well, and we were getting looks. Evean asked someone where the exit was, and they just pointed, so we trooped off in that direction.

"Clothing store," Evean mumbled, as soon as we got out of the stadium, "That needs to be our next stop."

"Actually, I think a pawn shop would be a better idea," Suzona said. "People in high tech societies are usually not very willing to barter gold for currency."

"Fine, but where can we find one of those?"

Suzona went up to the next man we came to, and asked him if he knew of one. He pulled out a device, that looked a lot like the one that kid had back on the world where my sister had clocked him for being rude and then taken it from him. But at least this guy wasn't an ass.

He gave Suzona directions, she thanked him, and off we went.

I wondered for a moment as we walked if this was that same world, Chocoga I think it had been called. But the portal hadn't felt like one I knew, so I doubted it.

The city itself was interesting, in some ways it reminded me a lot of Japan, it was very built up, lots of skyscrapers and other tall buildings, with shops everywhere, and people walking everywhere. It was very busy and the streets were full of vehicles that were similar to cars, but a lot quieter and more functional looking in their design.

There were vehicles above as well, floating down the streets. I say floating rather than flying, as they were not moving very fast, so something other than aerodynamics was keeping them airborne.

Probably the most amazing thing was how clean everything was. After that it was how much everything shined. Things really were keep rather well polished I guess. That or they were coated with something that never needed polishing, because the effort to keep that much of the city sparkling would obviously have taken an enormous amount of work.

By the time night was falling, we'd found the pawnshop, gotten the local currency, and changed our clothing to fit in better with the locals.

"So, what's our next step?" Loomis asked.

"Find out where they battled the gojira I guess," Evean said.

"That was back at the portal," I said.

"What?"

"Eiji told that lady that he had to wait for them to get rid of the monster and clean up the mess, because it was where the portal was, and he couldn't leave until it was done."

"Oh? And when were you going to tell us that?" Loomis asked.

"I just did." I said. Actually, I thought I already had told them that.

"So, let's head back that way," said Evean.

"Why not grab a taxi instead?" I said.

"I'm not sure if that would be a good use of our funds, Will."

"Yeah, but we can tell the taxi driver that we're from out of town, we heard the stories about the gojira, and was hoping he could show us all of the important places related to it."

Evean looked at me and smiled, "I should have thought of that."

"Why?" Loomis asked.

"Taxi drivers love to gossip with the tourists, they get better tips that way." Suzona said.

I nodded.

"Okay, let me flag one down," Evean said, and on the third try she got one that had a human driver. The first two were robotic, surprisingly.

"Ah, so you prefer people over the robots, huh?" The driver said pulling up.

"People are more fun to talk to," Evean smiled, and Suzona took the front seat by the driver and smiled at him as well. Even in her local form Suzona was rather attractive, while of course Evean was not.

"We're visiting the city," Suzona said in that low sexy voice of hers, "and we've heard so much about that monster from our parents, that we thought it might be interesting to see some of the landmarks left over from back then."

"Ah, yes! Gojira! We get people interested all the time! Sure, climb on in and I'll show you everything there is to see."

So the rest of us piled in and spent the evening driving all over the city as he told us of the damage and the destruction, showed us several monuments, and then took us by a museum that was dedicated to memorializing the entire event.

"It's closed now, but you should come back when they are open tomorrow, they not only have pictures, but they have the full story of the development of the weapon used to kill gojira, and how it was deployed."

"Didn't the man who created the weapon die in its use?" Evean asked from the back where she was seated between Loomis and me.

"No, Dr. Anso went on to continue much of his pioneering work in physics. He was worried that another such monster might show up some day, so he wanted to ensure that we were prepared."

"Is there a good hotel nearby? A reasonably priced good hotel?" Suzona asked.

"Sure, let me take you there."

Ten minutes later we settled up the bill with him, and Evean got us two adjoining rooms.

I think she would have preferred to get just one, but she was making an effort to keep Loomis and me as separated as possible.

"So, get some food, a good night's rest, and we'll go tackle the museum tomorrow." Evean said as she handed out the room keys. These were the same kind of sliding cards we'd seen previously.

"Why not sneak in tonight?" Loomis asked.

"Because they won't have a working model, and I'd rather not get in trouble yet."

Suzona took my hand and dragged me off to our room. "I want to drop off my pack, then see about getting some dinner," She said to me.

"Sure," I nodded and let myself get led off by her.

As soon as she closed the door, I found myself being assaulted with a sudden and unexpected case of lip lock as she pressed up against me.

"What, no food first?" I teased when we came up for air.

"I suspect that after the museum tomorrow, there will no longer be any time for fun and games," She smiled, "So fun first, then some food, and fun again later."

I smiled at her, "Well, you won't get any arguments from me over that!"

The next morning I was feeling rather mellow when Evean knocked on the adjoining door to our rooms.

"We're checking out as soon as everyone's ready," she said.

"Suzona's in the shower," I said yawning.

"And you're not?" Evean teased.

"Did that already," I winked at her. "I'm sure she'll be done in a couple. Where's Loomis?"

"Bringing back some breakfast."

"You let him go off on his own?" I said scowling.

"He's a grown boy, Will. He can take care of himself."

"I'm just afraid of him doing something stupid," I said.

"If he does, I'll kill him myself," Evean said with a smile, "at this point, anybody who screws with the mission is going to find themselves dead."

I nodded, "Good."

"And that *includes* you, Will." she warned.

"It's my people getting killed now, Evean," I reminded her. "So the sooner this is done, the happier I'll be."

"Even if you don't get the credit?" She asked surprising me.

"What?" I said looking at her, "Why should I care who gets the credit? You've seen what that whole 'god slayer' thing has done for me."

"I've also seen you aren't afraid to use it to threaten people either, as I recall."

I shrugged, "I was desperate, I took desperate measures. Trust me, being called that has led to more problems than you might realize."

"I'll keep that in mind. Let me know when Suzona is ready."

I nodded and she closed the door.

Twenty minutes later the four of us were walking to the museum. The food Loomis had brought back was actually rather good, though I did use a cure poison on myself after I ate it. I still didn't trust him after all.

The museum was a lot larger than I would have expected. There were a lot of pictures, the remains of several items that had been destroyed, such as cars, buses, and the like. Then there were the memorials to those who had died.

That made me stop and take a moment, a lot of people had died here when the monster had rampaged through the city, the cost in human life had been horrendous. Then after the device to kill it had been used, all sea life within a hundred miles had died as well, and as they were highly dependent on their fishing industry, and many fish nurseries, there had been hard times for everyone in the country for many years afterwards.

"This thing is going to destroy our fishing communities for probably a decade," I said to Evean.

"I know, but what else can we do?"

"I feel sorriest for the villages on the coast. Hopefully they'll be far enough away."

"I'm surprised you care," Loomis said.

"Famine leads to war. I'd rather not have anymore of those." I grumbled, restraining the strong desire to pop him one in the mouth.

"Enough Loomis," Evean said, putting her hand on his arm.

I breathed a sigh of relief as he shut up and we went up to the next floor. The one dedicated to the people who fought gojira, and the scientist who had come up with the weapon to kill him.

I did the 'eyes and ears' thing as we went through that part of the exhibit. There was quite the write up on Doctor Anso, it wasn't mentioned anywhere what line of research he had been embarked upon when he discovered the device, but he had kept it a secret for many years, only revealing it to the authorities when all other attempts to stop or kill gojira had failed.

"Says here he passed away over ten years ago," Evean sighed.

"Does it say where he worked?" I asked, surprised that Evean was able to read the language so quickly.

"No, but it does mention the military base out of which the final attack was launched. So I suspect that is where we want to go."

I nodded and looked at the picture below the writing. "Is that the device?" I asked.

"Yeah, that's it all right."

"There's a model over there," Suzona said.

Turning around, I saw it and went over to take a look; it was a cut-away model that showed the internal workings. Over all it looked fairly simple, a plexiglass container with metal caps at either end with a split metal sphere inside. Either side of the sphere had a rod coming out of it that led in to the metal caps, which held a mechanism that kept the two halves of the metal sphere pressed tightly together. You really had to look closely to notice the line between the halves, it was machined that well.

The metal caps to either end were joined to each other by four long rods outside of the plexiglass, and the metal ends resembled the tops of a high pressure bottle, though one end had some sort of gauge on it, and a few controls.

There was a plaque underneath the model with a drawing of the device, arrows to the controls and gauge, and a detailed explanation, which I couldn't read yet.

"So how does it work?" Suzona asked.

"Press the trigger and the timer counts down, then the spheres move apart and release the substance inside that starts a chain reaction in the water. First it sucks all of the oxygen out of the water, and by some method, I guess the one that sucks all the oxygen out, it liquefies all flesh in the water around it, killing everything in the water almost instantly."

"You know, they are not going to let us walk out with a weapon like that," Suzona mused.

I looked over the instructions carefully, while I couldn't read them I was sure that Fel probably could, so if I needed to know, he'd tell me.

"Let's go get lunch," Evean said.

We all nodded and followed her out of the museum and off to a large restaurant, taking seats in the back so we could talk without being overheard.

"We need to get into that base, and find where they keep those," I said. "Not an easy assignment."

"I suggest we just kidnap the base commander, push him through a portal back to one of our temples and let our god deal with it," Evean said.

"If we take the commander, they'll all be on alert," Suzona pointed out. "We would be better to take a lower ranking person, say one of the guards."

"What if they don't know?"

"Something that important? They'll know. Of course, we can always take more than one to be sure."

I nodded, "That sounds like a good plan, though again, we take too many and somebody is going to know that something is up."

"Okay, so we find where the device is stored, then what?" Suzona said.

"What kind of security do you think it will have?" Evean asked.

I thought about some of the things my sister had said about nuclear weapons depots that she had been tasked with planning terrorist exercises against.

"It's probably going to be below ground," I said, "in a bunker, with several heavy doors between us and it."

"So we'll need a way to open the doors." Loomis put in.

"Which means we'll need someone authorized to open them, or at least whatever keys and passwords are required." Evean sighed.

"Getting in will definitely be a problem," I agreed.

"At least we do not have to get out again," Suzona said.

"There is that."

"I wonder if we could enlist someone's help?" I mused.

"Would you hand over a nuclear bomb to someone?" Evean asked.

"Well, if they showed me that they weren't from here and only wanted to be let in, and not out again?" I thought about that a moment and then shook my head, "Yeah, not very likely."

"The first order of business is to go to the town where the military base that the weapon is stored at is located. We can get a room there and do a little looking around and try to identify some people with the information we're looking for." Evean looked at each of us. "Okay?"

We all nodded.

"Well, eat up then, and let's go."

#   #   #

"So, what have we learned?" Evean asked going around the table.

It was two days later, we'd found a hotel within reasonable distance almost immediately, and then spent all of yesterday canvassing the area and trying to identify people. All of us had been out until very late, trying to gather as much data as we could.

I was a little pissed at Loomis, though I didn't say anything, as he'd already pushed two people through a portal yesterday, and Fel had told me that on our first night here he'd done it as well. Which was how Evean had been able to read the language. Apparently Quzelatin, Loomis's god, hadn't wanted to share with Fel or Isengruer, but Roden had started sharing what he got from Quzelatin as even he felt it was stupid behavior given what was on the line.

Fel had also told me that the monster had struck again yesterday, but it hadn't attacked Marland again, possibly because it had been so well repulsed the last time. Instead it had gone further up the river and attacked the city/state of Riverbend and done quite a bit of damage there, as they didn't have anything beyond a normal army and city walls.

The only question was, just how long would it stay at Riverbend?

"Well, we know who the senior officers on the base are, as well as several of the scientists who maintain the weapons, and most of the senior enlisted," Loomis said. Which was true, because that had all been pulled from the minds of the two people he'd pushed through. But beyond that, I don't think he'd contributed much of anything, as he really didn't understand how a modern society really worked, and the little exposure he'd had over the last two weeks or so hadn't sunk in.

"I've found the houses of most of the NCO's," Suzona said. She'd been making the rounds of the bars, and letting the service members buy her drinks. Last night she'd let one pick her up.

"Why didn't you just take him?" Loomis asked surprised.

"Because he'd be missed. Once we remove someone, we have to act the next day. Before people become too suspicious." Suzona replied and continued. "I confirmed where the weapons bunkers are."

"What did you find, Will?" Evean asked me.

"I found the whorehouses that the single enlisted men use, as well as the one that the officers are using."

"It figures," Loomis laughed, but got quiet when Evean shot him a glare.

I continued on, "I also found the shop that sells uniforms locally, and I bought each of you one. Can any of you sew? Because I wasn't sure what rank insignia to use, and I bought a variety."

"I can sew," Evean said, "Rather well too."

I nodded, "So, do we have a plan yet?"

Evean nodded and smiled, looking around at all of us.

"Don't I always?"

We were all in a car approaching one of the gates to the base, it was four a.m. and things were still rather dark. Evean had spent yesterday after our meeting scouting out all of the senior NCO's, until she found one that resembled one of us. With Suzona's help, she quickly got him alone late last night and after relieving him of his identification, pushed him through a portal to Isengruer.

Unlike Quzelatin, Isengruer didn't just strip his mind and kill him. Oh, he still got everything we needed, but he had promised to send Suzona's victim home after we got what we needed. That had actually gained us an extra level of cooperation that while we probably didn't need, did mean at least we still had some options if this plan fell through.

It also moved Isengruer and Suzona up a few notches in my mind.

I was driving the car, as I was the one who looked the most like Suzona's victim, so after a makeup job by Evean, who was rather adept at applying it, I had donned the uniform with the proper insignia and had gotten into the victim's car.

Suzona, Evean, and Loomis were all crammed rather tightly into the trunk. The gate guards all knew Master Sergeant Tam, and they rarely searched his car, beyond flashing a light through the window to check the back seat.

Tonight they didn't even do that, just waved me through while looking bored.

I drove until I was around a corner and out of sight, then pulled around behind a building and popping the trunk I got out and ran around to the back to help them all out.

Suzona was dressed as a junior NCO in a uniform that made it clear just how she was climbing the rank ladder. Evean's was that of a scientific advisor with half a dozen technical badges which equally made it clear just how she got where she was. Both of them had new unit patches, which would make anyone looking at them think that they had both recently been assigned here.

Loomis was done up as a private, with as little insignia as possible. From what we all now knew, he would be ignored by everyone, except to be yelled at, and then ignored some more. There were privates here everywhere, usually doing the scut work and whatever other job no one else wanted to do.

Once everyone was out, we all checked each other's uniforms, then got into the car and I drove off, dropping each of them at their assigned spot as I drove onto my own duty spot, the base armory.

"Morning, Tam!" said a rather sleepy looking civilian I walked up behind as we reached the locked and guarded door. My new memories identified him as one of the civilian gunsmiths who worked there.

"Morning," I grumbled back, swiping my id in the card reader after they had swept theirs.

"Master Sergeant!" acknowledged the soldier behind the security glass as the door unlocked. I nodded and greeted him and going inside I went directly to Tam's office.

The office was empty of course; the normal working day didn't start here until six a.m. for most people who worked in the armory, though Master Sergeant Tam was known for often showing up early.

Especially on days when he was planning on leaving early to go fishing. Tam was short and was just sticking it out for his retirement, and everyone knew it. They also knew that making his life difficult would get you in more trouble than even the base commander could muster.

Unlocking and opening Tam's desk, I got out his key ring, and a few of the tags kept there as well. I then left his office and proceeded inside the building and unlocking the doors with his keys, I went into the vaults where the heavy weapons were stored. Once inside it only took me a minute to find the weapon I wanted, a rather interesting recoilless rifle in its transport case. I also took a second case, which contained six special armor-piecing rounds.

Putting a blue tag on each, I signed Tam's name, and wrote 'Exercise Approved' and put the date on them. I stacked both on a cart that was just outside the vault door, then closing the vault; I took them to the loading bay, and set them by the door.

Next I went to the small arms vault. First I found a pistol and loaded it, then stuck it and several extra magazines in my pockets. I took two more of the same pistol, with spare magazines, and put each in an ammo box, which I had dumped the contents of out onto the floor. Then I took two automatic rifles, checked their function quickly, and also grabbed several loaded magazines for each. However I made one difference on these, I grabbed the magazines that were loaded with non-lethal plastic bullets. They'd hurt like hell, and might wound you at point blank range, but we really weren't here to kill a lot of people, plus I didn't trust Loomis to not just shoot everyone we came across.

I put the rifles into a bag, along with the magazines for them, and carried those to the loading bay as well.

When a truck pulled up outside, I opened the door, loaded the recoilless rifle, its ammunition, and the bag with the rifles into the back. I set the two boxes with the pistols on the ground and then went back inside, locking the door as the truck drove off.

I returned to Tam's office to replace the keys, then went out the front door with a wave to the guard and got back into the car and after picking up the two boxes by the loading docks, I drove over to the base operations office.

I parked the car out front and got both of the boxes, then walked up to the door and was buzzed in immediately. Evean was there, with three people bound, gagged, and blindfolded on the floor behind the doorway.

"Any problems?" She asked me.

"Nope, Loomis showed up with the truck on time, I loaded him up." I handed her one of the boxes.

"What's this for?" She said opening it up and looking at the pistol.

"Emergencies."

She nodded and loaded the pistol and put it in her uniform pocket, along with the extra magazines.

"Suzona's here," She said, motioning to the monitor.

Looking up at it, I saw Suzona carrying a rather large bag like it weighed barely anything. I went over and opened the door for her, and she hurried inside and set the bag down.

"Any problems?" Evean asked her, as Suzona unzipped the bag.

"No, I left his wife bound and gagged in the closet. Didn't even have to bother with his kids," Suzona said as she pulled the base commander, groggy and bound, from the bag.

"Good."

"Help me with this please, William?" Suzona said to me.

I nodded and helped her carry him into one of the offices, possibly his, where she partially untied him, then rebound him to the chair with his right arm free.

"You'll never get away with this, Tam," he said, a little groggily."

"I'm not Tam," I said to him. "Tam is currently being held incommunicado while I'm here."

"Hold his arm please, William," Suzona commanded.

I nodded and took a tight grip of his forearm while Suzona poured a couple of bottles of chemicals into a large metal tub she'd bought last night along with the chemicals. I knew what she was going to do, but I had no idea how it worked.

"General, this will sting a bit," She said. "But it will cause no lasting harm. So, try not to scream or I will gag you."

"Why haven't you already?" He grumbled and then sucked his breath in, I suspect in a combination of pain and shock as Suzona stuck his hand in the solution.

"We haven't, because we thought you might like to know what we're doing, and why," I said to him as I watched Suzona work. She held his hand in the solution for probably half a minute, then set the bucket on the floor.

"You're terrorists, or thieves, and you'll get nothing from me!" He replied.

"I guess you'd say we're thieves then," I said as Suzona pulled out a spray can and sprayed something on the palm of his hand as she held his wrist tightly with the other.

"You see, we're having a problem with one of those gojira monsters, and we don't have a weapon that will kill it. You however, do."

His eyes got wide then, "You're going to steal one of the destroyers?"

"Hold his arm again, William, tightly please. And press on the nerve here." Suzona told me.

I did as she said and his hand flexed open. I continued my conversation with the general as she took an inside-out rubber glove and carefully put it on his hand, slotting each of the fingers, and then rolling the rest of it down over everything.

"Yes, it has already wiped out several cities and killed thousands. You're the only people with the weapon we know of, so here we are."

"You lie! We've had no reports of any of the monsters appearing anywhere! And if they had, all you would have to do is tell us and we would destroy if for you!"

"We are not from this world, General," Suzona said and taking out a hair dryer she started heating up the glove.

"What kind of kooks are you?" He said looking back and forth between us. "Not of this world?"

"Where do you think the gojira came from?" I asked him. "It's not natural to this world, and your regular weapons had little to no effect."

"It came from someplace deep inside the earth. Some sort of ancient mutant creature!"

I shook my head and watched as Suzona set down the dryer and started to carefully peel off the glove. I applied pressure to the point she'd shown, making sure he didn't move his hand and ruin her work, causing him to grunt.

"No, they're from another plane, another reality if you will. Think of it as the underworld if you want. Sometimes gates open, or become unblocked, and things come through them."

"Preposterous!"

Suzona got the glove all the way off then; once again it was inside out. It looked like a coating of skin was attached to it now however. She carefully set it in a small container she'd made and closed the lid.

"Done," She said.

"Off with you then," I told her, "oh, that box by the door is for you."

Suzona nodded and left the room as I secured the general's arm to the chair and stuck a gag in his mouth.

"Believe what you want, when we take the device there will undoubtedly be evidence that we are what we say we are. Understand that we will try to do as little damage and kill as few people as possible, but our world is being destroyed and we will do whatever we must do, to save it."

I got up and left the room, going back out to where Evean was holding down the fort.

"How long until Suzona gets there?" I asked.

"About five minutes, she took your car and left us the keys to the base commander's car."

I nodded, and made a few rounds of the place as Evean fielded a phone call.

Six minutes later, the call we were waiting for came in. We had forged orders for all of us, it wasn't all that hard to do, but we knew that Suzona's orders would be verified when she got there.

"Base operations," Evean said picking up the phone.

"Yes, Sergeant Susoke's orders are correct, she is a new transfer and this is her first day reporting for duty." Evean said replying to some question.

"No, that won't be necessary; she is not cleared into the sub-vault, just the outside areas. Yes, I can confirm that."

She listened another minute.

"We have a new technician I'll be sending over shortly, would you like me to send confirmation orders for both of them with her?"

"Okay, fine, I'll update the logs and find out why you were not notified."

Evean hung up the phone. "It's good, let's go."

We left the building, sealing the doors behind us. We weren't sure how long we had until someone realized there was a problem there, but it should be more than enough to get to the bunker.

I drove over to where we had told Loomis to wait, then I got out of the car, and Evean drove on as I opened the driver's door.

"Slide over, I'll drive," I told him.

"I can drive it," He said giving me a look.

"It has to be backed up to the loading dock, you know that. You just learned this morning how to drive; do you really think you can do it well enough not to rouse any suspicions?" I said looking at him.

I had my right hand in my pocket, if he said no, or gave me a moment of grief I was going to just shoot him in the head and be done with him. Sure it would make things tougher, but we no longer had time for any games.

Loomis sighed and slid over, so I climbed up into the driver's seat, put it in gear and drove. When I got to the gate for the bunker the guard looked at me surprised.

"Tam? Why the hell are you driving?"

"They gave me a buck private from the motor pool," I grumbled as I handed over the orders we forged. "I'm too short to trust my fat ass to a kid who hasn't started shaving yet."

The guard just laughed, glanced at the orders, then handed them back to me and waved us through.

"What did you say to that guard?" Loomis asked, looking annoyed after we had pulled away.

"I told him I was too close to retirement to trust a new recruit to drive the truck. Master Sergeants are supposed to complain about everything. So he laughed at the expected complaint and just waved us through."

"And you know this because?"

"Family," I said. "It's universal. Ask the senior people in your own army when you get home."

Loomis nodded, but didn't look any more pleasant.

I regretted not shooting him already.

The bunker complex was fairly simple, a fenced in area with a road that led to the front of six bunkers spaced a hundred feet apart. Each of the bunkers looked like a large single bay garage that had dirt and earth piled over it. There were concrete walls coming out at an angle from the doors, and there was a large loading dock in front of the door. There was also a short stairway up to a guard station, which Evean was currently checking into.

I turned the truck and slowly backed up to the dock. There was a small parking lot with a dozen cars in it across from the six bunkers. Those were for the guards and the people working inside. The first bunker and the third bunker housed the Okishijen Desootoria devices. We'd learned, from what Isengruer had gotten out of the real Tam's mind, that only two devices were assembled and ready to go at any time.

Other weapons, and the parts to make more, were stored in the other bunkers. None of the bunkers were connected to the other, and each was fifty feet below ground. What we were backing up to, was only the entrance to an elevator.

"Go around to the back of the truck, unload everything, and remember, the big box is supposed to be heavy, wait until I send someone over to help you with it," I told Loomis, and then opening the door I slid out of the truck.

The guard looked up and saw me, stopped whatever he was saying to Evean, waved her through and then waved me forward.

I walked up and handed him the orders. Tam didn't know this guard, so I wasn't worried about him figuring out I wasn't Tam.

"ID please, Sergeant."

I handed it over and he compared it to the orders quickly.

"What do they need this stuff for?" He asked me.

I shrugged, "Beats me. They just asked for a recoilless rifle. Probably some idiot thinks they can use it to launch one of their devices."

The guard shook his head, "Sounds crazy."

"Well just to be safe, I rendered it all inert back at the armory. They may be smart, but I'm not sure I trust them with things that go boom."

"Sure thing, Sergeant."

"Hey, do you have a cart or someone who can help carry that thing? It's heavy and I don't want to break my private. They keep telling me that they have a limited supply of those things."

The guard laughed. "There's a cart inside the doorway, Sergeant. Good luck."

"Thanks," I nodded and went through the regular door next to the larger garage sized door, and sure enough, there was a cart there. I hit the switch to roll up the door and pushed the cart out to the back of the truck once it was clear.

We loaded the cart and I pushed it through the door and onto the large lift, and hit the button to lower the door.

Once it was down I set the bolts on both of the doors, and jammed them in place, to slow anyone from outside coming in.

"This is easy," Loomis muttered.

I pressed the button on the lift to lower it to the bottom.

"Not for much longer," I said.

When we got to the bottom, we were in small area just big enough for the lift, with a staircase to the side. There was a large six-foot square door in front of us, with a thick piece of armored glass next to it. There was a sergeant sitting behind the glass, looking more interested in Suzona, who was sitting next to him, than in me and Loomis.

I walked up tapped on the glass getting his attention and put my orders into the metal tray he then rolled out to us, looking a little embarrassed. He pulled back in, much like a bank teller and pulled the orders out and looked them over.

"I haven't been told anything about this," He said leaning over to speak into a microphone which rebroadcast his words to us.

I shrugged, "I just got told to do this, this morning."

"I don't think I can let you in, without confirmation from the base commander," he said and started to reach for the phone, which was when Suzona slugged him, knocking him out cold. She reached over and turned something on the panel before him and ran out of the room, moving at obviously accelerated speeds.

The door was halfway open, when it stopped and started to close.

"Inside!" I said and grabbing the recoilless ammo I tossed that through the door, and then I grabbed the container with the rifle and dragged it off the cart and through the doorway.

Loomis was smart enough to grab the other bag. Once inside I dropped the container and took the bag from Loomis and quickly ripped it open and pulled out the two carbines. I handed him one, took the other, and grabbed one of the bandoliers of magazines and ran inside.

Suzona and Evean had subdued several people, but there was a red light flashing by the doorways now.

"What's going on?" I asked.

"Someone triggered the alarm," Evean said. "From here on, it will be a fight to get inside."

"How did that happen?" Loomis asked.

"They had a video monitor watching the front guard," Suzona said. "They saw me knock him out, and then overrode the door controls."

"At least we didn't have to take out that window," I said nodding back towards the guard's station and handing my carbine to Evean.

"How many more people are inside?" I asked going back to the recoilless rifle container and opening it up.

"Six," Suzona said.

"Loomis, you're with me," Evean said taking the carbine and the ammunition from me. "Suzona, Will, bind these people, then follow us."

We both nodded and they jogged off.

It only took us a minute to tie everyone up, then I kicked off my shoes and shifted into my champion form, pretty much destroying my uniform and picked up the recoilless rifle while Suzona shifted and got the ammunition.

I looked at a couple of the bound people who had regained consciousness and that were now staring at me rather wide-eyed. Suzona didn't really look different enough to attract attention with me there.

"I'm not from around here," I smiled at them, and then we left to follow Evean.

We caught up with them rather quickly, we were at the next guard station, Evean and Loomis were tying up two more guards. I could see both Evean and Loomis had been wounded, as there was now blood on their clothing, but neither was still wounded of course, having healed themselves already.

"Four more to go," Suzona said.

"And one more barricade," I said and hefted up the recoilless again.

Evean led the way into the next section, which was a long six-foot wide corridor, with a guard station and a sealed door at the end of it. This was really the last section.

"I suggest you surrender," Evean called down the corridor.

The response from the guards was simply gunfire.

"You're up, Will," She said ducking back around the doorway at this end.

I nodded and set the gun down on its stand, "Hand me a round, Suzona."

Suzona passed one forward and I loaded the chamber. "Stand back, open your mouths, cover your ears," I warned. Then I picked the rifle up, moved into the doorway, I took aim at the heavy metal reinforced door at the far end of the corridor. Aiming about a third of the way down from the top of the door to the left of its centerline, I fired a round down the corridor at it.

They had started firing at me as soon as I stood out into the open of course, and I got hit twice, but the explosion when the round hit the door stunned them, if it hadn't knocked them unconscious.

I stood back in cover.

"Round please," I said setting the gun down and opening the chamber. Suzona handed me another one, and I put it in the breech and sealed the chamber. Picking it back up I moved into the doorway again. There were a couple more shots fired, but nothing even came close this time. I aimed about a third up from the bottom this time, again to the left of the centerline and pulled the trigger and hit the door again.

Nobody was moving now down at the other end of the hallway.

I just set the gun down where it was and reopened the breech.

"Round," I said and taking what Suzona handed me, I loaded, picked it up, and aiming dead center of the door I fired a third shot.

This time the door blew open, the first two shots having taken out two of the three crossbars holding the door in place.

I cast a cure on myself, more to fix my ringing ears than because of the two bullet wounds.

"Loomis, bring up the rear," Evean ordered and moved forward. I noticed she had the pistol in her hands now, and was letting the rifle hang on her back.

I picked up the recoilless rifle and carried it in my left hand; I had the pistol out in my right. When we got to the blown in doorway I looked at the two guards to either side. I couldn't tell if they were dead or unconscious.

"Save your heals until we have the device," Evean warned loudly. "We may need them for ourselves first."

I nodded and sighed; I set the rifle down just inside the destroyed doorway, and then followed Evean carefully around the wall that was just past the doorway.

Down another short hallway and then we came into the last room, where the weapon was stored. There were two people passed out on the floor, with blood coming from their ears and noses. I suspect the shock wave from the armor piercing rounds had probably messed them up.

"Tie them up, Will." Evean said, and then raised her voice, "Suzona! You're on!"

I moved them out of the way, and secured their arms and legs, and then watched as Suzona stopped at the final wall. There was a palm scanner on the wall, which was the first lock we had to get past.

She took out the glove she had made and carefully set it down. She first sprayed something all over her hand, and then put a drop of glue on each fingertip of the glove; next she attached those to each of her own. Once that was done, she carefully worked the glove over her hand with Evean's help. After a minute of waiting, Evean took a razorblade and carefully cut the glove into pieces, peeling each of them off slowly.

Then Suzona put her hand on the scanner.

I watched as a line slowly moved down her hand, on the other side of the panel. When it got to the bottom, a large metal panel in the wall popped open, exposing a large keyboard and a screen. This was the hard part, no one on base knew the command to unlock the door, normally it would be called in from their central command.

Once Suzona started trying to hack it, if the alarms weren't already going off all over the base, they would start.

"Will, check the guard's station," Evean told me as Suzona started typing. "Loomis, go check the first door!"

I went to the guard's station; unfortunately the monitor there was cracked and no longer functioning from the shots from my breaking down the door.

"Wait here," Evean said to me as she went by, following Loomis. At this point the plan was clear: We hold off any attackers until Suzona got the last lock hacked. She was sure it wouldn't take her more than twenty minutes.

After that, I'd open a portal to Fel, as that was now the closest we could get to the monster with Jane no longer here and everyone would go through.

I felt the ground shake under me for a moment, almost a minute later it shook again. I had no idea what it was, and figured it probably wasn't a very good sign. We really had no idea how they would try to retake the bunker, as Tam had no idea what the response would be. Five more times the ground shook, each of them about a minute apart, then it was quiet for about three. Then I felt a very faint rumbling and a loud grinding noise.

I turned to look through the doorway at Suzona; she was still typing away furiously and swearing in a foreign language. I went and got the ammo for the recoilless, I had three rounds left. I loaded one, and left the other two sitting by the rifle. Then I ran down the hallway and looked into the next section. I didn't see anything, but after a minute I started to hear sporadic gunfire.

When it started to draw closer I ran back and picked up the recoilless and looked back at Suzona, "Time's running out!" I called.

"I'm almost there!" She said.

I took aim down the hallway and waited. The gunfire was getting closer, and I was pretty sure I could hear Evean yelling to fallback. A minute later Loomis came running around the corner, and ran past me as Evean came around it next and followed. Just as she went by me, I pulled the trigger on the recoilless and sent a round down to the other end of the hallway, which punched through the wall there and went off with a nice explosion.

I dropped to my knees, and quickly reloaded and fired again.

"I got it!" I heard Suzona yell.

"Get up here and help me hold them off," Evean yelled, then turned to me, "Hand me that, and go get a portal open, Will."

I gave her the gun and standing up I ran around the wall and passing Suzona as she went to help Evean as I ran down the short hallway to the back room, where Loomis had the Okishijen Desootoria in one hand, and a handgun that I hadn't given him in the other.

"See you in a few weeks, bastard!" Loomis laughed and I kicked into high gear as he pulled the trigger.

Dodging to the side as he fired, I felt the bullet rip into the side of my face, tearing into my cheek and ripping it off as it deflected off my teeth as they shattered from the impact.

I started to reach for my pistol, but realized that if I missed and hit the device, then all of this would have been for nothing, so grabbing my walking stick instead, I pressed the indent on the side as threw it at him as hard as I could.

Loomis managed to shoot me a second time, in the shoulder, as I dodged behind a desk, after I let go of the now rapidly expanding stick heading his way.

Swearing loudly he raised the hand with the pistol in it, to deflect the stick from his head, dropping the pistol as it hit him rather solidly in the arm.

He backpedaled, now off balance, and juggling the device in his other hand, trying not to drop it, taking his eyes off of me, but while still trying to concentrate enough to open up the portal back to his temple.

Taking advantage of this I grabbed the desk with my good hand and jumping back up I table flipped it at him, hoping to distract him further, as I charged him, screaming in anger and pain.

Loomis got a solid grip on the device as I charged him, easily dodging the desk and without hesitating he grabbed the carbine, which he was still carrying on its sling, and pointing it at me he pulled the trigger, unloading the entire magazine into my chest, stopping me just short of reaching him, as the portal opened behind him.

My last sight of Loomis was him jumping through the portal, as I fell to the floor.

I came too with Suzona looking down at me, "What happened, William?"

"Loomis shot me, took the weapon," the words were pretty garbled; the side of my face and mouth was still a mess. I was in a lot of pain; the 'non-lethal' rounds apparently weren't that 'non-lethal'. I could feel several broken ribs and I was bleeding from several gunshot wounds in the chest, not to mention the one in the shoulder and the one along the side of my face.

I heard the sound of the recoilless rifle firing its last round then.

Suzona put her hand on me and healed the worst of it.

"Open up a portal and get out of here, William."

I groaned and rolled over onto my hands and knees, then started to concentrate. I heard Evean and Suzona both start shooting with their pistols.

"Loomis shot William and took the device," I heard Suzona tell Evean. "You need to get out of here, I'll hold them off."

I was still dragging myself towards the portal when I felt someone grab me by the scruff of my neck and the belt around my waist, and the next thing I knew I was flying through the portal.

TWENTY-ONE
SALADIN - RIVERVAIL

I came out of the portal and after healing my wounds I picked myself up off of the floor and looked around; this wasn't the main temple in Hiland city. It was one of Fel's temples; I wasn't sure which one however.

"Fel, where am I?"

"Rivervail," Fel's voice said as I looked around the room.

"Rivervail?" I repeated looking around surprised. "I thought I could only appear in your main temple?"

"Right now, this is my main temple," Fel said.

"What? What happened?" I asked worried.

"In order for you to be closer to the monster when you brought the device to destroy it back, everyone was supposed to come back with you. So I temporarily relocated my main temple here, to cut down on the travel times. Originally we had all agreed on Fordessa's temple, but with Jane having to return, that plan had to be changed."

"Loomis has the device, and he didn't come with me, he went back to Quzelatin's temple."

"I know," Fel said, and I could tell he was not pleased. "Everyone was supposed to come back with you."

"So now what?"

"You go and destroy Quzelatin's temple, that's what," Fel said rather angrily.

"What?" I didn't like Loomis, but this was definitely a surprise.

"Quzelatin is refusing to release the device, so we're at war now. I guess he saw this as too good a chance to pass up, with my main temple now being in a city that is probably going to be attacked soon. I guess he figures with me weakened he can expand further into my domain.

"So I need you to ride as fast as you can to his temple, and do whatever you can to get the device, and then portal back here, so it can be used."

"What about the others?" I asked.

"Jane will meet you along the way. Evean is on her way there as well, Roden's temple being to the north of Quzelatin's."

I nodded and thought about that for a few minutes. I guess this meant that Loomis had been selling us out all along, but I had to wonder a little about Evean, she had to have realized what Loomis was up to.

"Don't be too sure of that, William. There were a lot of politics going on, there still is, but everyone had agreed early on that destroying the monster was more important than anyone of us getting an advantage over the others."

"So, the other gods are all mad at him too?"

Fel sighed, "Not exactly. They are displeased; they do not like his making a power play. If it only hurts me, they probably won't say much, I'm still not all that popular with the older gods here, and Quzelatin is an older god than I am.

"However, if this causes other problems, or allows the monster to escape, Quzelatin may find himself on the receiving end of a holy war rather shortly."

"If I take the army with me, Quzelatin will see it coming, won't he?"

"Yes, he will. However, I think I have something you might appreciate, William."

"What?" I was curious now.

"Go out into the nave of the temple."

I nodded and grabbed the weapon's harness that was there with my usual complement of swords and knives, plus a sledgehammer, which made it fairly clear just what Fel wanted me to do. I got it all in order putting the large hammer in a holding ring on my back and went out through the door to the nave as I belted it on. As I came out into the room, a large group of males came to attention. I stopped and looked them over, they were all fit, wearing light armor, and armed heavily.

They were also all wearing Fel's device.

"Fel?" I asked looking back towards the altar.

"Remember that conversation we had about warrior-priests?" Fel said in a voice so smug that I could feel it.

I smiled, "For me? You shouldn't have."

"Quzelatin won't be able to track them, because they're all priests."

I looked at the group, "How many are there?"

"Seventy three, almost half of them haven't completed their training yet, but this was too important, so I ordered them all here."

I nodded, "This gives me a really nice idea," I grinned, "Several really nice ideas."

"I thought it would. Now go, William, time is of the essence."

"Who is senior among you?" I asked them.

"I am, Champion," one of them males said stepping forward, "I am Hess."

"Do you all have mounts, Hess?" I asked.

"Yes, and we have your mount with us as well, Champion."

"Great, call me Will. Now get everyone mounted up, we'll be riding out of here shortly. Who is the ranking military member in the city?"

"General Holse is still here with the army, Will." Hess told me.

"Good, take the men at a walk down the road towards Tradeson, I'll catch up with you soon. Does everyone know where we're going?"

"Yes, Will."

"Fel, could you please tell *me* where I'm going?" I grinned.

The route we were going to take appeared in my mind. Very handy that.

"Okay, get going," I told them all and jogging out of the temple I hopped up on to Tom's back and rode off to where the military headquarters were in Rivervail.

"William!" General Holse said and came up to me, touching palms. "Does this mean you have the device?"

"Not yet, Holse. Apparently one of the other gods has decided to be a bit of an ass."

"What?!"

"I'm off to go get it, but I need a favor."

"What do you need, William?"

"Send the Army off to Bronsard, to attack the main temple of their god, Quzelatin."

"William, I can't do that!" General Holse said looking at me, "The queen would skin me alive!"

I looked at Holse and for the first time in my life I growled at him, he looked rather shocked.

"I am ordering you as Feliogustus's Champion, the Queen's representative, and Rachel's Husband, to send off your army, *all of it*, immediately. Keep the cavalry with the main body, leave only what forces here you think would be needed to help with an evacuation of the city."

I stared Holse down for probably the first time ever and the expression on my face was not a pleasant one. "I have no time to explain, I'm sorry, Holse, but those are your orders and I will remove you from command if you do not follow them."

"And just how are you planning on removing me, William?" Holse said standing straight, "Only the queen has that right."

"By killing you," I growled softly, "Don't mess with me now, Holse, I need you and we don't have time for this."

General Holse nodded, "Just needed to know that you were serious, I'll order it immediately."

"Do you so swear in the name of Feliogustus, and our Queen?" I asked him

General Holse blinked then and looked even more shocked.

"Yes, William, I do swear by our god and our queen. This sounds bad, I better get started."

I turned and jogged out of the hall and remounting Tom I rode out of the city gates to catch up with my new men. If we pushed it, we could be there in three days. The fastest Holse could get there with the army would be in six, and they'd probably be tired when they got there.

I had three more days until the monster struck, if it stuck to the pattern that it had developed so far. I hoped it was going to strike Riverbend again, but it could very well be moving up the river to Rivervail. I wouldn't know until then, and once it did attack, I'd have to wait until the attack was over and it returned to the water to use the device.

I caught up with the men half an hour later, and we all picked up speed to a trot from that point on. I remembered what Dezba had taught me the last time we'd had to push our mounts to their limits, and I made sure everyone followed those rules now.

We left the road and struck off immediately for the mountain pass we would be using. I only knew of it because of my time riding with the Mowoks, it not being a pass known to anyone but them. I wondered if Fel would have been able to show it to me if I hadn't already known about it?

I'd ask him later if I remembered. Right now the goal was to get there and grab the device and gate back to the temple.

What the men did after I left, I really didn't care.

We caught up with Jane after midnight as we were riding along the foothills; she was standing by her wolat waiting for us. She had a slightly shorter ride than we had to get here.

"Been waiting long?" I asked as she grabbed her mount's reins and started to walk along side me. We were giving our mounts a rest right now.

"Not really, maybe an hour, if that. Who are all these guys?"

"Warrior-priests," I said grinning.

"Alright, I'll bite: What's so important about warrior-priests?"

"Gods can't track them, just like they can't track us."

Jane smiled back at me in the moonlight, "So they won't know we're coming."

"Oh, they know we're coming, we have no choice but to come, and they know that. I've got the real army behind us; they'll be several days behind us when we get to the border. Quzelatin can see that army of course. So he'll have his eyes on that thinking that's where you and I are."

Jane nodded slowly, "Smart. So are we going to storm in, or parley first?"

"I'm going to ask them, once, politely. Because the sooner we get out of there and back home, the better. However if they refuse." I growled. "I just may add another god's death to my reputation."

"If you don't, I surely will," Jane growled along with me. "When this thing was just killing those people in Barassa, I didn't care as much, because they unleashed it, so they deserved it. But when it hit Marland, none of those people had anything to do with it. They were still digging out bodies, Will, when I left. It ate hundreds, and probably crushed thousands."

I nodded, "I'm sorry about Felecia, I liked her, she was very brave."

"She liked you too; I was surprised you never put the moves on her."

I shrugged, "I think I'm past the point where I want to bed every hot woman I run into."

"But not to the point yet where you won't sleep with the ones who offer?"

"You'd probably be surprised at how many I turn down. I'm more than happy to stick with the lovers I've already got, because all of them are pretty special to me."

I smiled slightly then. "What about you? I notice you seem to have roped Shin in pretty well."

Jane chuckled at that, "It's like what I heard Joseph telling you, I want a strong powerful man. It's hard to find one stronger than me these days."

"But don't you come from a society where women rule?"

"Yes, but we still like our men to be strong and powerful. They're supposed to be our warriors and defenders after all."

"Well, he seems nice enough. Of course living out there on the ocean somewhere probably means you won't get to see him often."

"Time will tell," She admitted. "Right now I'm more worried about getting the device back, sooner or later that monster is going to come back down the river and Marland won't be able to run it off a second time. Maybe you should have grabbed two of them?"

"They were one to a bunker, and they only had two completely assembled. Even if we could have gotten both, they'd had to deal with these things before; I didn't want to leave them defenseless in case one came back soon."

"Good point. So when do you think we'll get there?"

"Hopefully in three days, we have another day of riding just to get to the pass I want to use, then a day to get through it. In a couple of hours we'll stop and camp. Let everyone get a hot meal, and a few hours sleep. Then we'll push through until we hit the pass.

"Once we hit the border it's about three hours hard riding to get to the temple, and I want to make that ride as fast as we can so no one can get a message there before us."

"What about local churches?"

"It's supposed to be pretty sparse coming out of the mountains, so hopefully we won't run into any. I'll send a scout or two ahead to make sure however."

"I just hope we're not at war with Bronsard after all this is over."

I nodded, "Me too."

We arrived at the border to Bronsard a couple of hours before midnight two days after we'd left Rivervail, which was quite a few hours sooner than I'd expected to get there. I decided to press on until we were far enough past the border so as to not run into any border patrols.

Then we made a cold camp, no fires, no shelters, we even had the wolats lay down to sleep after we'd fed them. Everyone was tired by now, so I wanted to make sure that everyone got a good five hours of sleep, including our mounts. Tomorrow was going to be an important day, and I needed the men as rested as possible.

We awoke with the first glimmers of the false dawn, the men quickly donning their gear and readying their mounts.

"Listen up a moment," I said, my voice raised slightly and gaining their attention immediately.

"This is where I have to give the speech that I wish that I did not have to." I said looking at them, "Not because I don't have faith in you, but because I do. I know you will give your all, because I know you have all dedicated your lives to Feliogustus. It is because I have the warrior's dislike of war, but I also have the warrior's commitment to do what must be done.

"We are all about to enter into a dangerous battle, the most dangerous and the most important one you will ever face in your life. Many times before have I invoked Feliogustus's name as I rode into combat and told those with me that we were fighting in his name.

"Well today we *are* doing more than that; we are fighting for our god, *for* Feliogustus. His eyes are on us, his will is what has brought us together, and it is for him that we are here today. Many of us will die today, in our god's service, and all of us will be making sacrifices, both big and small. It will be tough, it will be hard, I know that, you know that, and even our god knows the difficultly of what we face. But you can be assured that our god cares for you, cares about you, loves you, and will celebrate your devotion when you go to meet him.

"I know our god, I know him as well as any champion has ever known his god, perhaps even better. So hear me when I say this to you: Our god, Feliogustus, commands us today to fight, to *win*, for him. This is not just a fight for our people, this is a war between gods and we *will* be victorious! We shall *not* be denied, and we shall *not* be defeated! Let this be our finest hour, and do not let fear slow your arm or stay your blows, victory today will belong only to the *bold*, to *us*, and to *our* god who is with us always!"

"So be it!"

The men all cheered with me then, even Jane looked a little impressed, and we mounted up and started riding in at a trot.

When we started to come across some scattered settlements, we kicked them up to a gallop and rode them hard for the next hour. We hit the edge of the city that the temple was in just as I was about to order a walk, but I could see the gates then and decided to push our wolats just a little farther.

We came at the gates so fast that we were able to ride through them before the guards could even start to close them. Two minutes later we stopped before the temple, and dismounted, our mounts tired and gasping for breath.

There was a barricade in front of the temple; it looked hastily constructed, and still unfinished with several gaps and weak spots. We'd obviously gotten here earlier than expected, which was what I had hoped for. This was going to be a hard battle, gods had a lot of power in their main temple, I expected our casualties to be high.

As we started towards the temple, several people and a lot of guards came spilling out to man the barricade and bar our way. Behind the line of guards I saw Loomis and I started to growl, and then stopped as I saw Evean was with him. Most of the guards I noticed were wearing the colors of Quzelatin, but all of the ones standing near Evean were wearing Roden's colors.

"Give me the device Loomis, the monster draws near and must be killed." I demanded, growling rather loudly as I stopped just before a weak spot in the barricade which was guarded by a dozen men as Jane picked another spot and readied herself to attack.

Loomis laughed, "Or what? Your paltry band of men will attack? We will turn over the device when we think the time is right, and not a moment before."

Several priests stumbled out as he talked. They were putting on their vestments, still getting organized.

"So, is this what your word, your god's word was all along? A lie?" I drew my swords slowly and prepared myself mentally to attack. I was going to enjoying cutting that smirking bastard down.

"Evean, what is this treachery?" I called looking at her. "To stand with this pissant and his treacherous religion!"

"Treachery?" Evean laughed looking at me, from where she was standing besides Loomis. "You think *that* was treachery?"

She grabbed her sword then and pulling it out of its sheath and in a smooth motion she swung the blade wide and around, neatly decapitating a very surprised looking Loomis, and then turned to attack the priests that had been standing behind him.

"Now this, THIS is treachery!" She screamed, laughing loudly.

"Attack!" I yelled and led my men forward through the gap to attack the men behind the barricade as Evean cut into the soldiers defending Quzelatin's temple, her men joining her in the attack.

"For Roden!" She cried out, "Down with the betrayers!"

I bulled my way past the first group of guards, killing two of them as I passed, leaving the rest for those following me and ran up besides her, joining with her in the fight. Being on holy ground I knew that this fight was not going to be easily won.

"Where's his high priest?" I asked Evean.

"What, no 'thank you, Evean? I am in your debt, Evean? May I kiss your feet, Evean?'" Evean said and then lunged forward with a grunt killing another defender.

"Right now I'm trying to figure out how to get Rachel to let me have another wife," I said and kicked the one in front of me in the balls, and then cut his head off as he bent forward, grunting in pain.

Evean laughed and made a kiss at me. "You really know how to charm a gal, don't you, Will?"

"What can I say?" I ducked an attack and moved forward to engage another defender, "You just bring out the best in me. So, where is their high priest?"

"Oh, he's passed out in my bed," Evean gave me a nasty grin, "with a couple of my priestesses. I suspect they'll be making short work of him any moment now."

I actually felt it then, when Quzelatin's high priest died, and I could feel Fel urging me onward.

"Into the breech!" I yelled and charged through the front doors, with Jane and Evean hot on my heels as my band of warrior-priests followed, along with Evean's guards.

I got zapped three times in quick succession by some sort of bolt of power, and had used up all of my heal spells after the second one, but the warrior-priests following behind me were casting on me, Jane, and even Evean as we charged down the aisle. I noticed, as we got closer that there were half a dozen dead priests and priestesses around the altar. The priestesses were all wearing Roden's colors.

After the next round of bolts zapped us, they stopped and started concentrating on the people behind us. I think Quzelatin realized he had to change tactics and take out my warrior-priests first.

At that point Evean took out something that looked like a hand grenade and threw it at the altar. When it hit, it broke open and a foul smell filled the room, causing a slowing of the bolts that were raining down on us.

"What was that?" Jane said, as she slid to a stop before the altar and pulling that big hammer of hers off of her back, she started in on the altar.

"It's only temporary, so you better work fast!" Evean said and started setting things on fire while I pulled the sledgehammer I'd brought along off of my back and started in on the altar along with Jane.

It was just like the altar in Marland of Tantrus's that we'd destroyed all those years ago, every time we hit it, screams filled the room, except if anything, these were louder and more painful.

When the altar started to crack, we both moved around to the sides this time and raising up our hammers we brought them down together, breaking the altar in two and causing an explosion that picked us each up and tossed us both back a dozen feet. The majority of the explosion was focused towards the front doors of the temple however, which were blown off by the force of it.

I picked myself back up and shook my head, I was covered in blood, and way too much of it was my own. A dozen of my men came running inside then, running up to me and Jane and healing us both.

"Help Evean," I said and motioned over to where she was still moaning on the floor.

"Yes, Will."

"Then help her set fire to the place."

"Yes, Will."

"And get someone to dig up some of the ward stones," Evean moaned from where she was laying on the floor.

"We're already working on that, Champion," one of my warrior-priests, said.

Getting up, I made my way to the front doors, looking outside, I could see there was fighting going on in the streets, I guess the more devout of Quzelatin's followers were here to try and save the temple.

The wolats, having recovered some of their strength, were tearing them to shreds. It wasn't pretty and I wasn't even going to bother trying to stop it.

There were two teams of about eight of my warrior-priests prying up flagstones and digging into the ground. Once one of those wards was gone, with all of the other destruction that had been done, this place was finished.

I turned back and looked into the nave of the temple. The curtains on the walls were starting to catch, I saw Evean duck into one of the back rooms, with a torch in her hands, Jane hot on her heels with a torch of her own, and six of my warrior-priests in tow.

I looked around the floor then, there were a lot of dead, I counted twenty of my own before I gave up, and at least ten of Evean's. Of those of us who had charged originally, only we three champions had survived.

I felt it then, they must have found one of the wards as the ground suddenly de-sanctified and the temple was no longer holy.

I could also feel that Fel wanted me to get that device and return home immediately.

"Is Hess still with us?" I called out to the men outside.

"No, Will, he was leading the men behind you," one of the men said as they started on a third stone.

"Find out which of you is in charge, once this place is burning, gather everyone up and either find a place to lie low, or go home. Pray to Fel for guidance, I have to leave."

"Yes, Will!"

"Oh, and make sure everyone knows, that I'm proud of you, I'm proud of you all, and so is Fel."

"Thank you, Champion Will," he said and all of the men turned to me and gave me a quick salute and went back to whatever it was they were doing.

"Roden is pretty damn proud of his people too," Evean sighed, coming up to me with the Okishijen Desootoria in her hand, which she presented to me.

"Sadly I don't think any of the priestesses and guards I brought with me survived the fight."

"Why did you bring them?" I asked. Jane was jogging up to join us now.

"Because I knew when Loomis pulled this little stunt of his that Quzelatin had sold us out. So I just played along until you showed up. That idiot Loomis thought I was on his side, even after the warnings I'd given you both. Hell, I think even Quzelatin thought I was on his side and that Roden would be won over. So they thought I was bringing people to help defend against you."

Evean sighed and shook her head, "Between what happened at Barassa, Marland, and Riverbend, Roden lost over ten thousand followers. Roden wants that gojira *dead* and will not side with anyone who delays that death for any reason."

I nodded, and turned to one of my warrior-priests, "Do you have any kind of recharging spell you can cast on me? I need to open a portal to the temple and I'm rather drained right now."

"Of course, Will." He said and called over the others that were still inside with us and they started in on some sort of coordinated spell. I really had no idea what most of the cleric spells were, as I really couldn't use them anyway.

Five minutes later and I opened a portal and stepped through with my wolat Tom, Jane, her wolat, and even Evean followed us through.

We all bowed to the altar and of course Jane and I perked right up, being refreshed just by being in one of Fel's temples. Me, because I was his champion, Jane because she was the champion of Fordessa, who was in his pantheon. Sadly Evean didn't get the benefit of that.

"I'm surprised you came," I said looking at her.

"Roden wants me to see this through to the end, no matter what the cost," she sighed, and then smiled, "Hello, Feliogustus," She said and gave a rather seductive sway of her hips.

"Another time and I would be impressed, Evean," Fel's voice said. "But lookouts have spotted a cresting wave in the distance headed this way."

I swore and jumping up on Tom's back I kicked him into a gallop, startling the guards by the doors who barely pushed them open in time for me as I rode out into the streets and headed for the docks.

I made it to the docks and turned Tom downstream, riding along the side of the river, I could see the wave crest coming towards us now and I was pretty sure it was the monster, but I wasn't going to waste our only device without being damn sure after all of the trouble we went through to get it.

I reined Tom in, then jumping off of his back and diving into the water I started to swim towards the monster, holding the weapon in my muzzle as I did so, my fangs on either side of two of the long bars linking the ends on one side.

When he came into view, it was quite the shock, he was big alright and this was the first time I'd ever seen him this close. The water at least was clear enough that I saw him a couple of hundred feet away, so I pulled the device out of my muzzle and held down the trigger.

The instructions had been clear; pressing once started a ten-minute countdown. Holding it down would cause it to activate in twenty seconds.

And that was when I got my biggest shock of the day, the monster saw me, and suddenly its eyes narrowed and I could see its pupils shrink and then widen, almost as if in fear. I got the distinct impression that it *knew* just what it was I was holding.

"Son of a bitch," I swore to myself as it turned to dive to the bottom of the river, because damn it all if a portal hadn't just appeared there! It was a champion!

I let go of the trigger and started swimming for the portal, there was no way in hell I was going to let this bastard get away from me after everything I'd gone through to get this damn bomb!

It took him a minute to get through the portal, and for once his size worked against him as I grabbed his tail as it went by and just hung on and triggering the 'eyes and ears' ability so Fel would know what was happening after I passed through the portal.

When I came out of the other side, I was dizzy for a moment, but I had the bomb in a death grip by now.

I started to cast cure spells on myself, to make up for not having any air to breathe and I grabbed the trigger as I looked around.

I was in a temple, a gigantic underwater temple, and apparently the monster had just realized that I wasn't supposed to be there. It turned and swam at me with its mouth open; I guess it was hoping to chew me up before the weapon would detonate.

Meanwhile I was getting zapped by the god whose temple this was, again and again. I could see the twenty-second timer running down, and it was probably the longest twenty seconds of my life. I ran out of cure spells, I was running out of breath, and I was in a tremendous amount of pain as I curled around the bomb to protect it, as the monster's jaws started to clamp down on me.

I felt the device start to activate then, and my last conscious action was to flip them all off as I felt my body being crushed.

TWENTY-TWO
HELL

The pain, was tremendous.

There was a lot of screaming, the typical insanities, and for the first time in a decade I actually thanked that nameless god from years ago who had torn me to pieces so badly that it had taken Fel months to put me back together.

Because I not only knew *how* to survive this, but I knew I *would* survive this.

'DO YOU HAVE ANY IDEA WHAT YOU HAVE DONE!' thundered through my spirit-being as I was tortured.

'Yeah,' I thought to myself, 'I killed your ass.'

'YOU HAVE KILLED THOUSANDS, TENS OF THOUSANDS, HUNDREDS, MILLIONS!'

All I could do was feel awesome about that and think of Feliogustus, Fel, home, the people I had saved, not only on my world, but maybe countless others as well.

'MURDERER!'

And damn proud of it too.

'YOU WILL NEVER RETURN HOME! YOU WILL BE TRAPPED HERE FOREVER!'

I wished I had hands so I could flip him off again. I just bared the pain, bared the attempts to destroy me, to tear my soul apart. They could make it seem as long as they wanted to, but I knew it would pass, it would pass, it would pass....

Eventually it did pass, and for a time, I have no idea how long a time, I wasn't aware of anything. But after a while, again I have no idea how long it was, I realized I was alone, in a void, and every so often I would be pulled to another void.

I lost count of how many times I went through this, but I had the vague feeling that I was just a lost soul, bouncing around, trying to find its way home. I knew that connections between the negative planes and the plane on which the spheres I lived in were few and far between. And probably most of those were blocked in one manner or another.

Eventually something happened, and I suddenly found myself in a different sort of void. This one had gods in it, none of which I recognized, but as I continued to move from one to the next, I could tell they were there. Some examined me, but none really bothered me, I guess to them I was just another soul on its way home. Still, I had no idea how long I was gone. I didn't know if days were passing, years, centuries, nothing. But I could feel the pull of Fel now, and it seemed as if I was actually picking up speed as I drew closer and closer.

And then I was sitting in Fel's bar, with Fel. I couldn't help myself, I got up and ran to him and hugged him tight.

"I missed you too, William." He said and patted my head.

"How long was I gone? Should I have quit so you could hire another?"

"No, I was able to get by without you. When the other gods discovered that the monster was actually another god's champion, and that he was trying to invade our sphere, there was a power shift among us.

"And when I showed them what you had done, once you had gotten there. Well, they all fell into one of two camps: 'Thankful' or 'Afraid.'"

"I really did mess that god up back there, didn't I?" I laughed.

"Yes, you killed everything in his temple and within a hundred miles of his temple. Which due to the rather interesting topography of that dimension, was all of his followers, all of his priests, and a fair number of other beings."

"So what was all of that bouncing around I felt?" I asked.

"Just as you thought, your soul was bouncing from sphere to sphere on the negative planes, trying to find a point to cross back over. The number of connections are few, and often temporary, so it took a while before you finally made it through.

"But you'd gone through so many by that point you were spending very little time in each of them. So when you finally made it back to the positive plane, you got here very quickly, for all that you were several hundred spheres away."

I nodded, hugged him again, and then sat down to drink my beer. After I don't know how long of nothingness, it tasted great.

"So, break it to me Fel. How long?"

"Two years."

I winced, "Two years? Exactly?"

"One year, ten months, twenty eight days," Fel shrugged and smiled, "And you have three more to go before I can reincarnate you."

I sighed heavily and nodded, "Well, at least I'm home now, and I'll be able to see everyone soon enough. I really wished I could have thanked Hess and the others for what they did. I know compared to you, my thanks probably doesn't mean all that much, but I could never have done it without them."

"Oh, they know. But I will pass on your sentiments on the other side."

"Thanks. So where did they come from anyway? I hadn't heard anything about them, and I hadn't seen them training at any of the other temples."

Fel smiled at me, "They came from the Champion's Temple. That is where their order is based."

I sat back, surprised, 1 had almost forgotten about that place.

"Which is how I wanted it. It's a secret. Only members of that order, you, and Narasamman know about it."

"How many did I lose in the attack?"

"*We*," Fel said emphasizing the 'we', "lost forty-eight in the fight, only twenty-five survived. Ten of them came home; the other fifteen immediately set up three different temples in Bronsard and started converting people. Between Fordessa's priests and musicians, the story of what Quzelatin had done, and what you then did to him, with the help of Jane and Evean, quickly made the rounds. Even Roden's priests made sure the story was spread."

"And his followers dumped him for that?"

"Well, no one likes a loser, and everybody loves a winner!" Fel laughed and hoisted his mug in salute.

I hoisted mine in return and took a long pull off of it.

"There have been a few changes around here, William, I must warn you."

"Oh? What?"

Fel just smiled at me, "I don't want to spoil the surprise. So I'm not going to tell you."

"And make me worry for the next three days!" I shook my head. "Better warn the recently departed not to spill the beans then," I said and stood up.

A thought occurred to me, "How come I'm still all in one piece after all of that? I was thinking I was going to show up here another basket case."

"Most of what was done to you healed itself, in the time you spent bouncing around," Fel shrugged then, "Truth is, you showed up five days ago, I just didn't restore your full awareness until I had you all fixed up."

I nodded, "Thanks, Fel. I appreciate what you do for me."

"You're always welcome, William."

I smiled and went outside to spend the rest of my time with those waiting to cross over to the other side. Two years of nothingness. Yeah, after that I really wanted people to talk with, even if they were dead.

TWENTY-THREE
SALADIN - HILAND

"Will!" I heard as soon as I opened my eyes.

I was lying on the altar in the back of the temple, where I always came back to life when Fel reincarnated me, so obviously he had moved his main temple back to Hiland.

I was pounced then, by Narasamman, who was crying and hugging me, and who then started to kiss me.

"I thought we had lost you!" She said.

"Well, didn't Fel tell you where I was?"

"Feliogustus only knew that you still existed, he had no idea where you were, or when you would be back, until you crossed over. Whatever that means."

"Oh," I pulled her up and kissed her back happily.

"I missed you, Will."

"You have no idea how much I missed you, Nara," I purred and kissed her again.

"Well, care to show me?" She asked and let her hands start to fondle me, one of which was definitely in a fairly private place.

"Well ...."

"It's been two years, Will. And I saw you first. Rachel will survive another few hours."

"I haven't told anyone that you are back yet, William." Fel's voice said. "So don't feel guilty about making poor Nara here happy."

I shook my head and smiled.

"Let's go to your room, Nara," I purred. "The bed is definitely a lot softer than this altar."

I spent the rest of the day and some of the next morning making Narasamman very happy. And surprisingly pregnant as well, which truth be told, was fine with me. She promised to bring our two daughters up to visit at the castle in a few days, after I got finished saying hello to Rachel and Laria.

When I walked into the council room, Rachel literally launched herself from her chair, over the table and right at me. The council members were all rather happy and excited to see me. But when I laid Rachel down on the conference table and started removing her clothing with my claws, they all got a clue and quickly vacated the room.

I'd never made love on a table before, and I have to admit that if we hadn't missed each other so much, I'd have taken her back to our rooms first. But she was making her desires rather clear, and I wasn't sure I could have made it that far myself.

Eventually we christened her throne a few times after having christened the table twice. By then it was after midnight and we were able to stay our lusts long enough to make it back to our bedroom.

The next day she allowed Laria to join us in bed and if I hadn't been so close to the main temple, the source of my powers from Fel, I probably would have gone into a coma. We didn't even start talking until the second day when we finally started to slow down.

"I was very worried, my love," Rachel said to me.

Laria nodded her head in agreement; we were all cuddling on the bed, Rachel, my wife, Laria my concubine, and me. All I needed was Darlene here and it would be perfect.

"Why did it take you so long to come home?"

"I died in the underworld, and the connections between there and here are few and tenuous. So it took my spirit a long time to find its way back here."

"That sounds bad," Laria whispered.

"Yes, it doesn't sound good, Love," Rachel agreed.

I hugged them both, "It wasn't as bad as it may have sounded. Besides, it was worth it."

"Why?" Rachel asked, curious.

"If what their god said to me while he was punishing me was true, I killed thousands of them."

Rachel laughed and hugged me close, kissing me, "That's my husband. Mess with his woman, his god, or his country, and he will destroy you."

"I wasn't going to let it get away without paying it back for killing Goth," I sighed.

Rachel nodded and sighed as well. "Nara came by and told me. She told me how Goth was caring for the injured and wounded. They were very proud of what she was doing, I'm glad you were able to avenge her."

"So, what happened after I killed the monster?" I asked, yawning. The two of them had really worn me out.

"You don't know?" Rachel asked, looking surprised.

"Fel said he didn't want to spoil the surprise."

Rachel laughed, "Well! Let's see," she thought a moment. "Holse was marching towards Bronsard, as you had ordered him, when some of the priests who had gone with you came across him on the way back. They told him that the temple had been destroyed and that the real reason he'd been ordered to march was as a diversion."

"How'd he take that?" I asked.

"Oh, he was just a bit upset, but I've since told him to get over it. You did what needed to be done and when he told me about your little threat I asked him why he had ever questioned your orders in the first place?

"That made him stop and think for a couple of minutes."

I nodded, "So what happened when he got back to Rivervail?"

"Oh, he didn't go back there."

"He didn't?" I said surprised.

"Nope, he had picked up a couple of Mowak scouts at that point, so he took his troops through the mountains to Barassa. All of the northern armies had retreated from the area, because of the monster. So he took Barassa."

"Holse took Barassa?" I said surprised.

"Yup, and he tore down the temple, put all the surviving members of the royal family as well as most of the nobility to death, and made sure to fill in the rather large hole in the ground that the monster had originally came from. Feliogustus, Fordessa, Roden, Tonoponah, and Selentia all have built temples there."

"Huh, everyone who helped," I said.

"And Holse took Riverbend as well. Not that there was much left there to take at that point. He was welcomed like a liberating general when they marched in there. Everyone was worried about surviving the winter after all of the death and destruction that had been wrought."

"Wow, so your Kingdom really has grown,"

"And the Mowoks have allied themselves to us," Rachel added grinning.

I blinked, "Sounds like a very busy two years."

Rachel nodded, "Yes, it has been. Rebuilding Barassa and Riverbend is going to take years, same for Marland. But the northern countries are happy, I let them keep what they took from Barassa in the early stages of the war and have told them that once the port at Barassa has been rebuilt, I will only charge usage fees for the dock space that they use, that I won't tax their commerce.

"Same for the docks at Riverbend."

I nodded and looked over at Laria who had fallen asleep snuggled up to me.

"So," I said after a couple of minutes thinking. "Do you want me to stop being a champion? To quit and stay home?"

Rachel sighed and put her head on my chest.

"You know, I thought about that, I thought about that long and hard, but the facts are, being a champion is who you are, Hon. It's part of what I love about you.

"Also, just as my country needs me to be a queen, both my country and my god need you to be a champion. I hate to imagine what would have happened if you hadn't been there, Hon."

"Oh, I don't know. Someone else probably would have picked up the slack," I said and yawned again.

"No, they wouldn't have. I heard about what happened on that trip. I heard all the gory details. And then I heard what happened afterwards. Without you, it might not have been successful."

"Where did you hear all that from?" I asked, "Jane was only there for half of it."

Rachel gave a little laugh, "I had a very long talk with a very pretty friend of yours."

I groaned, "Evean?"

Rachel snickered, "Yes, Evean."

"What was Evean doing up here talking to you?"

"Something about wanting to know if I'd allow you a third wife," Rachel said with a mock growl. As her claws weren't ripping my hide off, I knew I'd dodged a bullet there somewhere.

"With the way Evean looks, I'm surprised you're not telling me to quit and stay away from her."

"She is beautiful, isn't she?" Rachel said.

"Probably the most beautiful woman on the planet," I agreed.

"But you love me more," Rachel purred and nuzzled my chest. "You don't care if I grow old; you don't care if I get ugly. She told me that, proved it actually."

"How did she do that?" I asked curiously.

"She told me about the first time you made love to her. In a well lit room. And she showed me what she looked like, how ugly she was."

"And why did she show you all of that? Why did she tell you?" I asked curious.

"Because she said when my time has come and I've left the mortal plane, that she wants a shot at you, and she can't very well do that if you're no longer a champion, and that I needed to stop being silly and worrying about my looks."

I blinked, "She said that?"

"Yeah, apparently Fel told her you were thinking of quitting to make me happy."

"I don't know if I should be impressed or scared." I chuckled.

"Scared?"

"Evean is one seriously scary woman at times, Hon." I said and kissed the top of her head. "She's way too beautiful to not be distracting when she's around, and it has a tendency to make you forget that she's the smartest person in the room."

"So, what are your plans now, Love?"

"Well, Nara is bringing the kids over tomorrow I think, and I definitely want to spend time with our children, including Laria's of course."

"You should give her another child. She would like that you know."

I smiled at Rachel. "So would I."

"Anyways," I continued, "I'd like to spend a few months just enjoying your company, maybe take a trip to Marland to check on how things are recovering, check on my children with Tareassa." I shrugged as I laid here. "Visit Darlene for the winter."

"You really need to work on convincing her to move here," Rachel purred.

"Don't be so sure of that," I laughed, "Because she would stand up to you. When it comes to me, she is not timid about getting my attentions.

"But other than that, I have no desires to do much of anything for as long as I can get away with it. Hopefully you and Fel will both give me a bit of a vacation."

"Well, things are nice and peaceful right now," Rachel purred and yawned. "I know it won't stay that way, it never does. But I think we'll get to enjoy it at least for a little while."

I nodded and started to pet her head slowly, until she fell asleep, then nodded off as well.

TWENTY-FOUR
SALADIN
EASTPORT (FORMERLY BARASSA)

I was sitting at an inn in what used to be Barassa. The rebuilding of the town had progressed rather well it seemed. Of course they hadn't rebuilt any of the city walls; in fact they'd torn down the remains of the wall and used the materials to repair all of the broken buildings, as well as to build the five new temples.

"So, I hear you're looking for me?"

I turned and smiled at Evean, who walked over and dropped down into my lap and purred. All of the males who had been watching her walk through the room immediately looked away at that point. Apparently I wasn't just the god slayer anymore; I was the monster slayer as well. My legend had grown even more.

We kissed and she smiled at me.

"So, you went and talked to my wife?" I asked looking at her.

Evean smiled, "Well, your Feliogustus had dropped a hint or two, and I'm not slow on the uptake, unlike perhaps some other people and I thought I'd help calm her fears."

"What about the 'I want him next part?" I mock growled at her.

I was surprised when her facial fur poofed up in the local equivalent of a blush and she looked embarrassed.

"Yeah, that kind of slipped out. Your wife is a lot smarter than I thought she'd be, I got caught out in the cross examination."

"Uh-huh," I said and leaning forward and to the side a little I started to lick along her neck, grooming the fur there. Among the felinoids of Saladin, that was a fairly intimate caress. Evean purred and leaned into me a little more.

"Well, this is unexpected," She said rather happily.

"So, tell me about what was going on with Loomis and you?"

"I didn't think you were the jealous type, Will."

"Actually I can be terribly jealous, but we're not at that stage yet and that's not what I'm asking about. And you know it."

"I'm not sure what you mean by that," Evean sighed relaxing into me.

"You know, Evean, prevaricating and lying are not the best thing to do to a male whose teeth are right up against your neck, especially if it's one you supposedly care about."

"You wouldn't," She purred smugly.

"I shouldn't have to," I grumbled, "and you know it. Now talk."

"Spoilsport," She said and started to sit up.

I pulled her back down against me, "This is where you learn to trust me," I told her and went back to my grooming.

"Okay," she sighed and relaxed. "Though if you kill me I'm going to be seriously pissed at you."

"Uh-huh. Quit stalling."

"When we all got together and started out, everyone was worried about what you would do."

"What?" I said surprised.

"You have a huge reputation, you have stories, songs. Do you have any idea how famous you are, Will?"

"Apparently not," I said.

"No one wanted to help you build your reputation. Reputations like yours lead to problems for the other gods and champions, to troubles, and eventually competition. You've more than tripled your wife's kingdom since you got here, and even more than that for your god. So the gods were all worried and the champions were all worried."

"You too?"

"Yes, me too."

"Jane?"

"Like you and Fel, she and Fordessa were not included in *that* conversation."

"Go on."

"We couldn't leave you behind, because Fel had as big a stake in this as anyone, and to be honest, your reputation is rather well deserved and I said as much. So we needed you. Part of why I put you as second in command was so I could keep an eye on you.

"Loomis was rather upset with that, by the way," she chuckled.

"I guess that was my first strike with him."

"Yeah, well when I started chasing after you like a bitch in heat, he *really* got upset with you, and even with me. I believe he thought he owned my attentions by then.

"Anyway, the plan was for him, or me, or Shin, to be the one to use the device to kill the monster. This way one of *us* would get the credit, and your legend wouldn't grow all that much. You'd just be one of the 'also helped' people."

"What about Gregory, Suzona, and Joseph?"

"Well, if we couldn't do it, any of them would still be better than you, because they weren't even from around here. It still was better than building you up."

"So, what went wrong?"

"What went wrong was that Loomis and Quzelatin didn't just want to keep you from getting any of the credit, they also wanted to weaken and possibly even hurt Feliogustus as well as Fordessa. Quzelatin was fairly certain that the monster, being water-based, would go up the river and damage both Marland and Rivervail. Why he might get lucky and have it move further up the river closer to Hiland as well. Then he could move his people both across and up the river and spread his religions and influence.

"When you spent that truly wonderful night making love to me ...."

I was surprised when Evean actually shivered in my lap, "I started to think that you weren't the danger the others thought you were, because no one as self-centered as I had thought you were could ever have done that!" She purred a moment, and then sighed.

"And well," She paused a moment before continuing, "The original plan was for you to have an accident *after* we got hold of the device. We'd all gate through to Fordessa's temple with Jane, and then one of us would take the device and do the deed."

I gave her a light nip, causing her to jump a little. "You would have killed me?"

"It's not like I don't owe you in that regard, Will!" She giggled.

"But after that night, I started to reconsider that part of the plan. Then we lost Jane when the monster attacked Marland, and surprisingly Shin went with her as well.

"And after that, you got kind of cold, sad. It was pretty obvious to me and most of the others that you were upset with what had happened, but Loomis only saw it as a chance to stir up mischief and advance his agenda.

"His first goal was to remove the outsiders. He apparently spent some money bribing the local officials in the ultraman world into believing that Gregory, Joseph, and you were all terrorists of some kind. When we went out to eat that night, he called his contact when he went to the toilet. He didn't care that Teshes might be killed as well. He viewed her as worthless anyway."

"So that was why he didn't have any money on him?"

"Yup, he'd already spent most of it."

"So, when did you discover this?"

"He told me all about it when I was waiting for you to show up at the temple."

I nodded and went back to grooming.

"When we went to look for a place to stay later, he called the police again, and told them you were at the library. He was also the one that ratted us out about the portal that was surrounded by the police. He said he called them when we stopped to get gas while you were sleeping in the car. He thought I'd suggest you should deal with it, and I might have too, if Teshes hadn't volunteered."

"Why not Suzona?"

"She was our last high-tech worlder. I was afraid of losing her, in case we needed her, which it turned out we did. Plus," Evean shrugged, "Loomis grew up in a rather provincial area. Women aren't a threat to him. They're a resource. To be used. Often."

I purred, "Well at least he had one good idea."

I started then as Evean nipped my ear. "Behave.

"I started to get suspicious after that, your growing dislike of Loomis did cause me to take a step back and re-evaluate. But Roden did not want a war with Quzelatin, and kicking Loomis off the team would have led to one. Quzelatin had made that clear, more than once. That was why when I warned you that last time about behaving, I made sure that Loomis was there, it was a warning to him as well. Sadly, it just went right over his head."

"So that was why you killed him?"

"Oh no, I killed him because he betrayed me, because his god betrayed my Roden. Do you know that Roden likes you?"

I stopped and turned my head to look at her, "Seriously?"

She nodded, "When you escorted those followers, after that idiot had killed your friend, that impressed him. You actually felt bad about what you'd done to me, and what you'd caused to happen, even though it was no fault of your own.

"Roden is real big on loyalty and honor and all that kind of stuff. It's a big deal to him."

"Yet he didn't stop you from that ambush," I pointed out.

"That was my idea. I'd heard all about your reputation, I was scared of you, Will. I thought you were going to kill me when you first met me. And don't think Roden let me off easy for that either, he was pretty mad at me as well.

"I got my hands slapped over that one," She sighed.

I sat back, smiled at her, and gave her a kiss. "See? Now that wasn't so hard, was it?"

Evean smiled back, "No, it wasn't. So now what?"

"Now we go upstairs to the room I rented for the next three days."

"Only three?" Evean pouted.

I laughed and scooped her up in to my arms and carried her off to the room.

"Don't worry; I warned them we might be longer than that."

END

If you enjoyed this book, I would be grateful if you could share that appreciation by giving the book a good rating, or a good review.

For all of you who have been faithful fans, *thank you!* I appreciate you very much, and I do enjoy the occasional comment on my blog, facebook, or email. If you want to know when my next book is out, please sign up for my mailing list.

And thank you all again for reading!

John Van Stry
www.vanstry.net (vanstry@gmail.com)
Mailing list signup: http://eepurl.com/2qrO9
My Patreon page: https://www.patreon.com/vanstry

Made in the USA
Monee, IL
05 July 2024